I0557885

Also by Daniel Rider

Dreams in Shadow: Seventeen Stories All Told (also featuring short stories by Clinton Boomer, Torah Cottrill, Darrin Drader, Scott Gray, Ty Johnston, Uri Kurlianchik, Colin McComb, and Darren Pearce)

Daniel Rider

Monumental
WORKS GROUP

Copyright © Daniel Rider 2012

All rights reserved. No part of this book may be reproduced or transmitted in any form or by any electronic or mechanical means, including photocopying, recording, or by any information storage and retrieval systems, except by a reviewer, who may quote brief passages in a review. Any members of educational institutions wishing to photocopy part or all of the work for classroom use, or publishers who would like to obtain permission to include the work in an anthology, should send their inquiries to Monumental Works Group, 1642 W. Edgewater, Chicago, IL 60660.

FIRST EDITION

ISBN-13: 978-0615650470

Monumental Works Group
1642 W. Edgewater
Chicago, IL 60660
www.monumentalworksgroup.com

Cover by Jason Walton

This is a work of fiction. All names, characters, places, and situations appearing in this work are either the product of the author's imagination or are used fictitiously, and any resemblance to real persons, living or dead, events, past or present, or locations, urban or rural, is purely coincidental.

For Hyunji and David

Yeh ladka hai deewana,
hai deewana
(This boy is mad.
-Mad… Mad… Mad…)

—Kuch Kuch Hota Hai

…his brains dried up…

—Don Quixote

Nyonyowu!

—The Epic of Son-Jara

PROLOGUE

KHADIATOU CAMARA WALKED down the unpaved street toward the theater, her sandaled feet kicking up small clouds of dust. In one hand, she held two 500-franc coins her mother had given her, enjoying their slippery feel against her sweating palm. The fingers of her other hand were wrapped around her little brother's wrist, pulling him along behind her. Sekou was only seven years old, and he followed absent-mindedly, staring wide-eyed at all the people walking by.

Khadiatou—Khadi—was thirteen, and she was excited.

Once a week, her mother, who ran a small rice and soup restaurant, would give her money to see a film, and there was nothing she liked better than walking into town to see a movie. Usually, she would bring one of her four younger brothers or her sister with her. Today was Sekou's turn.

As they walked, the sun beat down on them, and Khadi noted her shadow. It looked wonderful. That morning her mother had done her hair in typical Malinke fashion, shaping it into long spikes that shot straight up. This made Khadi proud, as did the fact that she was wearing her new dress, which her mother had made for her from yellow and orange fabric. She hoped there would be many of her friends from L'École Moyenne at the theater so that they could see her like this. The all-gray uniforms of the school were fine, but it was fun to be seen on the weekend in regular clothes, especially when those regular clothes were something new and special.

After passing a few huts and metal-gated enclosures, Khadi saw what she was looking for—two small buildings facing each other across the intersection, both with movie posters taped to their dried-mud fronts.

The first theater had a big poster with a picture of an American action hero, Arnold Schwarzenegger. In yellow-rimmed letters under his picture, the title read "L'EFFACEUR." *Eraser.*

Khadi had to drag Sekou past it, his glance locked on the image. He loved these Hollywood movies with their strong, muscular action heroes who fought with superhuman strength to defend their country, les Etats-Unis. Schwarzenegger, Stallone, Willis, Segal… they were fine with Khadi, but she always found something lacking in their performances.

These American action heroes could do anything, it seemed, stopping bombs, killing terrorists, piloting planes, and falling from mountains with no more than slight scratches. They could save the world in an easy hour and a half, but…

They never danced.

And they never sang.

Khadi liked the next theater because it played "les films Hindi," movies from India, where heroes usually fought for love. They sang, they danced, and they loved.

Also, with the exception of her schoolmate, Sidiki, whose family owned the theater, and who usually ran the movie, the audience was almost all women, and Khadi had a chance to hear some of the local gossip, which she always brought back to her mother.

The best gossip, though, came from outside the theater, so, after a quick look at the poster for the film inside, which showed a good-looking Indian man and woman smiling at each other on a black background, Khadi pulled Sekou across the street to where several vendors sat at shaky, weather-beaten wooden tables, selling groundnuts, plantains, cookies, and Vimto.

She went immediately to Aissatou's stand.

Aissa was Peulh, not Malinke, and had lighter skin than Khadi. She also had a large, friendly smile and sparkling, humorous brown eyes that made Khadi happy. Khadi liked her a lot.

Aissa sat in front of a bowl of oranges, using a small knife to cut the orange exterior of the skin away, leaving the oranges in the white pulpy layer underneath. She then laid the shaved oranges in a pan of water in front of her where they bobbed up and down, looking like miniature footballs.

"Inike, Khadi," Aissatou said, greeting Khadi in Malinke as she always did. "Tanate?"

"Tanate, Aissa." Khadi smiled.

"Qu'est-ce que vous voudrais aujourd'hui?" Aissa asked, switching to French.

"Des oranges. Trois."

Aissa pulled three oranges out of the pan and sliced off just the top of each one, then handed them over. "Merci," Khadi said and handed her one of the coins.

"Merci beaucoup," Aissa said, storing the coin in a metal box and returning four to Khadi.

"And the American?" Khadi continued in French. "He is here today?"

Aissa rolled her eyes and motioned across the street to the theater. "He's there. You know. Every Saturday he's there. I don't know about other days, but if it's Saturday, he's there."

"Thank you." Khadi felt a little excitement bubble up inside her. She was looking forward to seeing the American. "I'm going now, Aissa. The movie will start. Goodbye."

"See you next time, Khadi." Aissa's expression showed that she knew why Khadi was so eager to go, as did the shaking of her head.

Crossing the street quickly, Khadi handed an orange to Sekou and paid six hundred francs to enter the theater. She pushed through the sheet hung in the open doorway to keep the light out, and they were inside.

The space within the theater was smaller than her classroom at L'École Moyenne, filled with closely situated wooden benches in two sets of rows. At the front was a single television on a stand, with a VCR underneath it. Sidiki's father was a professor at the nearby university and had enough money to own a generator, so while families like Khadi's own only watched TV when the local electricity came on at night, Sidiki's family had been able not only to watch TV, but to set up a side business showing three films a day.

The movie had already started when Khadi entered. On the screen, the hero, a man with a big nose, was speaking loudly in Hindi to a woman. The film hadn't been translated into French like all the American movies were, but these Indian movies were easy to understand: the man and the woman were going to fall in love, and, more importantly, they were about to sing and dance.

As she sat, Khadi put the orange to her mouth and sucked on the opening at the top, drinking in the juice. She sucked in a couple of seeds, too, and as she spit them onto the floor, she looked around the theater. The room was full of mostly middle-aged women, some cleaning their teeth by chewing on small sticks, others talking excitedly about what was happening on the screen.

In the middle of one row, though, between two women holding babies, was somebody different: the American.

He had a high forehead, blond hair parted at the side, and a big nose like the Indian hero on the television screen. He was wearing a simple T-shirt and blue jeans, and, like American movie stars, he had blue eyes. Khadi had seen him many times and was always curious.

The American seemed so out of place here among the women. He never spoke to anyone, just stared at the TV screen as if he were learning deep secrets from it. Even now, his intensity seemed to make him transcend his surroundings. It was as if he couldn't tell where he was, only caring about what was on the screen. He leaned forward, putting one elbow on his knee and holding his chin in his hand.

Khadi noticed that all the women had become quiet. Onscreen, the song had started. The hero was dancing in a circle around the woman, smiling. He held his arms wide and began to sing. The heroine acted annoyed, but it was almost certain that by the end of the song she would be singing too. Obviously, they loved each other.

Khadi had seen many films like this and knew that it was obvious.

The women in the theater were quiet, but their bodies were moving, heads shaking side to side with the music.

Khadi took another look at the American. He was still in the same concentrating pose, his blue eyes focused on the screen, taking it in.

Khadi knew a little about him. He was friends with the Peace Corps teacher, Mademoiselle Jamie, who had disappeared so abruptly a few months before. She had taught English to Khadi's L'École Moyenne class for the past year, but then one day she was just not there. She had apparently gone back to America without telling anyone what she was planning or why. That's what the headmaster, Monsieur Diallo, had told Khadi's class. But Khadi could not understand why her teacher would go without saying goodbye.

Before she'd left, though, Khadi had asked her about the American man who used to ride his bike up to see her. Mademoiselle Jamie had told her that his name was Don, that he knew about medicine and was living in a small village 15 kilometers to the south of the city. She said that he was not her boyfriend, as Khadi had guessed, but only a friend, and she enjoyed his visits. Sometimes Khadi had seen him on these visits, riding through the streets on his bicycle or eating at a Riz Gras restaurant with Mademoiselle Jamie, but now that her teacher was gone, she saw him even more. Almost every week he was at the theater, and he was always looking this intense.

Khadi wondered...

"Oh!" The woman next to her gasped and Khadi turned back to the screen to see what had happened.

The song had finished and a bad man had grabbed the heroine. He was yelling at the hero. Then, he slapped the hero across the face.

The hero staggered backwards, and the bad man came and hit him again.

He punched and pummeled the hero relentlessly, from side to side of the TV screen, and then hit him squarely in the chin, sending him flying into the air, where the hero did a complete 360 degree spin and then landed hard on the ground, blood covering his lips and face.

The bad man began to kick him.

The heroine stood by, eyes wide, holding her hand to her face in anguish. Her eyes moist, she yelled the hero's name: "Ravi!"

Khadi looked at the American. Through all this, he was entranced, staring at the screen fiercely.

The theater was silent except for the thump of the bad man's boot hitting the hero's ribcage.

It did not seem that the hero could survive. He was down, blood all over his face, dirt in his hair, gasping.

But Khadi had seen enough of these films to know that the hero would survive. There would be a turnaround and he would be victorious.

Khadi didn't watch to see. It was the American's reaction she was interested in.

Onscreen, just barely in Khadi's sight, the hero suddenly reached up and caught the bad man's foot. For a moment, the two men stayed in that position, frozen, the villain paused in the middle of his hostile action, the hero's fingers clutching his boot.

Still, Khadi watched the American, who leaned forward

even further. His hand dropped from under his chin and hung loosely over his lap. His neck stretched out. His head jutted forward. He was mesmerized.

Then, back onscreen, with a shout, the hero pushed, and the bad man flew backwards into the air, landing on his back with a jarring thud.

A cheer erupted through the audience of women. They clapped. A few shouted. This was the moment. This was where the tide turned.

The hero jumped up and strode toward the bad man, his fists ready, his face set in angry determination. The soundtrack rose to a victorious, swelling crescendo.

As the music continued to support the hero, the bad man pulled himself backward, trying to stand, his eyes wide in fear.

The men's eyes met, just long enough for the bad man to see that there would be no mercy.

The hero moved...

and suddenly...

Suddenly, there was a shout.

"Yes!"

It came from within the theater, not from the movie.

Everybody turned to where the American was standing, staring wide-eyed at the screen as if it had given him a revelation.

"Yes!" he boomed again, and his eyes didn't move from the screen for a moment.

"Yes!"

And then, without looking at the people around him, he stepped down the aisle and out of the theater.

Immediately, there was an explosion of conversation.

The movie had been forgotten as everyone remarked on the strange foreigner.

Khadi, however, watched for signs of the American's return, a shadow perhaps to fall at the bright, day-lined edges of the sheet in the doorway...

But no shadow came, and he never came back.

Khadi paid little attention to the rest of the movie, lost in her own thoughts even after all of the other women's chatter had quieted down. So lost was she, in fact, that she only registered that the movie was finishing by the fact that all the women were starting to stand up and leave. She gave the TV one last look to see that the hero and heroine were singing again, this time at their wedding, a clear sign that everything had wrapped up in a satisfactory, audience-pleasing way, and then she, too, like the other women, stood up to go.

That night, Khadi continued to think about the American, wondering why he had reacted the way he had. Perhaps, she thought, she might talk to him the next time. Mademoiselle Jamie had, after all, taught her enough English that she could ask how he was.

But when she went to the theater the next week, the American was nowhere to be seen.

Or the week after that.

Or even the week after that.

The American Peace Corps was gone, it seemed, and, just like Mademoiselle Jamie, who had assigned homework on a Wednesday and been gone on the Thursday, nobody knew what had become of him or why he had left.

Khadi's mother said that maybe all white people were crazy, but Khadi wasn't sure. He was gone, said her mother, and that was all there was to it.

Khadi guessed she was right, but still, every week, as Sidiki started the VCR at the front of the theater and the music swelled, she cast her eyes about for a glimpse of the sharp, rapt features of the enigmatic American.

PART ONE

"DOST" MEANS "FRIEND"

CHAPTER ONE
ALL ALONE AND FRIENDLESS

SEATTLE, WASHINGTON, USA

OH, DON, WHY aren't you here?

What do you do when your best friend leaves you and goes off to Africa during the worst year of your life? When he joins the Peace Corps and searches out adventure and you... well, you get kicked out of your house and take a temp job at some huge, but lame, company like misterbook.com?

And what do you do when he stops answering your letters, which you so desperately need to have answered?

And what do you do when all of a sudden this sucky life that you've gotten started and don't know what to do with and don't know how to get out of... What do you do when all of a sudden it gets suckier?

These are the questions I pondered as I stared into the bathroom mirror in the "temp" section on the third floor of misterbook.com's main Seattle building.

Really, I was hiding out.

My lunch break had ended five minutes ago, but I didn't want to go back.

Just before lunch, Donna, my supervisor, had come by my cubicle with a big smile to inform me I was doing a "great" job and they would like me to stay on for another three or four weeks.

"Shayla," she'd said, "we're really enjoying having you work here. Do you like working here?"

I'd smiled and nodded, and ignored the tendril of nausea unfolding in my stomach. Donna was going to ask me to become a full-time temp, I just knew it. She was going to ask me to become the person I was pretending to be… *permanently.*

Ugh.

But I had to pretend because, quite frankly, what else did I have? Other than going from temp job to temp job until I could finally do what I really wanted with my life?

Unfortunately, I had no idea what I really wanted.

Other than I wanted Don to come back.

I looked more deeply into my reflection. Or, well, I looked more deeply into what should have been my reflection. This particular bathroom mirror, the "temp" bathroom mirror, had a problem. It had one of those big distortions that make people's faces seem all out of whack.

The distortion ran right across the mirror from right to left in a big solid line.

Anybody unlucky enough to be in this bathroom saw part of herself seem to melt bizarrely into the mirror. Like, for shorter people, their foreheads might smudge so they looked like one of the little aliens off Tim Burton's awful *Mars Attacks!*, or, for taller people, their chins might seem to be clanking from side to side like a broken manual typewriter as they washed their hands.

As for me, well, the mirror showed me for what I was—a temp, a ghost in the hallway, unfinished, half a person.

And the other half? Well, actually, the more I looked,

the more I thought that mirror made me look like a clam!

The distortion was right where my face was, and it made my face into a big, round, clammy blob. There was my pale skin, ashy white like a clamshell. There were all the little lines and wrinkles and pockmarks looking like the grooves of that clamshell. There was my mouth, clenched and uneven and sharp, just like a clam, just like it'd need a fork to pry it open.

Maybe I'm a geoduck, I thought.

I turned my face sideways and stuck out my tongue. Strangely, this made my brown eyes melt into my mousy-brown hair in the mirror, creating a sedimentary blur. Yes, I really did look like a big clam under murky mud water.

Ugh!

Shayla the clam. Twenty-three years old and hiding under the sand. That sounded like the misterbook me, all right!

"What would you do, Don?" I asked the mirror. "Would you stay here? Oh, I know, you'd run off to Africa and leave me behind."

This was depressing.

I wanted somebody to step in so that I would have to act normal, so that I would be forced to go back to work. To stop thinking like this.

But nobody came, which was even more depressing because I had to find the motivation to leave the bathroom and go back to work all by myself.

If Don had been there, he would have made me feel better. He would have listened to me explain my odd behavior, and he would have given me some good advice, or at least he would have told a joke, or said something really random to make me laugh.

I stared at the contorted Shayla in the mirror.

"Don isn't even on this continent anymore," I told her.

Then I went back to work feeling sad and lost and alone, just like I had when my lunch break began.

***

Who is Don Smith?

Don Smith is my best friend.

He is also, like me, a freak.

Well, maybe he's even a little bit freakier.

The first time we ever talked was in 7th grade Homeroom class on Halloween. He'd been sitting at the desk behind me and Jennifer Abrams since the school year began, but we'd never spoken, not even a brief "hello." This didn't seem strange at the time. Unlike Jen and me, he had come in from a different elementary school and, while Jen and I were always talking, he always seemed aloof. He never talked to anyone. Usually, he spent his time with his head down, intently writing in his notebook.

It was easy to forget he was there. He seemed to just melt into the air behind us.

Until Halloween, that is.

Not many people had dressed up, certainly I hadn't, and those that had had made a coordinated effort—three jocks dressed as women, and all the cheerleaders dressed up as little girls. Other than that, there was one group of alternatively popular kids that had gone for the hippie look, but that was about it. For those of us who weren't part of some major clique, wearing a costume in seventh grade seemed out of the question. If you weren't dressing up in a collective, then you weren't cool unless you were ignoring the holiday.

Don Smith, however, did not ignore it. Alone, all by himself, he had come dressed as a Klingon. And not just any old lame Klingon outfit. He was in full regalia, bony exoskeleton head, sharp teeth, and a silver and black costume. He honestly looked like he had just walked off an episode of *Star Trek: The Next Generation*. I was stunned when I walked into the room. I think my jaw actually dropped. Don was scribbling in his notebook, so he didn't see my shocked look, but Jen Abrams did, and she rolled her eyes in acknowledgment: *What a freak.*

As I walked to my desk and sat down, I saw that I was the only one who really seemed to notice the Klingon behind me. For everyone else, Don Smith was still just melting in, still being ignored. For me, though, something fundamental had changed.

I needed to talk to this person.

He was... different... from everyone else.

"Hey," I said, smiling the guarded, sarcastic smile that I used at the time. Still use, to be honest. "Interesting costume."

The only part of Don that reacted was his eyes. While his mouth stayed set in a grumpy look of concentration and his face remained tilted down toward his notebook, his eyes rolled up to look at me.

...and look.

...and look...

Just when I felt my own smile was going to shatter from forced use, he made one short, simple nod of acknowledgement. Then, with a blink, he changed his focus back to his notebook.

Jen Abrams just stared at me when I turned back to her, the clear message being *Why are you talking to him?*

There was no time to think about it because Mr. Murakami stood up from his desk with a stack of papers in his arms. "Happy Halloween," he said. "I hope that you're all ready for your test." He handed them out with the typical charming Murakami smile. I didn't think it would have been possible to dislike Murakami because of that smile, even if he were failing you and making you stay one more year in seventh grade.

When I got my row's tests, I turned to pass them back to Don, who took them with the same stony face as before, his eyes now unreadable. But as I turned back to my own test, I heard his voice, calm and monotone, saying: "Qapla'." I didn't know what it meant, but he said it in such a way it sounded like "Good luck."

As I worked on the test, I was aware of him behind me, hearing his strong, steady breathing, feeling a little itch between my shoulder blades as if the rustle of the paper and the movement of his pencil behind me were tickling my skin.

It's the feeling you get when somebody you care about is about to touch you, like when I used to pretend to be asleep to annoy my brother and he would eventually stop whining for me to wake up and just grab my arm. Waiting for that moment was a certain form of frightening desire. The Klingon behind me had created that feeling, that insecurity in everything but the fact that I *was* insecure: he could grab me, stick his pencil in my back, whisper terrible things. Essentially, at twelve years old, I had found my first enigma in Don.

I could hardly finish my test, thinking of him behind me, but I finally filled in the last blank just as the bell rang. Beside me, Jen Abrams was still desperately scribbling answers, but not fast enough because Mr. Murakami swiftly came and picked up every test.

"How'd you do?" I asked her.

"Stupid test. Mr. M sucks!" she said, ruining my theory about everybody liking our teacher. She picked up her bag without looking at me. "Later."

As she walked off, I was about to ask Don how he'd done. He was standing up, his books under his arm. Suddenly, somebody shoved the books out from behind him. They leapt briefly into the air and then went crashing to the floor.

"Nice costume, Smith," Erik Anderson sneered, continuing past me in his new junior high letterman's jacket with a big jackass smile. His two friends, wearing similar jackets and sneers, grouped around him toward the door.

"Ha'DIbah!" Don said, between clenched teeth, but loud enough for everybody to hear. Anderson and his friends just sniggered and strode into the hallway, not even caring enough to look back.

Don glared after them for a second, then bent to pick up his books. I knelt down and helped.

"What did you say to him?" I asked.

Don looked at me, very serious, a book half lifted in his hand. "It's Klingon," he said, without a muscle twitching in his set face, "for 'asshole mother fucker.'"

I stared at him, feeling my eyes getting rounder.

Then, for the first time, Don Smith smiled (a big dopey smile, awkwardly offset by his fake fangs) and spoke words that I understood: "Thanks for helping me pick up my stuff."

And the Klingon winked.

DON SMITH
   Latest orders
   The Complete Unofficial Guide to *Deep Space Nine*
   The Bailey Book of Medical Terms and Diseases
   The Iliad
   The Lonely Planet Guide to West Africa
   The Lonely Planet Guide to the Middle East
   The Red Badge of Courage
   The Koran
   War and Peace

My job at misterbook.com was to answer simple email questions about customer's orders and to help them find different products—or, if the question was more complicated, to pass it along to a full time employee.

There were five unanswered messages in my inbox, but I didn't feel like working. Instead, I checked Don's name on the misterbook database.

Again.

The result left me with a dull, dead feeling. It had been May 12th, almost a year and a half ago, that Don had ordered his last book. I had looked at his records maybe a hundred times since working at misterbook, but nothing ever changed. Of course, I knew it wouldn't. He wasn't ordering books from Africa. But I couldn't help myself.

"Hey, Shay," came a voice from above.

I clicked off my screen immediately. For a moment, Don's orders hung there like ghosts, then popped way out of existence, to hide deep down amidst all the other almost-forgotten records crunched together in the misterbook database.

I looked up at the head staring at me from above the cubicle. "Hi, Patel."

"Good lunch?"

"It was all right."

Patel's perfect-toothed head bobbed up and down. "I just got back myself. Let me tell you… that Jack in the Box down the street is good, but their idea of customer service…"

"Service with a crack," I gibed, not thinking.

"Huh?"

"Nothing," I said, hiding a smile. That was one of Don's old sayings: *Wow, that server's really showing us her backside. Service with a crack.* "I know what you mean, Patel. That's why I eat here."

"Oh, eating here… much too depressing, Shay."

"It's all right."

"Well, you'll have to come to lunch with me sometime."

"I know, I know… I'm missing out."

"No, I am. I'm the one being deprived of your company!"

In the world of misterbook.com, Patel was one of my few saving graces. He was Indian, outgoing, kind, and always able to bring my mood up, even if it was only for just a moment. He genuinely wanted to be my friend and I was grateful, even though I wasn't sure I was worth it. That's why I always said no to going to lunch.

He didn't seem to mind. He was always just as friendly, and he always kept offering.

Patel was descending back into his own workspace now, but suddenly stopped, remembering something. "Hey, get your call?"

"Huh?"

"On your cell. I heard it coming from your bag. You must have left it when you went on break."

"Okay. I'll answer it later."

"Righto."

But really I answered it right away, as soon as Patel's head disappeared into his own cubicle, because what else was I going to do? Otherwise, I would have to do my job.

One message, said the screen on my cell phone. Did I want to listen?

Not if it was my mom again. She was always asking when I would come down to visit, even though she was the one who had kicked me out of the house.

I clicked on *Missed Calls* to see who the message was from. The numbers of all the callers flashed up and…

No.

I had to stare at the number for a while to see if it was true.

Don's parents' number.

Which must mean Don, right?

A moment ago I had sent Don deep into misterbook purgatory, and here he was popping up again.

Although it couldn't be him.

Could it?

He was in Africa, wouldn't be back for another year…

Nervously, I clicked to listen to the message.

A deep, nearly monotone voice started up: "Shayla, this is Robert Smith."

Don's father?

"Please give me a call. It's about Don."

Click.

I stared at my phone.

Don's dad? Why would he call me? He didn't even like me. He'd had a plan for Don's future—becoming a doctor— and that plan didn't include a friendship with me.

For Dr. Smith, I had always been a distraction along Don's path to success. There was absolutely no reason he would call me.

Unless…

Terrible possibilities popped up in my mind.

I hit *Call Back* without even thinking, held the phone tight to my ear with my eyes closed. It rang once, twice…

"Hello, you have reached Dr. Bob and Anita Smith. We

are…"

I clicked off my phone and set it down with my heart shaking inside me.

CHAPTER TWO
HOME AGAIN

"DON'S HOME."

These were the words I wanted to hear, but I was afraid to make the call.

What if the words I wanted weren't the words I got?

Don had assured me that Biribiri was a totally safe country, but it was a lot different from America.

Who knew what might have happened?

I was sitting on the Number 48 bus coming home, staring at the cell phone in my hand. The bus was crowded and I was pinched between an art student, who was grasping an unwieldy 3-D model of a building that kept bumping my thigh, and a bulky businessman who wouldn't stop grimacing, as if his day had been worse than anybody else's.

I'd listened to Dr. Smith's message again, but still couldn't make heads or tails of it. It was impossible to tell if he had good or bad news.

As we passed through the University District, with its newsstands and Chinese restaurants and grunge clothes shops, I tried to put the bad possibilities out of my mind. Then, getting off the bus in Greenwood and walking the two blocks to my duplex, I listened to Dr. Smith's message twice more. I wanted to see if there was any clue in his voice that would give me an answer. There wasn't. Not a hint of worry, anger, sadness, or happiness could be discerned in the strict, measured tones of Dr. Smith.

I would have to call.

But I wanted to do it from the comfort of my home. In my bedroom. Where I would have somewhere soft to roll if the news was good.

Or, if it wasn't, somewhere safe to fall.

I shoved the cell phone into my pocket.

By now, I'd reached the driveway of my duplex.

Ugh.

It was a pretty ratty place.

Even though it was a sunny day, the duplex managed to retain the image of rain that Seattle is known for. There was mildew scattered at random intervals across the chipping white paint, dry but droopy leaves hanging from the gutters, and frayed, soggy duct tape patching up our neighbor's window, where somebody had thrown a rock through a month before...

Some people say that you will always remember your first apartment fondly. Not me.

The only nice thing was that my car was there in the driveway to greet me. It was a brown 1988 Hyundai Excel that my mom had bought used right around the time I started high school, but it was in great shape. I smiled to see it now... but...

Drat.

My roommate's mud-spattered Jeep was parked right behind it.

That meant she was home, which was not good news.

My roommate, Heather Swyne, was not an easy person to live with. I'd found her in an ad in the *Seattle Times* the previous October, and rooming with her had offered the benefit of cheap rent and a place a little far away from home. I hadn't considered the negative effects a roommate who was rude, dirty, and overwhelmingly promiscuous would have on me. Unfortunately, now I was stuck with her. Until October, at least.

Luckily, she was hardly ever home.

Usually she was at one of her boyfriends' places.

But not today.

Not when all I wanted to do was get in and call Don's home in peace.

Great.

Despondently, I climbed the three steps to our door and pushed it open.

Heather and her current boyfriend, Aaron, were sitting on our chewed-up sofa, beers in hand. She was sitting sideways on his lap, her heavy arms wrapped around his neck to keep gravity from pulling her down. Poor guy; she was no lightweight. He was looking deep into her eyes.

"Hey," I said.

"Mm," they mumbled, without looking up.

It was obvious from their flushed faces that they'd been up to something, so I was happy to bend away from them to say hi to Heather's cocker spaniel, Noodle, who hobbled over to me from the corner of the room. She was only a year old, but she acted like a senior citizen.

That, I guessed, was the effect of living with Heather. She wasn't exactly the kind of person who would be known as a caregiver. She pretty much only cared about her own needs.

Like now, for instance, I thought, when I straightened up to find Heather and Aaron in the middle of a very deep, embarrassing kiss. Tongue and all.

Disgusted, I tried to sneak past to see the Caller ID box behind them.

Yet, somehow, from deep within Aaron's mouth, Heather saw me. "Oh, yeah…" she mumbled. "I was supposed to tell you. Don's back."

I turned. "What?" I said.

It was hard to believe Heather had really spoken. She was still staring into Aaron's eyes, not looking at me.

"Don's back," she said. "There's, like, five messages.

He says he really wants to see you."

My jaw dropped. So he'd actually called himself!

Don was back!!!

"Who's Don?" said Aaron, indolently, his hand gliding over the arc (mountain?) of her stomach and resting in the deep valley under her breasts. "Her boyfriend?"

"No." Heather arched her back in a stretch that conveniently ended with her breast in Aaron's hand. "She doesn't have a boyfriend."

"Oh."

Aaron bent his neck to kiss her again.

My stomach flipped.

This wasn't right. If I was going to hear that Don was back, I wanted it to be a moment of celebration. This was more like a voyeuristic nightmare!

"Could you move your Jeep?" I blurted. My voice sounded as irritated as I felt.

For the first time, they both looked at me, seemingly shocked that I could be so rude.

"I really have to be somewhere," I said.

I hit traffic as soon as I got on I-5, but I didn't care.

It was a beautiful day. To my right, the Space Needle shone whitely in the sunny August daylight. To the left, a line of cars made their way north, windows open, music playing. Above the cars, beyond the highway, the spectral image of Mount Rainier hung majestically in the sky, its icy peak etched in white and aqua lines.

And 40 miles south, in my hometown, Don Smith was home.

For the first time all day, I felt good.

I put on my sunglasses and pulled out my cell phone. Now was the time to call Don.

There was only one ring at Don's house.

Then, "Hello?"

It wasn't Don.

It was Dr. Smith, sounding uncharacteristically out of

breath, as if he'd run to grab the phone.

"Hi, Dr. Smith?"

"Shaay-laa," he said, drawing my name out longer than necessary. "I'm glad you called."

This was strange. Dr. Smith never called me "Shayla." He only called me "Ms. Yost." And he was never glad I called.

But now he actually did sound happy to hear from me. Hmm...

"Uh... may I speak to Don?" I said.

"You know he's home then? Did you talk to him?" His voice was like a greedy child grasping for sweets, rushed and surreptitious. He was anxious about something.

"I haven't talked to him yet. I think he may have left a message at my house, but I didn't have time to listen..."

"Oh."

"Listen, if you don't mind, I'm driving down now from Seattle. I just wanted to say hi and make sure Don was there."

"Oh, he's here all right, but he's... indisposed... at... the moment." His hand rustled across the receiver and I thought I heard him say something to someone else.

"Is everything okay?" I asked. He was beginning to make me nervous.

A zip as the hand moved away. "Excuse me?"

"Is Don okay?"

"Shayla..." Uncomfortable pause. When he spoke again, it was in the polite, but impersonal, computer monotone of an answering machine message. "...Don's here. I know he will be very happy to see you. Please come soon."

"Uh, okay, but..."

"Drive carefully. We'll be waiting for you."

"Okay..."

The conversation had gotten weird, so I decided not to say anything else. I just waited for Don's dad to say goodbye. But Dr. Smith did not hang up. Instead, there was a long silence and then he asked a question that was so uncharacteristic and random that I almost didn't stop in time to avoid rear-ending the new VW Bug in front of me:

"Shayla, did you ever watch any kind of foreign films with Don in the past?"

"Um…" I paused to check my rear view mirror. The guy behind me had stopped pretty fast too, but there was no damage. "I'm not sure what you mean."

"I mean like films from the Middle East or India?"

"No. The closest we ever got to that was Klingon," I said, allowing myself a smile.

There was a brief pause and then Dr. Smith, the real uncensored Dr. Smith that I knew, muttered in a grumbling voice, "I hate Klingons." There was another pause, and then he spoke again in his nice Dr. Smith voice. "No, no, don't worry about it. We'll see you soon."

And he hung up.

I called my mom.

Sure, she'd kicked me out of the house a year before, and, sure, I hadn't liked it.

But I understood why she'd done it. I'd been graduated from high school for four years and I'd never once talked about leaving home or getting a job. I was stuck in a holding pattern. And she'd put up with it, at least until my younger brother Jack got into his second year and started talking about moving up to Auburn and getting an apartment so he could be close to his classes at Green River Community College. I guess my mom had decided she'd better push me on a little bit, too.

She'd suggested it gently, in a "You know, Shayla, your brother's going to be moving out. Maybe it's time you thought about that, too" kind of way. But I'd responded in anger. Fine! If she wanted me out, I was getting out! I drove to the store right away, bought a *Seattle Times*, and started calling potential roommates. In Seattle, no less, an hour away just to spite my mom.

And that's basically how I'd ended up in my current awful situation.

But I couldn't really blame my parents. They'd been trying to help me, not make my life worse.

They'd failed, but the thought had been there.

The bottom line was they loved me. And I loved them right back.

And if I needed something, I knew they were there to help me.

Especially my mom.

So when Dr. Smith confused the hell out of me on the phone, I didn't hesitate to dial home.

"Oh, Shayla," my mom said when she heard my voice, "I'm soooo glad you called. I've missed you a lot this week."

She was certainly happy to hear from me, much more than Dr. Smith had been, and she wasn't faking.

"Are you coming home this weekend?" she asked.

"I don't know. Don's home," I said, cautiously.

"I know!" Mom gushed. "He called. I gave him your home number. Did you talk to him?"

"No, not yet."

Of *course*. Of course Don had called my mom first. Why hadn't I thought of that? He'd been in Africa when I'd moved to Seattle. When I'd got my new cell number. There was no way he could have known how to reach me. I rolled my eyes at the irony of my wasted day of worrying about the Smiths' call.

"Don's mother called, too," my mother continued. "She sounded urgent, so I gave her your cell number. I hope that's okay."

"It's fine. But, Mom… You talked to Don? How'd he sound? Did he sound okay?"

I knew I sounded a little too eager. My mom was the absolute opposite of Dr. Smith. Where Dr. Smith had always worried that my relationship with Don would be a bad influence, taking away from his son's time to study and join academic clubs, my mom had always looked at Don and pictured some kind of starry-eyed romantic future for us. I don't think I really noticed until somewhere around the ninth grade, but my mom was always looking for signs that I might be interested in a relationship with Don. Getting so excited about his being back must have sounded like one of those signs. But I couldn't help myself.

"Well, he sounded fine, happy... but..." My mom paused. "Well, there was one thing..."

"What?"

"He said 'Yah' a lot."

"'Yah?'"

"Yeah, 'yah.' Like 'yah' this, 'yah' that. 'Have a nice day, yah.' I've never heard so many 'yahs.' He must have picked it up over there."

It didn't sound all that serious to me. "Maybe he joined the Sisterhood," I said.

Mom laughed; she'd read the same books as I had. For four years, we'd borrowed one book a month from the library and taken turns reading them.

"Oh, honey, I miss you. Please come this weekend. Bring Don. Your father and I would so love to see him. He's such a nice bo—young man."

It was pretty obvious that Mom didn't know anything. She'd made me feel better, but it was clear she was about to go into one of her rants about how great Don was and how he'd make some girl happy someday (wink wink nudge nudge). I decided to cut the conversation short.

"Listen, Mom, I'm going to talk to Don now. I'll see if he wants to come up this weekend. I'll let you know tomorrow."

"Okay, hon." Now it was she who sounded eager. "Say hi for me."

"I will."

"Kisses."

"Kisses."

Click.

I looked to my left. There was the Wild Waves theme park, not quite closed up for the day, a small cluster of swimsuit-clad people standing at the top of a wooden tower waiting for their chance at the purple, red, blue, and yellow water slides.

I was getting close to home.

As if to prove me right, there was a light bump and the road smoothed out. Now I was definitely in Pierce County.

Only thirty more minutes and I could see Don… and figure out what on earth was going on.

CHAPTER THREE
CRAZY HEART

DON'S PARENTS LIVE in Yettikum, a small town just outside Tacoma. They have a three-story gray wooden house up on a hill overlooking the Puget Sound. Standing on their porch, one can see the Sound, whitecaps rising across it in furious motion on windy days, and beyond that the islands and a sketchy outline of the Olympic Mountains. Many times, I had pulled into the Smiths' driveway to see Don's parents enjoying a glass of wine on the porch, watching the sunset. This was the one thing that really impressed me about them. They always, always, caught the sunset together.

When I arrived at their house that night, the sun was just disappearing behind Haricot Island and the sky was turning a burnt pink color, but nobody was on the porch to watch it.

Strange.

But I didn't waste much time thinking about it.

I ran for the door. I didn't even bother to lock my car. It was Yettikum after all, not Seattle...

I knocked, my heart pounding. Would Don answer?

A figure appeared behind the glazed glass of the door.

There was a soft click, and the door opened inward.

Not Don.

It was his mom.

"Shayla," she said. "It's a pleasure to see you. Come in. It's been a long time."

"Yeah, it's been a while."

Despite wanting to see Don, I couldn't help the big smile that crept over my face. Don actually didn't like his mom's attitude in front of me, said that it was feigned, that whole June Cleaver thing to impress the few friends he had, but still it made me go all warm inside. It was so unconditional, and so different from my parents. Sure, my parents had always been optimistic around me, but their optimism always seemed to have unspoken dreams for the future behind it. "Oh, you're doing so well" or "You'll get it," or "I'm sure Geometry can't be all that hard. I bet Don will be able to help you a lot," or "Oh, well. Geometry was never really my thing, either, and look at me. I turned out just fine." Really. Compared to Mom and Dad's way of speaking, Anita Smith was a delight.

"Go ahead and take off your shoes and come say hello to Dr. Smith. He's in the living room."

I wanted to go downstairs to Don's room right away—the door to the stairs was right in front of me behind Don's mom—but politeness made me slip off my shoes.

I padded into the living room, where Smith sat on one of the sofas bent over a glass of red wine. He looked at me with a grumpy, I-don't-want-to-be-bothered expression, but then he seemed to realize something and stretched his lips quickly, and briefly, into a smile. I mouthed the word "hi" silently.

Anita Smith followed me in with two glasses, one wine, one ginger ale. She handed me the ginger ale and sat on the sofa across from her husband.

I stood awkwardly between them, wondering what to do. I shot one look back at the door to Don's downstairs room, then took a brief, nervous look around the living room. The Smiths had apparently fallen in love with crystal since the last time I'd been here: crystal decorations were everywhere, from the coffee table to the bookshelf to the shelves above the fireplace. I also noticed the muffled sound of what seemed to be Arabic music coming from somewhere in the house, and wondered if Mrs. Smith was going through some kind of eastern phase. She was always switching up hobbies and decorations like this.

Mrs. Smith patted the sofa, and I was obliged to sit down next to her.

"What are you doing these days?" she asked, in a joyful, interested voice that, to give Don credit, sounded remarkably false.

"Well, I've got a place up in Seattle. I'm working for misterbook.com."

"Oh, misterbook.com. Aren't they the book sellers on the computer?"

"Yeah, they are."

"Oh, that sounds interesting, doesn't it, Robert?"

Dr. Smith glared at her. He put down his wineglass and turned to look at me, pressing his fingers together as if praying. "Listen, Shayla, Don…"

He paused, cocked his head. I noticed it, too. The music had stopped.

"Shayla." Dr. Smith's voice was urgent. He spoke quickly, as if he were afraid he would be interrupted. "Don is—"

He was interrupted.

At first the noise was soft, hardly discernible. It came from downstairs, a repeated slapping sound that came in quick bursts of two, and quickly gained in volume and tempo. I knew what it was immediately, remembered it from the many visits I'd made in high school after Don moved to the basement—Don, running up the stairs two at a time in his socks, coming to greet me.

And here he was.

He dashed into the living room like a star into the spotlight, completely oblivious to the serious mood of his parents. "Hey, Shay! How are you? Come downstairs." He turned around and ran back, his feet beating a return journey down the stairs.

I stood… and Mrs. Smith stood with me, grabbing my ginger ale arm. "Shayla, I need to tell you…" Her voice was a whisper: "Don has really changed."

"What do you mean?" I asked. He'd seemed about the same to me. Hectic and irreverent. Just the way his dad didn't like.

"Well, he's all right… in one way…" Anita said.

"Physically," grunted Dr. Smith.

"But in other ways, well, we're concerned about him."

"Mentally," was Smith's contribution.

"For one thing, he says he doesn't want to be a doctor anymore. He says that's not what he thinks his destiny is any longer."

So that's what this was about, I thought. Don was breaking off from the path they'd designed for him. He was finally rejecting the idea of doctorhood. Good for him, I thought.

"And right now, Don—"

But the voice from the bottom of the stairs cut in. "Shay, come on!"

I felt harassed, and completely uncomfortable. I looked to the door, then back to Don's parents. "I'd… better go down," I said.

Anita Smith moved her hand from my arm to my shoulder. "Shayla, we think Don's going to ask you to do something…"

"What—?" I started.

But Dr. Smith interrupted. "Don't even think of doing it."

"Dr. Smith's right, Shayla," said Mrs. Smith. "It will be best for everybody if you say no."

She gave my arm a meaningful squeeze and let me go.

I got my first good look at Don as I came down the stairs. He was wearing a button down shirt, the color of smoked salmon, with large bleach-stained patches, and a mismatched pair of some kind of blue, billowing African pants, something like oversized pajama bottoms, but made of a fabric I'd never seen before. Also, he looked like he'd lost weight, although he'd been thin to begin with, but otherwise, he was the same old Don: blonde hair, blue eyes, and a bent, pointy nose that jutted out like an armadillo's. Without the nose, he would probably have been very handsome. As it was, his looks were striking, in a decidedly Sherlock Holmes way, but he fell between Average and Modestly Good-Looking.

At that moment, his hand was on the doorknob of his bedroom door, ready to twist. As I came down the stairs, studying him, he turned with imploring eyes: *Hurry up.* I rolled my eyes at him—*what's the rush?*—And he broke into that great, big, wide unaffected smile that he has.

And—

Oh God—scratch everything I've just said.

It's the smile. That smile lights him up and makes him handsome. It got me that Halloween behind a Klingon mask, and it still had me right then at that moment. I had missed Don so much it hurt.

Afraid my face, a great traitor to me, might show all this emotion, I quickly said something disparaging:

"I thought the Peace Corps was *two* years," I said.

Ouch! That was too much. I didn't even know why he'd come back. Judging by his parents' attitudes upstairs, something could really be wrong with him. And here I was saying that.

But he didn't even seem to notice.

"Shay!" he bellowed, and pounced up the three stairs between us. He wrapped his arms around me and spun me in a crazy circle, nearly bashing me against the wall and ceiling. It was a miracle that my ginger ale managed to stay in its glass. Finally, he set me down in front of his door, and pulled me close again in a cellophane hug. "I am so glad you're here!"

Okaaaay…

He unwrapped me.

"When did you get back?" I gasped.

"Yesterday."

Yesterday. That made sense. He'd probably sent from Africa to tell me, but his message hadn't arrived yet... but...

"What's up with your parents calling me?"

"They called you?"

"Yeah. It really freaked me out. I thought something had happened to you."

"Something *always* happens to me." He winked and smiled at my face, then saw how concerned I was. For a moment, his smile faltered, but he shrugged it off. "My parents... Ignore them. I just told them something that I shouldn't have. I should have known better than to mention it." He shook his head to free that thought, then clapped his hands on my shoulders. "Come in my room. I need to talk to you about something."

I remembered what his room had been like the first time I'd seen it when we were seventh graders: there had been a full-sized cardboard standup of Worf (his absolute favorite), various posters of the *ST:TNG* crew, and a model replica of the Starship Enterprise hanging from the ceiling. He was absolutely a *Star Trek* fan. It was like entering a shrine to the series. Through high school, the move downstairs, and his time away working on a pre-med degree in Georgia, the posters had begun to disappear and the Enterprise had found its mission in the closet, but every time I had been here since that first time, Worf was always there, standing stolidly in the corner.

Now Don opened the door and beckoned me to go in for the first time in over a year. So many times we had spent here talking and talking about nothing and everything, while his parents worried upstairs that we might be doing something else.

Even once...

But no... it was better not to think about that now...

I focused on Don's room, and the differences I saw there.

The first thing I noticed was the music. It was the same Middle Eastern sound I'd heard upstairs. Don had turned it down, but it was definitely coming from the surround sound stereo of his entertainment center, slightly jazzy music in a foreign language, but I swear I heard some English in there, something like "You are great, ya, you are great, ya, ya ya aap mahan hain." The second thing I noticed was that Worf was nowhere to be seen. And the third thing I saw was that Worf had been replaced.

Big time replaced.

Everywhere there were posters of dark-skinned, dark haired people, ladies with thick eyelashes and wraparound dresses and men with big hairdos doing their best to look cool in leather jackets. One man with round lips, and a nose almost as big as Don's, seemed to be the center of the poster collection; I also saw his face on the TV, which Don had on, but with the volume turned off. On TV the man didn't look so good; he was lying on the ground beside what looked like a country train station, his face ripped and bruised as a group of guys with guns kicked, punched, and threw him flying through air and space to reality-defying altitudes. He was unconscious, and the gun-toting thugs were giving themselves high fives when I turned back to Don.

"Who are these people?" I asked.

"They're stars," he said, approaching one of the posters (a good-looking but heavy eye-browed lady in white muslin) with what very much seemed like lust. "This is Kajol, and Salman Khan, and Aishwarya Rai and... (here he paused, reaching out to the middle poster reverentially, as if he could hardly believe)... *Rahul Ghosh*," and then, for no good reason, he began to sing. "He is great, ya, he is great, ya…" Then he looked at me expectantly.

"Okaay," I said, slowly.

"Oh, ya ya ya, yes he is great," Don sang, and I had the feeling that I'd been supposed to join in with him for that last line.

"All right, but where is this Raoul from? He's definitely not African."

"Ra*h*ul!" Don corrected me exuberantly. "From India! He's a Bollywood star. An action star. A true star."

A numbness spread up my back and concentrated at the nape of my neck. I shivered. There was something definitely off here. Don had gotten lost in things before, like his fascination with Klingons, but this felt different. This felt like more than a hobby. And did I detect a hint of an Indian accent in those last few sentences?

I reexamined the room. Everything pointed to Don's infatuation. Besides the posters and the TV, Don's shelves were cluttered with stacks and stacks of ratty-looking video tapes, many of them labeled in handwritten Arabic-type script. On the bed was a half-full suitcase which seemed to have exploded. What was inside was folded or packed badly, but around the suitcase was a pile of unfolded, unkempt clothing, and on top of these unhappy clothes lay a magazine called *Stardust* with more Indian people on the cover. Finally, on the bed stand, was a—thankfully unopened—package of sandalwood incense.

"So," I said, letting the idea roll around my brain for a second, before bouncing it out as a confused question. "You spent a year in Africa with the Peace Corps and now you love Indian movies?"

Don didn't answer. What he did instead was something that came as a total surprise. I would come to gather later that it wasn't such a strange thing to find Indian movies in other countries. In fact, as Don would later tell me, more people worldwide watched Indian movies than American movies. But I didn't learn that until later.

Because this is what Don did...

He spread his arms wide above his head, gave the broadest, wildest smile he could have given, and pronounced: "I am in love!"

He clasped my shoulders abruptly with his hands and looked at me with eyes that expressed hope, joy, and very possibly malaria.

***

"What?" I asked after a considerable pause. "With Indian movies?"

"No, no, no," Don laughed and to my surprise picked up a pair of crumpled pants from the discarded pile on his bed and began to fold them. "With a woman." He set the folded pants in the suitcase, and looked up to gauge my reaction.

My head was reeling with non-sequiturs. "Are you *packing* a suitcase?"

"Of course. I told you, didn't I, yah? I am in love. That's why I called you here." He sat on the bed and gave me his most sincere look. "Shay, the fact is that I need you. I need you badly."

I felt dizzy. Don needed me. Badly. This almost made up for the fact that he was turning into an Indian before my very eyes. He really had just said "yah," hadn't he? With an unmistakably Indian accent.

I sat down next to him.

Who could he have fallen in love with? What did he mean by "love" anyway? He'd been away for a year and a half. He'd left me here in Washington all alone for a year and a half, left me to suffer the worst year of my life alone, and now he was in love? It was impossible.

But seeing his clear blue eyes focused on me, imploring me, I couldn't say these things.

"What do you need?" I asked.

"I want you to come on an adventure with me, Shay."

His accent was now full-blown Indian.

I took a sip of my ginger ale, stared at the TV. Rahul Ghosh was now dancing about in front of a windmill with some beautiful Indian lady in a sari and a whole crowd of people as if he were in a Broadway musical. Even the guys with guns who had beaten him earlier were there, smiling and dancing as if nothing had ever happened.

"What adventure?" I asked, finally. There were other questions in my mind, of course, but this was the only one I felt remotely comfortable asking.

"I need you, Shay. I'm going to meet my love and I need you with me."

His *love*?

"Your *what*? Who… Where are…?"

"Her name is Devi Chakraborty… no relation to *Disco Dancer*… and she lives in Atlanta."

I nearly choked on my ginger ale.

The sky over Haricot Island looked as if somebody had hit it. As I pulled out of Don's driveway, I noticed that the pink and red glow had deepened into a big bruise, dark, purple, and swollen, hanging over the Puget Sound. By the time I drove past our old high school and out of Yettikum, it was completely dark.

I'd had to get out of there, had to leave Don. I'd been trembling, had had to clamp my hands on the steering wheel so I didn't lose control as I pulled away from his house. What he was asking for was too much. I told him that, but then it had gotten even worse.

"Come to Atlanta with me, Shay," he said. "I want you to be with me. I need you." He wanted me to drive to Atlanta with him, to tell this girl, this Devi Chakraborty, that he loved her. I'd never even heard of her.

All I could say was, "When?"

And that's when it got worse.

"This Sunday," he said.

"Sunday!" It was only three days away. "Are you crazy?"

"It has to be Sunday. Sunday is Raksha Bandhan."

"Raksha what?"

"Raksha Bandhan. The celebration of brothers and sisters. I've never had a real sister, but I feel like you've always been there for me. I very much want you to be with me on my trip."

"Oh… so I suppose it doesn't have anything to do with me having a car when you don't."

For all I knew, it may have been true. Don had sold his car right before he left for Africa and I hadn't seen any sign of a new one. Nonetheless, Don seemed genuinely hurt and surprised. "Not at all," he said, wide-eyed.

"Do you know what you're asking me to do?" My voice was rising and I couldn't control it. It was the first time I'd felt this frustrated in a long time. "I've just gotten my life back. Do you know I've been living with my parents for four years! Four years! And finally I'm out, I'm doing something, I've got a job, I've got an apartment, and a roommate, and you expect me to just drop everything to help you go meet some girl in the South? Do you think that's reasonable?"

"Shay, it wouldn't be reasonable if you liked any of the things you have now, but you don't, do you?"

"What?"

"I know. Your mother told me: you're miserable."

Oh Mom, thank you. Thank you so much. That really helped.

"I need to work," I said. "I need the money."

Don flashed a brief smile, lifted the clothes pile to reveal a wad of hundred-dollar bills. "Peace Corps savings. It's enough to get to Atlanta and back and to help you pay your rent until you get another job."

This was going too fast. I put my hands to my head and squeezed my temples, not because I had a headache, but to keep my head from exploding. "I can't do this," I said.

"Think about it, Shay," said Don. "I want you with me. I could buy a car if I wanted, but I want you with me. And anyway, you need this. You need an adventure."

I pulled my fingers from my forehead decisively. "What I need," I said, staring him in the eyes, "is to go home. I've got to work tomorrow."

"Think about it, Shay." His blue eyes were worried, pleading, innocent, as he sat on the bed watching me.

I already had my hand on the doorknob. "I'll call you tomorrow." I pulled the door open and then looked at him one last time. "You're insane, you know that, Don?"

He smiled... a soft, lovely smile.

"Dil deewana hai," he said. "The heart is crazy."
And I left.

Driving home, I thought about all the things Don had done for me.

Ever since we'd met, he'd been there to help me if I needed it. When I was having trouble with Geometry in the eleventh grade, he'd spent hours and hours explaining different equations and functions to me, and I'd ended up with a "B" in the class, which, for me, was very good. When my grandmother died, he'd held my hand and let me cry. He'd even put up with all the chaos that was my relationship with Brad Newton, and when I broke up with Brad right before senior prom, Don had been the one to take me. We'd even managed to stay friends after what happened the night before he left.

Don's plan was a crazy one, but by the time I got home, I'd made up my mind.

I had to go.

It was lunatic, but it was like Don said.

The heart is crazy.

CHAPTER FOUR
THE GIRL WHO'S LEAVING

THE NEXT MORNING, I shook hands with Donna and returned to my desk, trembling. I'd felt like she might be hurt. After all, just the day before she'd thought she might have me as a full time employee, and here I was saying today was my last day. But no, she'd taken the news surprisingly well.

This was going to be easier than I thought.

I logged onto my computer and checked the time. 7:55. Five minutes to just kick back before work started. I leaned way back in my chair and closed my eyes, taking in those last few minutes of relaxation—

"You are great, ya, you are great, ya, ya ya aap mahan hain!"

This familiar bit of song came at me like a barrage of artillery fire from the next cubicle. I jumped, and both I and the chair fell over backwards. When I opened my eyes, I was staring up at the ceiling tiles. I was still in the chair, but on the floor now, and my head was sticking out in the hallway. I flailed my arms and legs to maneuver my way off the chair, feeling for all the world like an overturned turtle.

I'd managed to get on my hands and knees by the time Patel popped his head out of his cubicle. "Shayla! What— Are you all right?" He leapt to my side and helped me up, one hand on my arm, one on my shoulder.

How embarrassing.

Patel bent to pick up my chair. "What happened?"

"I got surprised. I fell down."

He followed my eyes back to his cubicle, where the song was still playing, but much quieter. "Oh, I'm so sorry. My sister sent this video file to me. I didn't realize the volume was all the way up."

"That's okay. Rahul Ghosh, right?" I stepped past him, and looked curiously at his computer screen. It was the same Rahul Ghosh, all right, the same guy who had so miraculously survived a savage beating on Don's TV screen the night before and then done a group dance in front of a windmill. In the RealPlayer video on Patel's screen, Rahul was shown on numerous stage sets, each time his costume changing to match his new environment, and to show him as a great man. A bevy of women—whose clothes also changed accordingly—followed him singing the "You are great" line, then Rahul would sing something in Hindi that I didn't understand, something that presumably dealt with how "great" he was. I watched him change from being Napoleon in the Alps to some guy wearing what I think is called a Nehru suit to Michael Jackson doing "Bad," and hummed along with the tune when he became Gandhi.

"You know Rahul Ghosh?" Patel asked. He'd been watching me quietly. Maybe he was trying to assess whether or not I had a concussion.

"Oh, I've got a friend who likes him. A *lot*."

"Yeah, he's my sister's favorite." Patel closed out the video just as Rahul Ghosh was donning an Italian suit and pointing a gun for a James Bond impression. "Ya ya aap mahan—" Click.

"Shayla, I'm really sorry I surprised you. Let me make it up to you. How about lunch today? My treat?"

"Lunch?"

"Yeah, you know, food. That stuff that makes the human body go."

"Oh, Patel, I'm sorry, but I can't. This friend—I promised I'd call him on my lunch break."

His eyes narrowed. "Nothing too serious, I hope?"

"Well, it's weird, that's all."

He smiled. "Oh, well. Another time, I guess. I promise I'll get you out to lunch sometime… I owe you now. As long as your friend wouldn't object."

"Uh…"

"Maybe next week, huh? I see I'll have to schedule ahead."

It had gone easy with Donna, but Patel was going to make this hard. What was with him and lunch, anyway?

"Listen, Patel, this thing with my friend—"

"Mm-hmm."

"It's kind of serious."

"Oh."

"No—it's just—About lunch. I can't do it because I'm leaving. I told Donna this morning."

"What do you mean?"

"I mean this is my last day."

Patel stared at me a while. Finally:

"You're… leaving?"

"Yes."

"*Leaving* leaving?"

"Yes."

"As in you've quit and you're leaving?"

"That's right."

"But I thought—Didn't they offer you—They said—"

"Yes, they offered me the job, but… Well, this is more important. I've got to make sure Don—"

"Don."

"Yes, Don."

"That's your friend."

"Yes. I've got to make sure that he's okay."

"Of course you do."

Patel looked at the wall, clucked his tongue, shook his

head a bit.

"Patel, I'm sorry." I didn't know why I was sorry, but I had to say something.

He shook his head more vigorously. "There's no need," he said, then stuck out his hand. "I wish you all the luck in the world." He gave my hand two quick pumps and let it go. "Okay, I'll let you get on with your work. I know you've got things to do." He sidestepped into his cubicle with a curt little nod.

I stood in the hallway for a second holding my hand out in front of me like an injured puppy. What was that?

Then I ducked back into my own cubicle.

I'd felt like a ghost my whole time temping at misterbook.com, but now that I was leaving, it was as if I'd become some kind of a celebrity. I'd never gone out of my way to get to know anybody, except for Donna and Patel, but suddenly people I had never even seen before were coming up to me to congratulate me and wish me well. I was the one that was getting away, so everybody wanted to talk to me.

Everybody except Patel.

He never once popped his head over his cubicle to say hi, and the one time I went to talk to him, he was on the phone and waved me away. He even stood up and left when I entered the break room, leaving me to talk to another tech guy, Billy, who immediately said, "Man, you're brave. I wish I could quit."

Then, an hour and a half before work was over, Patel left his cubicle and didn't come back.

Fine. If he wanted to spend his last day sulking about me leaving, it didn't matter to me. It didn't make any sense. We'd had a lot of conversations at the cubicle and ended up in the break room together many times, and he was the person I'd been on friendliest terms with, but if he wanted to end it this way, I didn't care. It wasn't like I was ever going to see him again.

I picked up my paper bag full of all my cubicle stuff and headed out, giving Patel's space an acid glance on the way.

Goodbye, misterbook.com. Good riddance. I will never be back.

I pushed the down button on the elevator, tapped my foot, looked straight ahead.

BING! The door slid open and I found myself facing Patel. His breath was coming in quick bursts as if he'd been running and he held a Safeway box in his hands.

"Shay!" he gasped. "Thank God you're still here. I was afraid I'd miss you."

I stared at him. The elevator started to close and he rushed out.

"Listen, I'm sorry if I was a jerk today. I was just surprised to hear you were leaving."

He handed me the box. I looked down through the clear plastic window on top to the chocolate cake inside. In pink cursive icing on top, it read: GOOD LUCK TO A GREAT FRIEND.

I blushed.

I hadn't been much of a friend, great or otherwise.

Unbidden, the lyrics to the Rahul Ghosh song played in my head. "You are great, ya, you are great, ya..."

"You didn't need to—"

"Sure I did. Listen—You've been like a ray of light sitting next to me." I gave him a disbelieving look. "I mean it," he protested. "The guy before you was always picking his nose. It was DIS-gusting."

I laughed. Patel smiled.

"Listen, I know you're on your way out. Go home, enjoy your cake, but don't forget—" He extracted a business card from his wallet. "I still owe you a lunch."

"Okay." I pretended to look at the card, then deposited it in my purse. "Thanks, Patel."

"Absolutely. I honor my obligations."

An elevator was opening and I took my chance.

"Bye, Patel. And thanks for the cake."

"See ya, Shay. And really—feel free to call whenever."

The doors slid closed and Patel, misterbook, that whole lifestyle, slid closed with it.

The cake was nice, but now it was time to really *be* a great friend.

To Don…

No matter how crazy his plan seemed…

CHAPTER FIVE
PEPPERMINTS AND PAPRIKA

DID I SAY Don's plan seemed crazy?

Forget that.

It was Don himself who was crazy.

I saw that immediately when I pulled into his driveway on Sunday morning.

He may have been out there when I visited him on Thursday, obsessed with Rahul Ghosh and finding his Indian "love" and speaking in a fake Indian accent, but none of that prepared me for what was in front of me now.

Don was at the end of the driveway, sitting Native American-style behind a small polished wood coffee table that he had liberated from his parents' den. He was wearing the same blue pants he'd worn the night before, but now he had completed his costume by including the top, a large loose-fitting plastic-looking affair whose bottoms hung down close to his knees.

The table before him seemed all arranged for some bizarre magical ritual. In the middle of the table was a strange wooden bowl, and on both edges stood incense sticks, thick smoke streaming upward from their tips.

Hazed in the smoke, Don's face was a study in serious concentration, his eyes hidden under a pair of sunglasses. He was sipping from a steaming mug that might have been tea or, judging by his set up, could have been eye of newt for all I knew.

I'd met Klingon Don and Indian Don. Now, apparently, I was getting my introduction to Voodoo Don.

It was with some trepidation—and the firm knowledge that I had parked ten feet away—that I opened my car door.

As soon as my feet touched the pavement, Don hopped up and spread his arms wide, as if he could embrace me from there.

"Shayla," he boomed. "My sister!" He was still using his Indian accent, but it wasn't as pronounced as it had been before.

I followed the incense smoke upward with my eyes to the deck where, as suspected, his parents sat. They had pulled their chairs up close to the railing and were watching us with the kinds of stoic expressions I imagine are reserved for when a family member shows public signs of insanity.

I quickly turned my attention back to Don.

"Don, what is this?" I said, attempting to put a little laughter into my voice so that he thought I was feeling *Oh you wacky guy* instead of *Uh-oh, my best friend is really going cuckoo for Cocoa Puffs*.

"Raksha Bandhan. I told you the other night. It's an Indian ceremony. The celebration of sisters and brothers. Come on over here."

"Okay, but I mean what are you wearing?"

"Oh, this? It's a boubou. I brought it from…"

He paused and then, instead of saying "Africa," he said…

"…while I was in the Peace Corps."

His eyes got distant for a moment, troubled, and then he smiled again: "It's really comfortable. I was going to go to the Indian store to get something Indian to wear, but my father wouldn't let me borrow the car…" He looked venomously up at the deck where his father's stare was returned impassively. "Anyway," he said, "the important thing is Raksha Bandhan."

He took my hand and led me to the table. The bowl in the middle turned out to actually be a wooden fruit and nut serving bowl with three compartments, but there was no fruit or nuts inside. Instead, Don had filled the individual compartments with first little mints, then a long and ugly hand braided bracelet, and finally a colorful red powder. I leaned closer to see what the red powder was—paprika?—and took in a whiff of sandalwood incense. I sneezed and red powder puffed across the table.

Don quickly took my hands. "Shayla, like I said before, Raksha Bandhan is the celebration of the brother and sister. It shows that we care for each other, and that we will protect each other from any danger. Here's how it works. First, tie the rakhi to my wrist."

I looked at him blankly, and he held up his wrist.

"Oh, the bracelet?" I picked it up. It was made of hideous thick blue and yellow yarn and it was obvious that Don had done it himself, probably pillaging his mother's drawers for the material. I tied it to his wrist.

"Next, the sister puts the kumkum powder on the brother's forehead."

"Huh?"

"Like this." He dipped his index finger into the red powder and put a streak on my forehead. I sniffed. Definitely paprika. But if Don wanted to believe it was some special Indian powder, I wasn't about to disillusion him. It was obvious that he'd read about the ceremony somewhere and put it together the best he could from what was in his parents' house.

"Now you do it to me," said Don, indicating the paprika.

"Do I need to?"

"Please."

I did as he said.

Finally, Don picked up two of the little mints and unwrapped them. "Now, something sweet. You give me a sweet and I'll give you the other." He handed me one of the mints and then held his up between his thumb and index finger.

And then, before I could lift my own mint, he was leaning toward me… very close toward me… holding the mint right up to my lips. A warmth spread through me. He was so close I could feel his heat, his face so near mine that our kumkum powder—or paprika patches—almost touched, and between our faces was his hand, pushing the little mint gently toward my still-closed mouth. Suddenly, softly, the tip of his index finger made contact, brushing my upper lip, and I opened up quickly and accepted the mint. As its sweetness washed over my tongue, I felt his fingernails slowly withdraw from my closing lips.

"Uh…" I said.

What were his parents making of this, I wondered.

"Oh," said Don, "you dropped your mint."

I had.

"Oh, whoops—"

But Don wasn't done. He leaned in even closer, his eyes wide and blue and sincere, his lips slightly parted.

Oh my God…

Was Don going to kiss me?

And could I let him kiss me?

My best friend, my potentially crazy best friend?

The answer, apparently, was yes.

Without thinking, I let my head tilt back.

Above me, an image swirled: Don's father, standing at the railing looking down at me, his mouth open to speak; Anita Smith's hand touching his elbow, stopping his mouth.

I closed my eyes.

Don's minty breath moved closer. I smelled both mint and incense at the same time, the fragrances mixing delightfully. I felt his breath now on my face, warm and wonderful. His forehead was touching mine now, our spices really coming together. My heart thumping. His hands clasping my shoulders. His sweet breath warming my lips, my lips parting to take the kiss, but not yet… the warm

breath moving now, caressing my cheek, my hair, my...
ear....

What?

Then: "Shayla," he whispered in my ear, soft and deep and meaningful. "Shayla..."

"Mmm," I breathed, my eyes still closed, the heady incense seeming to curl within my brain and make me numb.

"I want you to know that I love you..."

My heart skipped a beat.

"...and that you really are like a sister to me."

My heart tripped and fell.

"I want you to know," Don continued, "that I will always protect you, under any circumstances, that I will always take care of you."

He gave me a gentle squeeze on my shoulder and stepped away, leaving me there with my tilted head, closed eyes, and beating heart.

I don't usually swear, but...

Dammit.

I snapped my eyes open, feeling embarrassed and cheated and...

There was Don with a huge smile, rubbing his hands together in glee. "And that's the celebration of Raksha Bandhan. We have recognized each other as brother and sister now." He held up his wrist and admired the bracelet. "You have shown you wish me well, and I have promised to care for and protect you."

I wanted to rip that bracelet off his wrist. Wish him well? After that?

I opened my mouth; he held up his hand.

"No time to chat. We've got to go." He bent quickly and pulled his suitcase from under the table. Then he fast-walked to the trunk of my car. "*Really*. Let's *go*."

It didn't take long to figure out why he was in a rush.

A low, angry voice assailed us from above. "What's going on here?"

It was Dr. Smith. I looked up to the deck where he was still standing, glaring down at us, his face reddening. I suddenly noticed that I was standing completely in his shadow.

"I—" I said.

Don's hand was on my shoulder.

"Get in the car, Shayla," he said, softly. I stood, petrified to the spot.

"Well?" demanded Dr. Smith. "What is this, Don?"

Don stepped in front of me, taking the full force of his father's shadow and enveloping me in his own. "It's all right, Papa-ji," he said, the Indian accent suddenly back and fully in control and probably way over the top. "Shay and I are just going on an adventure. Goodbye, Ma!"

Anita Smith raised her hand and gave a weak wave. Dr. Smith did not move at all until Don turned and, his arm over my shoulder, steered me toward the car.

That's when Dr. Smith lost control. "You're not going anywhere. I demand to know where you're going! Tell me right now where you're going!"

Don turned very slowly. "Papa-ji," he said, softly and remarkably reasonably, "it's really quite simple. I have fallen in love and I'm now going to find this woman and bring her back to you. You may not approve of my going, but it is something that I must do. Love is more important than anything. Thank you for understanding me, and letting me go. Your support means everything to me."

Don turned and grabbed my hand. "Let's go, Shay."

As he pulled me to the car, his father shouted, "I'm not supporting you. You don't have my support!"

Don opened the driver's seat door and gently nudged me in, then ran to his own side.

"I forbid you to go," his dad was yelling. "Do you hear me, Don? I forbid it!"

"Key?" said Don.

My mind numb, my eyes on Dr. Smith, I turned the key.

Now Dr. Smith was looking straight at me. "Don't do this, Yost!" he screamed. "Can't you see he's sick? He needs to be here with us! He needs help."

"Go ahead and take off the emergency brake and back

up," said Don calmly, imploring me with his blue eyes. All attention was on me now, Don paying no attention to his father, just looking at me, and his father glaring down at me, his voice getting louder and his face getting redder and redder, a whistling tea kettle. Mesmerized by Dr. Smith's face, I obeyed the words at my ear and let up the emergency brake with my foot. I put the car in reverse and began backing up.

Now Dr. Smith was moving. He ran to the porch stairs and bounded down toward the driveway, yelling, "You're not going anywhere!"

Beside me, gently, Don said, "Shay…" I looked at him out of the corner of my eye, noticing that Dr. Smith had now reached the driveway. "Go," said Don, just as gently as before. "Fast."

I pushed my foot down on the accelerator, not too much, but enough to bring us out of the driveway and into the street. I jerked my car back into Drive.

"Wait a second," said Don and I paused. His dad was running quickly down the driveway, almost to us. Don rolled down his window, stuck out his arm… and waved. "Bye, Ma. Bye, Papa-ji. I'll see you soon!"

"Don't you call me Papa-ji," yelled his father, still running.

"All right, Shay," said Don, leaning back in his seat and calmly pulling on his seatbelt. "Drive."

I didn't need to be told. I hit the accelerator just as Dr. Smith's outstretched fingers came down on the roof of my car. I heard them squeak across the smooth top and saw him jump away as the car moved.

"Ms. Yost!" he screamed angrily and pathetically as we sped up the street, and then, "Come back!" he screamed in a questioning, and defeated, tone when I stopped twenty feet away at the stop sign. But, other than observing the law, I didn't hesitate. We turned onto the main street out of Yettikum and Dr. Smith tilted out of view in my rearview mirror.

"All right!" said Don.

"What?" I said. My fingers were wrapped tight around

my steering wheel, my knuckles white. My heart was pounding like hip-hop.

"That was really great, Shay." Don was laughing and slapping the dashboard. "Really great, yah."

"What?" My heart was still pounding, but the fear was changing... into anger. Anger specifically for Don. I scanned the side of the road.

"What you did. You are really terrific." His voice took on even more of an Indian rhythm... if that was possible... the emphasis joyfully cresting on syllables that just didn't sound right coming from Don.

"Oh yeah?" I said, seeing my opportunity on the left. It was the gravel parking lot of Frontier Junior High School, our old school. I veered across the street and brought the car to a jolting halt in front of the old playing field.

"What are you doing?" Don asked in surprise. "What's wrong?"

"What's wrong?" I said. "You tell me what's wrong. What was that back there? What is wrong with you, Don?"

"I—"

"Tell me this whole Indian thing is an act like what you used to do with that Klingon costume. Tell me that much. Tell me because I'm starting to think your dad might be right and you *are* sick. You're definitely making me feel crazy. So what is up with you?"

The whole time I'd said this, I'd been facing straight ahead, staring at my fingers wrapped around the steering wheel. Now I whipped my head around and looked at him.

Don was giving me his most intense look of concentration, something he always did when he was listening hard. Although most of the time he got carried away by his own thoughts and interests, he had the most disarming way of becoming absolutely selfless when he realized that other people needed help, which was really his most magical quality, and one that I loved.

"Shay," he said, and his accent softened to somewhere between Indian Don and normal Don. He reached out and placed his hand on my shoulder. In spite of myself, I felt a tingle go up my spine. "I am really sorry. I didn't mean to freak you out." He gave my shoulder a squeeze, and looked into my eyes. I didn't want to, but I nodded; as if this was some kind of an answer to my question, which it wasn't. "Listen, Shay… do you trust me?" Don said.

His face seemed so innocent. I studied it for a moment, watched his unwavering eyes, his smooth forehead, his slightly parted lips. He was being patient, giving me time to answer, thinking only about me now and not Rahul Ghosh or India or Raksha Bandhan… At least I don't think those things crossed his mind. I nodded slowly.

"Good," Don said. "You know, Shay…" and here he broke contact, looking down just briefly, his forehead creasing with a passing concern, but it was only a very brief moment because he was looking at me again in an instant, his face as smooth and bright as before… "Some things happened while I was gone… I don't really want to talk about them… they were bad things, very bad things… and if I'm acting a little odd, that's why…" He touched my hand. "But please don't worry. I'm alright. I'm doing the right thing, and I'm happy with who I am now. Everything is good with me, and I won't let anything happen to you. Okay?"

I watched him carefully. I had a ton of questions, but something told me that Don was being as open as he could. Something bad had happened to him while he was gone. What? But his eyes told me that I was dealing with a spirit of glass. The wrong question from me could make him shatter before me.

"Okay," I said.

"Do you trust me?"

"I do. Don, I always have. You know that."

His smile was immensely grateful, and his eyes were wet, as if I had just saved his soul. "Thank you. Shay, thank you so much! Come here." He opened his arms and I slowly leaned in and hugged him.

He rocked me softly.

I don't know if his answer satisfied me or not, but this

sure did.

If you haven't guessed by now, I had feelings for Don. Old, old feelings.

I first realized my crush when Don asked me to the Spring dance.

I had gotten used to Don's strange ways over the course of seventh grade, his silences bursting into excited outpourings of energy, his shyness disappearing when he was in front of a class, his flashes of confidence and bursts of Klingon… so it was no surprise whatsoever that he didn't ask me in any kind of normal way.

"Hey, Shay."

I was sitting in front of Mrs. Wycliff's portable, which is where we had Choir practice. I didn't play any instruments; Don played the piano and trumpet and his band class met in the portable next to ours.

"Can I talk to you for a second?"

"Okay."

I excused myself from my friends: Darrin, Andrea, and Kim. They were all totally normal just like me.

Jen Abrams, who was not totally normal, had not talked to me very much since Halloween when I went a different way from her and started to hang out with Don. She was now in junior cheerleading and was Homeroom rep for Student Government. Our paths excluded friendship.

Don and I had to pass her and her "cool" friends to go around the portable, which was no problem because they totally ignored us. We walked sideways to skirt around their group.

Don led me around to the side of the portable, not looking at me.

When we were alone, he leaned back against the brown wood and finally faced me.

"Shay…" he said, "… would you… go to this seventh grade dance with me tomorrow?"

I was surprised that he asked—he'd made fun of me for

going to the *Dashing through the Snow Dance* in December—but I was happy.

"Okay," I said.

Don looked away, grimacing. "My Dad said I have to go. He said it's good to be social. You've got to be social to be a doctor."

"No problem. I'll go."

"Thanks, Shay."

That afternoon, in homeroom, he passed me a note. I DON'T KNOW HOW TO DANCE, it said.

I wrote back: I CAN TEACH YOU.

That afternoon, Don and I practiced in my living room, my mom peeking in from time to time with a "Good work" or a "You're getting it now!" and trying to keep my eight year old brother, Jack, away from us, because he was always laughing and making faces.

As it turned out, Don wasn't bad at the actual dancing. He was bad at getting close. I realized that as soon as I put my hands on his shoulders and he backed off.

"Look, my parents made me learn how to dance," he said, "but I just don't know how to act at a school dance."

The Smiths had enrolled Don in ballet for six years and, no matter what he had done to get out of it, nothing had worked. "I pretended to be sick a few times, but they never bought it," he said. "They'd just buy me a box of lemon or cherry flavored cough drops and say I could suck on them during practice if I had a cold. If it was my stomach, they'd say 'Just dance half an hour; if you're still not feeling well, we'll go home.' The only reason I got out was because my mother made my father agree that if I could get a part in *The Nutcracker*, they'd let me decide on another activity." He'd played one of the mice when he was ten years old and when that was done, despite all of his father's efforts to push him into boxing, he had chosen to learn karate.

I decided to start with fast dancing.

This didn't help much because Don's idea of fast dancing was a strange mix of his ballet and karate training. He gave me a frantic display around my living room that sent our cat running to the basement.

"No, it's more like this…"

I stuck in my Roxette cassette and swayed side to side, bouncing just a little to "The Look." He joined in, shifting from foot to foot self-consciously.

"Now that's more like it," my mother said, popping her head in from the kitchen. Jack peeked at us from under her arm and went into a giggling fit. My mom reshut the kitchen door.

"You can move your arms if you really want to."

I did, and we danced like that until the end of the song.

"Okay," I said. "Now for the slow dancing."

I put on the Bangles' "Eternal Flame."

Don put one hand on my shoulder and then took my other hand and stretched out our arms as if he wanted to do a tango.

"Uh, not that way," I said and gently pulled his arms around me. "Wrap them around my waist," I said, "and then just sway."

He wouldn't look at me this close, but instead turned his head to the side.

"If you're not going to look at me, then put your head next to mine."

He did and I wrapped my arms tighter around his neck.

I'd only been asked to slow dance twice at the winter dance, both times by guys who were really awkward, one who kept bumping into my feet as he danced and the other who smelled slightly of beef stew, and I hadn't been comfortable then.

Dancing with Don, I was comfortable.

He followed my movements carefully and left a warm, tingling feeling on my cheek every time he breathed.

It was the first good dance of my life. I closed my eyes and enjoyed it.

Don apparently didn't, however, because as soon as the song was done, he pulled away from me.

"Thanks, Shay," he said hurriedly. "I think I got it."

I wanted to ask if we could try again, but looking at

Don, I stopped myself. He was jumpy, moving from foot to foot, hardly looking at me.

I watched him shuffling there, and it made me smile.

He was actually acting shy…

And it was cute!

For the first time, I realized that I could like Don. That it might be nice to be more than just friends.

He could actually be my boyfriend!

I just wondered if he could feel that way, too…

He continued to fidget. "Hey, let's do something else for a while," he mumbled.

I thought.

"You wanna play Mario?" I asked.

"That sounds good," he said.

Don had asked me to trust him, and I did.

Even more, I cared for him.

It's true that there were times when I wished he would consider me differently, that his love would be for somebody other than just "Shay" the friend, but I had pretty much come to terms with the fact that this was our relationship.

And he cared about me, I knew that.

So I put the car in gear, pulled back onto the road and headed out of Yettikum.

Five grocery stores, four McDonald's, one mental hospital, and innumerable used car lots later, we were on our way: going South on I-5.

Toward Devi.

CHAPTER SIX
PLAYING PEEK-A-BOO
WITH MOUNTAINS

THE TRIP DOWN the west coast on I-5 is a nice one. The highway runs parallel to the Cascade Mountain range, and every once in a while an enormous snow capped mountain appears and dominates the eastern horizon. For an hour or more, this mountain can be your companion, sometimes disappearing from view as you take a corner or go down a hill, sometimes getting tucked away behind tall pine trees, but always popping back up to offer an amazing view, especially on a clear day.

This particular Sunday was a very clear day, and Mount Rainier was still on display for this first part of our trip. I had my window down, and I was feeling happy, the way I always did at the beginning of a road trip, even one that had such a crazy goal as this one. I watched the mountain until it sank behind some buildings on the side of the highway, then rolled up my window and turned to Don, who had his sunglasses on and was admiring the scenery on his own side.

We hadn't really had a chance to catch up yet, so now was the time.

I considered.

He'd said he didn't want to talk about Africa so I wouldn't. Not yet, at least.

Instead, I asked about Devi Chakraborty.

"So, who is she?"

This was something Don was happy to talk about. He'd met Devi in the medical program at Emory University, the program he'd first gone to Georgia to be in. Devi was three years ahead of him and "absolutely brilliant."

"She's going to make a great doctor," he said. "She's almost finished. She's doing her residency now at Emory University Hospital."

He told me she was kind, always had a smile for everybody, and had been a good friend. She was also beautiful, he said, and instead of describing her, pulled his wallet out of his back pocket and had me look at the pictures inside.

Keeping one hand on the steering wheel, I took the wallet and glanced at the girl in the first photo.

In the picture, which Don had obviously cut out of a larger group photo, Devi was wearing a white lab coat and giving a soft, slight, closed-lip smile. She was a good-looking lady, with a skinny oval face and big brown eyes, but going off my first look, I didn't think she was the drop-dead beauty that Don obviously regarded her as. Her face was just a little too skinny, her eyes just a little too big to make her truly beautiful, I thought.

But then again, I could have been biased.

My second glance was a bit kinder because I realized that her thick, glistening black hair (done up in a bun for the group photo) probably really made her face look stunning when it was down, and her nose, just slightly out of proportion to her skinny face, really gave her character. I couldn't help admitting that she had a certain class, although I was happy to think that I was just a little better looking in comparison.

Still, to Don, I just said, "Wow, she *is* beautiful."

He nodded enthusiastically.

I flipped to the next picture and almost dropped the wallet.

It was me and Don at a Mexican restaurant from my twenty-first birthday. Don was smiling and looking fine. I, on the other hand, was wearing a sombrero and leaning over a strawberry margarita with a strange smile on my face and one eye half-closed.

Ugh.

I quickly flipped through the plastic sleeves for more pictures, but those were the only ones of either Devi or myself.

I handed the wallet back, shaking my head.

"So, did you and Devi ever date?"

"Once. We were more like friends, though, really. Anyway, I was going away… She wrote to me a lot."

So had I, I thought, but kept it to myself.

Don told me about how he had met Devi in a particularly hard class, how they had studied together, how they had always gone to movies and restaurants together, even how they both loved tortilla chips.

Tortilla chips made me think of my photo at the Mexican restaurant again, and I had the painful realization that every time Don had thought of me in Africa, that was the picture he probably would have looked at. That was how I was remembered. Picture-wise, Devi scored a lot of glamour points over me.

Ultimately, Devi and Don had eaten one last meal together in Atlanta, and he had left for another continent, and she had stayed to finish her medical degree. It wasn't much of a love story, and there wasn't much in Don's story that made me think he had really been romantically interested in her when he left, but he certainly was now. He kept talking about how beautiful and nice she was, and how he couldn't wait to see her. He actually used the word "yearn." I really wondered if the only reason he yearned like this was because of his new-found love for Indian movies (was he going to Atlanta to live out his own personal Hindi movie???), but I was afraid to ask.

Instead, I said, "So what got you interested in Indian movies anyway?"

Knowing Don, I readied myself for a flood of information.

Before, any mention of the *Star Trek* universe would send him into a long, rambling, but often very in-depth, monologue about the show, of which he seemed to know and have an opinion about everything: why Wesley Crusher was an ineffective character, how Klingon culture resembled Japanese feudal society, how the saucer section could disconnect from the Enterprise at times and what this would mean for the body of the vessel.

It was all fascinating...

...for Don.

Although I had at one point been convinced to go to a convention (where Don had participated in a frenzied Q&A with Jonathan Frakes), I had eventually convinced him that I could not be converted.

Still, there were always times when he would look distant or agitated in conversation and, almost always, it turned out that some minor plot point or some technical faux-pas in a recent episode of *The Next Generation*, (and later, in high school, *Deep Space Nine* and *Voyager*) was slow-boiling in his brain. So, if Don liked Indian movies as much as he had liked *Star Trek*, and it sure seemed like he did, I knew I would be in for a really long conversation.

I was surprised, then, by Don's simple, but breathlessly delivered, answer:

"Oh, Shayla, they're great! You're really going to have to see one; I meant to show you one the other night but you left so fast. I mean I can't really describe it. I guess the best way to put it is that they are action musicals."

"Action musicals?"

"Yeah, action musicals. I mean, imagine this: you know Arnold Schwarzenegger? Well, imagine him in a truly vicious fight scene, yah? After a major fist-fight, he finally wins. Then, immediately after winning, he flips on some sunglasses and goes into a dance number singing about how much he loves some lady. That is an Indian movie."

"Hmmm…"

I didn't know what to say. From the little bit of Indian movie I had seen on Don's TV a few nights before, everything he said matched up.

"I promise I will let you see one. Promise."

He went totally quiet then for a few moments, enough time that I was compelled to look over at him.

He was staring at the glove box absorbedly, or maybe he was staring through the glove box. He seemed suddenly very serious.

"Don…?"

He snapped out of it immediately, a smile spasming instantly to his lips. He gave the glove box a sharp pat.

"That's enough about all that. I want to know about you. I read all your letters; I know it's been a strange year for you. But I want to hear all about it… I want to know what's been going on."

He followed up with a barrage of questions, asking about my mom and dad, Jack, my roommate, and my co-workers at misterbook.com. It was a relief to talk about these things with Don. Nobody else would have understood.

I opened up in a way that I hadn't for months, and it seemed fitting that we were talking about the really bad stuff when Mt. St. Helens, that poor, decapitated, pitiful mountain, loomed into view ahead of us.

It was this mountain that we peered at as I told him all about my four-year depression, how I had hardly been able to get out of bed some days, how Mom and Dad had tried to cheer me up with trips and movies and surprise presents. I told, too, about Dr. Ripples, my psychologist, who, after two and a half years of clinical help and bizarre baseball metaphors which were supposed to explain my state of mind, told me that he thought I was fine, that I understood myself well enough to go out in the world. This was, of course, three months after I had unwillingly been forced back into that world by my parents, who for some reason thought that my leaving home would help me conquer my feelings.

I told Don all about that, and even about how the depression came back all the time, when I had to clean the stacks of dishes my roommate used but refused to wash, when I went to work, when I thought of Don off in Africa, when I thought of the future which I no longer knew what to do with. I told him how the depression paralyzed me, sometimes for days, and how I would walk around in a haze hoping to be ignored. I told him that I had really missed him, that as bizarre as it seemed I hadn't felt down since he came back, that I wasn't quite happy yet, but that his being there made me not sad, which was wonderful.

Don listened to it all very carefully, nodding, encouraging, asking tons of questions, but always skirting around the big one... never coming close to what both he and I knew was the cause of these worst years of my life, never once even mentioning the name that had come up in every single one of my sessions with Dr. Ripples.

Just like I knew it was not time to talk about the Devi Chakraborty-Indian movie connection, he knew not to talk about Brad.

Still, I felt relieved to talk, happy to be able to laugh as I explained some of the things that had happened, overjoyed to be able to connect with somebody so well, like I had always connected with Don. It was only hunger that made me finally stop talking, and by then we had reached Portland, Mt. Hood off to our left. We stopped and ate at a little family restaurant, staring out the window at the distant thin-necked white mountain, so different from the bulky Mt. Rainier of home.

It was only later that I realized Don had not answered my question about Indian movies.

He had told me what they were, not how he had gotten interested in them.

He had started talking about me to avoid answering that question, and it was going to be a very long time before I discovered how significant that was.

***

After lunch, Don took the wheel and popped in a cassette of Indian music called *The Best of Rahul Ghosh*, telling me I would love it.

I made it through about a song and a half before the throb of the speeding car and the odd melodies put me to sleep. After that, the day floated by without a care. I woke up, I fell asleep, I had an orange that Don had been nice enough to bring along for the ride. We listened to Indian music, we listened to the radio and kept flipping whenever we got out of range of a station and it started to break up. We had nostalgic conversations about the past and the good times we'd had, and we managed to abridge everything so nothing bad or painful could pop up. We laughed and reminisced as only good friends who have shared much can, and nothing of any weight disturbed us.

At some point, I fell asleep and stayed that way for a long time. When Don woke me up to look at Mt. Shasta, I was surprised that we had even crossed into California. The last thing I remembered was watching the attendant filling our tank in Medford, Oregon (crazy Oregon, where they won't let you fill your own tank!)

Mt. Shasta was beautiful and huge (though not quite as tall as Mt. Rainier, according to a sign at the highway viewing area), and it kept me stimulated for a full twenty minutes before I cruised back into sleep.

When I awoke, it was to Don's voice and the smell of eleven secret herbs and spices. We were next in line at the KFC drive-thru.

"Wake up, sleepyhead," Don said.

"Where are we?"

"A little town called Dungannon, but I thought it might be wise to stop for the night. After all, you've been asleep for hours, and I could use some food myself. Anyway, there's something I want to show you."

I shook my head to wake up. It was still pretty light, but the dashboard clock informed me it was 7:20.

Don had already scouted everything out. With our meals in a bag on my lap, we drove over to a small motel that said in chipped green letters DUNGANNON MOTEL.

We checked in to a room with two twin beds and when we got inside, Don snapped open his suitcase and pushed aside some clothes to reveal his secret possession: a VCR.

"It's time to watch Rahul Ghosh in action," he said.

So, with the VCR hooked up to the motel TV and our KFC meals before us, Don fulfilled his promise and showed me a complete Indian movie. It was called *Pyar 101 (Love 101)* and I was happy to see that it had subtitles, unlike the film I'd spied a bit of in Don's room. In the film, Ghosh played a college professor who strongly believed in the power of love and taught his students to pursue and enjoy relationships. Ultimately, what this meant was a lot of singing and dancing as different students, and then Ghosh himself, hooked up. I was surprised by the lack of fighting other than some lengthy scenes where Ghosh and the female Dean of the university, who apparently was anti-amour, talked to each other with stern looks on their faces. (Not surprisingly, it was this female Dean whom Ghosh ended up falling in love with.)

"Fantastic, huh?" said Don, clicking off the TV two and a half hours later when the credits began to roll.

"Hmmm…I don't get why everything happens in India, but suddenly for all the dance numbers, they seem to be singing and dancing in the Swiss Alps or something."

"That's Bollywood," said Don. "It isn't really romantic unless the musical numbers are over the top. Rolling hills, wide open spaces, impressive backdrops, men and women running toward each other against the wind, clothes rippling…"

"Windmills…" I said, remembering the scene from Don's bedroom.

"Sure."

"It was pretty good."

"You should see one with fighting!" said Don, and started to hunt around for a different video.

I held up a hand.

"Nah, I don't think so. Not tonight, at least. These

movies are pretty long, and I'm actually kind of sleepy."

The moment I said it, I realized how true it was. I was exhausted. With Don coming home, quitting my job, a drive down the West Coast (even if I'd slept a lot of it), and two and a half hours of Rahul Ghosh behind me, there was nothing that sounded more appealing than sleep.

"Okay, why don't you clean up first, then?"

"No, no, you go ahead."

"I'll be right back."

Don went into the bathroom, and as I waited, I pulled my cell phone from my purse.

Three messages.

The first two were from Don's dad. In the first one, he was yelling about how Don was crazy and we should come back. In the second, he was still yelling, but this time he included the thought that I must be crazy, too. I erased both messages.

The third message was from Patel.

"Hi, Shay," he said. "I just wanted to make sure that everything was going okay with you and your friend, Don. Oh, well, that's it, I guess. Goodbye. Oh, and if you're wondering how I got your number, don't worry. It was still on my caller ID from work from that day you were running a little late a couple weeks ago. I noticed it and thought I'd give you a call this weekend. Take care. Adios. Sayonara. Auf wieder—" He hung up.

That was nice of him, I thought. I'd have to try and remember to give him a call sometime.

I saved Patel's message, and then fell fast asleep to the sound of running water as Don brushed his teeth in the bathroom.

Sometime later, I awoke with a start from a falling dream, my heart trembling.

Where was I?

For a moment, I stared about me, not comprehending, but then I realized.

It was okay. I was in the motel, in my bed. I was safe.

Don was still awake, sitting on the edge of his bed, watching the TV with the sound turned all the way down. He had put another Indian movie in the machine—the action movie—and was so focused on the screen that he didn't notice I was awake.

On the TV, a young woman, maybe one of the ones from Don's wall, was walking alone down a dark, shadow-lined street. As she walked, several idle, leering men disengaged from the shadows and began to trail her with loping, ominous strides. When she noticed and sped up, so did they, and finally they formed a circle around her, gaping and licking their lips obscenely. She tried to make a dash for it, but the men blocked her, and one wrapped his arms indecently around her, pawing at her as she struggled and the others laughed.

Don reached for his blanket and pulled it close to his face, twisting it nervously in his hand.

Off screen, a voice yelled a long drawn-out "Rascaaaaals!" The men—and the lady, too—looked about in wonder. Where was that scream coming from?

And suddenly Rahul Ghosh was on the screen, jumping straight up in the air from the darkness and landing on top of a parked car.

Don dropped his blanket.

Ghosh shouted at the men, who stared dumbfounded, which seemed normal. What else can one do when a man appears from nowhere and immediately begins defying the laws of gravity?

Ghosh then catapulted himself from the car, legs outstretched, and knocked one of the baddies to the ground. The others looked at each other and, in a concerted motion, ran for the attack. Luckily for Ghosh, they didn't make it at the same time, giving him just enough of a gap to punch one down before the next arrived. They kept coming, though, falling down and then getting back up to try again. Each time, he valiantly fought them back.

Rahul Ghosh, defender of women.

Don followed all of Ghosh's actions intently, giving the air a little uppercut once in a while as if it were he and not Rahul Ghosh who was fighting.

I smiled lightly, my head nodding.

When Don got into something, he really got into it.

I fell asleep blinking at his intensity.

My last thought, though, was, *Wait a minute—did I ever brush my teeth?*

CHAPTER SEVEN
TRUCK STOP TROUBLE

IT WAS JUST a little after eight o'clock the next morning that we left the motel and pulled into the Albeiro Truck Stop/Restaurant, which sat right before the entrance to I-5. The sky still had a peach-colored tinge to it, and I could just make out a gathering of white cows grazing in the flat meadow immediately beyond the highway.

Albeiro, apparently the only restaurant in Dungannon, looked like a cross between a Denny's and a Hooters, with a typical boxy family-restaurant shape, but a tall white sign in front that showed an illustration of a long-blonde-haired woman carrying a tray of food and drinks and wearing the kind of maid outfit usually only seen on French maids, with the skirt cut far up the thigh, the top cut low down the cleavage, which was amply drawn, and a large white headpiece in her hair.

"Classy," I mumbled.

"Let's just hope the food's good," said Don.

I was surprised upon entering to find that the waitresses all actually dressed in the French maid outfits, although not a one of them was blonde. Our waitress was a cute but chubby almost-twenty with a nametag that read MISTY on her chest and a pimple on her breast that I could see clearly when she leaned over to take our order. I was proud that Don didn't seem to notice.

There were three waitresses in the restaurant and only about four tables taken, all by what appeared to be truck drivers who were drinking coffee and already looking ready for a good night's sleep. Across the aisle from us, though, was a group of three truckers who seemed to be looking for something else. These three were all unshaven and two of them seemingly hadn't seen exercise for years. Every time one of the waitresses passed by them, they would all stare, turning in their seat if they were on the wrong side for ogling, and each time one of the hefty ones would let out a "Whoo-ee" or a "Now that's what Papa's ordering" loud enough for us to hear. The waitresses ignored them.

Don voiced my own feelings. "Disgusting," he whispered. He leaned toward me, using his eyes to indicate the direction of the three men. "Can you believe that?"

I couldn't, but Don was taking it harder than I was, sitting tense and straight with his fingers gripping the table as if he wanted to flatten it. I had never seen him look so angry.

Misty came and placed our drinks in front of us, but our thanks were drowned out by the skinnier truck driver calling out "Hey, sugar, can I get some service?" He seemed to be enjoying looking at her from behind, his eyes making slow trips up and down her legs and hips.

"Excuse me," said Misty sweetly to Don and me and went to the truckers. I took quick glances to see what would happen. Don didn't even look. He squeezed the table even harder, as if he were afraid it was going to leave us.

"Yes, sir?" Misty asked the driver.

"Can I get some sugar over here, darling?" He looked up at her cleavage through thick glasses and stirred his coffee provocatively.

"Yeah," sniggered one of the other truckers, "You can never get enough sugar."

For a moment, Misty looked confusedly at their table,

searching for something. Not finding it, though, she said, "Yes sir. I'll be right back with that."

She walked off and all three focused on her behind as she did. "Whoo-ee," said the one who always said "Whoo-ee." The thin one reached beside him and picked something up, the sight of which put his fellows in convulsions. It was a full container of sugar. That's what she was looking for, I thought.

I turned back to Don, ready to say something derogatory, but forgot to speak when I saw his face. He had his teeth clenched together and I could see his jaw muscles moving as he ground them together. "Don, are you okay?" I asked.

"It's not right," he said, in an angry whisper. "Somebody should tell these guys to stop. Somebody should help her." I was alarmed to see that the vein on his neck was clearly visible now and it was throbbing.

"She's alright," I said. "She probably knows how to handle them."

"It's not right," Don said again, this time glancing over at the truckers, who didn't seem to notice.

"Here you are, hon." Don jumped and spun his head back, but it was only Misty with our food. "One Albeiro Slam for you, sir, and ma'am, here's your Cheese and Tomato omelette."

"Thanks," I said, lifting my silverware.

"Thanks," Don mumbled, not lifting his.

"You're welcome," said Misty, and, pulling a full canister of sugar from her front pocket, she spun around to the truckers.

"Oh, now, honey, that's not the kind of sugar that I wanted," said the thin truck driver.

Don's head shot up and he looked straight at me, his blue eyes angry and worried and pleading at the same time.

"I can't let this happen," he told me. "I can't. Not again."

His knuckles were white and each of his fingernails had a hot pink arc across the top from him gripping the table.

"I've got to do something."

Teaching Don to dance in my living room had made me realize that I could like him, but it wasn't until we were at the actual dance that I discovered he might like me too, and that's when the crush really developed.

It all started out innocently enough. Don danced to fast songs with me and a group of friends for the first half hour, and even slow-danced with me once. I was happy to dance with him, but I had my eyes on other guys, too. In fact, I would have been delighted if Erik Anderson had noticed me and asked for a dance, despite the fact that he was what Don termed "the biggest ass in the school." That was true, but he was also really good-looking.

As it was, half an hour into the dance, Don was leaning up against the wall by the open door to the cafeteria, in a heated conversation with Brent Mellner about whether or not Leonard Nimoy would appear in the next night's episode of *Star Trek* or not. The conversation went something like this:

Don: "Spock's father's going to be in it. I bet there'll be a surprise cameo."

Brent: "They would have publicized it!"

Don: "Not if they want to surprise the audience."

I stood next to them, barely listening, looking about the dance floor and getting occasional glimpses of Erik Anderson dancing with some girl that wasn't me.

The debate had subsided into a general conversation over which one was cooler—Worf or Data—when two new people dressed in faded blue jeans and blue jean jackets strode into the gym, right next to Don, looking around cautiously. Brent Mellner immediately stiffened and Don turned around swiftly, eying them suspiciously.

The first one, who had a pinched face and squinty eyes and Jon Bon Jovi hair, said to Don, "Hey, Book-dude, you seen the Vice Principal or any teachers around?"

"I don't know. Allerman's around somewhere," said

Don. "Why?"

"Hey, Hair," the guy now said to me.

Brad Newton had somewhere picked up the habit of referring to people not by their names but by the first thing he had noticed about them. For Don, it had been reading, for me it was my hair, which I had let grow out so that it now rivaled his.

He kept talking to me, ignoring Don's question.

"That is some nice hairstyle you got there, Hair. I bet it's nice and smooth, huh, Bear?"

Brian Wrczic was a big, burly guy, who everybody was afraid of, except for Brad. People called him the Bear. He shrugged his bear shoulders and said, "I don't know, dude. Let's go."

"Hold on, Bear," said Brad. "Hey, listen," he said to me, "Would you mind if I just touch your hair one time? It's really kicking." He kept his distance, but looked at me expectantly, waiting for an answer.

To be honest, I was flattered. My palms all of a sudden were moist and my heart was jumping. I could feel the blood in my cheeks. I don't know what I would have said if Don hadn't suddenly stepped between me and Brad.

"Listen, Brad, leave her alone."

"What's it to you, Star Trek?" Brad's voice took on a more threatening tone and the fact that he had switched from the affectionate "Book-dude" to the supposedly demeaning "Star Trek" seemed like a bad sign.

"I'm just telling you… Be cool. This is my friend."

Brad raised his hands in a motion of surrender, but the rest of his body shouted that he could take Don if he wanted. "Hey, okay… I don't want a fight," he said, although he was a good half a foot taller than Don and much tougher looking. "It's good. C'mon, Bear." He turned and walked out, followed by his friend, but then he popped his head back in and with a cocky smile, said to Don, "See you in Metal Shop, Star Trek!"

"I hate that guy," Don said to no-one in particular when he was gone.

"Oh, he's not that bad," I said. "He was just messing around."

"That guy's a bigger ass than Erik Anderson," said Don. "He always takes my books during class."

"Does he give them back?"

"Yeah…eventually."

"So, he's not that bad."

"Shay!" He looked hurt. Brad Newton was what was considered to be a "stoner" in our school, somebody who didn't care about learning and hung out with other tough looking people, probably getting high on marijuana and listening to metal bands like Metallica and Motley Crue and Judas Priest. I'd heard all of the stories, knew all the rumors, even believed them, but there was something oddly cute about Brad… and he hadn't hurt Don; that was good.

Don's betrayed look didn't last very long. After a pause, "Isn't this the Bangles?" he asked.

"Yeah."

"Well… come on. I can dance to this one."

I let Don lead me out to the dance floor.

As I turned to him and saw him with his arms out waiting for me, I suddenly realized what had happened.

Don had protected me.

I'd always heard that Brad was a bully, that he got in fights and never lost. Don had surely heard the same things I had, but he had still stood between us.

I was impressed.

Now I moved toward him, but I'd only just put my arms around Don's neck when there was a nasty smell and acrid blue smoke rose up from the front of the gym.

"Smoke bomb!" somebody yelled, and people made a rush for the outdoors.

"See… it was Brad," Don said. "I told you he was an ass."

Don never told me but I know for a fact that on the following Monday, Brad took his *Star Trek* book again… but this time he never gave it back. In fact, it wasn't too long after that I first saw it sitting on the floor in Brad's bedroom taking up space because he had no idea what to do with it. But by that time, Brad had switched from calling me "Hair" to calling me "Lips," and other than a little pang of guilt that made me nudge the book under Brad's bed, I had other things to think about…

Yet one thing I never did forget was that Don had stood up for me, and even though it was Brad's room I ended up in, I never got over the feeling that I had for Don that night.

That was how the crush got started.

"AAAAAAHHHYAAAAGGHHHAAAARRRRRRRR….."

That was the sound Don made as he leapt up from his seat.

I don't know what I was expecting, but this was not it.

One moment, he was clenching the table, staring down at his plate, mumbling about how he couldn't let this happen. The next moment, he had flown up into the air as if he had a spring in his butt, as if he were a man who could say, with no irony, "I'm a Tigger, and Tiggers like to bounce!" It was fast enough that it seemed impossible that he could have used his legs. He just shot straight up at a 180 degree angle as if he were wearing a rocket pack.

Maybe I'm wrong. Maybe he didn't really jump straight up—I was a little preoccupied by Don's plate of food which his knees had sent flying from the table toward my face; I only very narrowly missed being brained by a sausage—but that's how it seemed.

When the sausage had ricocheted off the back of my seat and plopped onto the pleather beside me, and when Don's plate had stopped clattering back and forth on the floor, I was able to take stock of the situation. Don was standing—actually standing—on his seat with his legs spread like a cowboy and his hands in two fists by his sides, his karate pose. I'd seen him use this once when he had shown me how he could break a piece of pine wood in half with his hand back in junior high. Around his plate and scattered across the floor were the remains of his breakfast, scrambled eggs and ham making a little trail across the aisle toward Misty and the truckers. Standing above the spoiled food, Don was looking action-hero tough, his eyes cold and hard, his fists clenching, his mouth a cold, hard line. He looked like Schwarzenegger, or Bruce Willis. He looked like...

...well, Rahul Ghosh.

Really, he did. This looked exactly like the fight scene I'd woken up during in the middle of the night before.

Don looked like he was ready to kick some ass.

As if to prove my frenzied thoughts right, he jumped off the seat and strode across the aisle to the truckers, his steps confident and sure. I followed his feet as they moved past the greasy ham and quivering eggs to the table, looked up at his fists, looked past them to the truckers... and it was only then that I suddenly realized how wrong this all was.

It was as if somebody had suddenly turned off my adrenaline's Fight faucet, and now it was all coming from Flight.

The scene that met my eyes was a strange still life: Misty, her eyes wide, half holding the sugar container out to the thin trucker, the three truckers each staring at Don with whatever expression they'd had when he'd jumped up, none of them knowing quite what expression was appropriate for the situation, the quietest one frozen with his fork right before his open mouth, a piece of pancake dribbling a slow thread of thick syrup, the thin one reaching out for the sugar with a leer, the "Whoo-ee" guy still wearing a broad, lascivious grin, but with a look of disbelief in his eyes now. None of them had seen or heard of Rahul Ghosh before and they hadn't expected to discover him in a truck stop just north of Sacramento. It certainly wasn't where he belonged, and certainly not wearing Don's face.

Suddenly I was scared, really, truly, terrified.

How long had Don stuck with karate? It didn't seem like it had been all that long.

The inappropriateness of the setting didn't slow Don down a second. He stopped in front of the three men and slammed his palm down on the table. The trucker's plates bounced and rattled. Still holding his pancake before his mouth, the quiet guy put one protective arm around his plate and stopped it shaking. The other two altered their frozen expressions into looks of irritation and annoyance.

"You rascals!" Don boomed... and I'm not making this up. He actually said "rascals" and he said it just like Rahul Ghosh had said it to the gang members in the movie, with a long "a" so it sounded much more Indian, like "You ros-kuls." A little tremble went up my spine.

"You absolute ros-kuls! Is this how you treat a lady?" He made a sharp gesture toward Misty, who took a quick step back. "You owe her an apology."

"Kid," said the thin trucker, leaning toward Don, "I don't know what in hell you're on, but I suggest that you back off."

The Whoo-ee guy's smile brightened and he nodded. This was the way to deal with a little punk like Don. The quiet guy, seeming to see a quick resolution to the situation, started eating again, popping the piece of pancake into his mouth. Don's attention flashed to him.

"Don't eat while I'm talking to you!"

He leaned across the table and shoved the man's plate away from him. The man must have been hungry, though, because he shot his arms out immediately to reclaim his breakfast, and in doing so, he caught Don a blow on the forehead that sent him stumbling backwards. This wouldn't have been a problem if there hadn't been the trail of Don's breakfast behind him. Without it, he would have regained his balance in an instant; as it was, one backward step landed his foot in a pile of egg and he fell completely on his back.

"Don!" I said.

"Don't worry," Don said and jumped back to his feet in a fluid motion that showed he'd learned a little more from his karate lessons than just breaking wood in two. I hoped he'd learned a *lot* more. "That was nothing."

He stepped back to the table.

"Hey," said the thin trucker, "dipshit, cut it out. We

don't want to hurt you."

Don laughed. "It won't be me that gets hurt if the lady doesn't get her—

"Oof!" He staggered back.

Apparently bored by Don's dialogue, Whoo-ee guy had punched him in the stomach, just a few inches above the groin.

"Don, stop," I said, "What's the matter with you? This is crazy."

Don staggered a little, holding his stomach. "Don't worry. I'm all right."

He straightened.

"Gretchen?" Misty called out to another maid-outfitted waitress. "Call the police."

Don looked over to her, completely missing her point. "It's alright, ma'am. I'll take care of these losers for you."

But in the time he took to say that, the thin trucker had assessed the situation, realized that Don wasn't going to back off, and had hit upon a plan. When Don turned back to the table, he was already standing in front of him, with his fist raised.

"You—" said Don…

…and the trucker hit him right in the face.

CHAPTER EIGHT
MADNESS

"WE'LL GO."

There was nothing else I could say. Don was lying on the floor with an odd grin on his face, senselessly rolling his head from side to side, his cheek slapping a piece of ham with each roll. "Come on, Don," I said.

"Shay," he mumbled, drunkenly, with a smile that looked ghoulish next to his half-closed black eye and split lip. "That was great, yah?" He closed his eyes again and rested his head fully on the ham, as if it were a pillow. "I'm just going to take a little nap now."

I looked around at the aftermath of the recent mini-battle. Misty was standing with her arms folded, breasts crushed together, all sense of sugar drained from her face. The thin trucker and the Whoo-ee guy were both half standing, the Whoo-ee guy rubbing his fist, which he had apparently injured on Don's gut. The other trucker was still sitting and eating, his eyes moving from me to Misty's breasts between bites of pigs in blankets. On the periphery of the recent violence, life went on; other waitresses and diners went about their routine, but more slowly, staring at us and whispering. It was obvious that I was going to have to pick Don up by myself.

I reached over and grabbed his hands and gave a heave that brought Don to an almost sitting position. He blinked his eyes open somewhat. "Hey, Shay! Did I win?"

"We need to get out of here."

"Time to go already?"

"Yeah, time to go. You can help me, you know."

"Don't wanna go," he mumbled, closing his eyes again. "Sleepy." He leaned back and I almost lost my grip on his hands.

"Come on!" I said sharply.

"Do I have to?"

My adrenaline was wearing off. Now I was just getting embarrassed, and angry, too. "Yes, you have to," I hissed, then changed to a nicer tone, realizing that I had to be encouraging. "You want to see Devi, right?"

"Devi?" Don's one eye eagerly opened wide; the other squinted at me.

"Devi."

"Let's go!" Don gripped my hands and hoisted himself up in a fit of energy that got him to his feet... and then left him so that he had to lean on my shoulder. "But let's go slowly."

With Don's arm around my shoulder and his body leaning against me, we stumbled past Misty to the doors and pushed out into sunlight. I dragged Don to my car and negotiated him into the passenger seat, where he immediately opened the glove box for his sunglasses. When I got to the driver's seat, he had already put the seat back and was lying down with his hands behind his head.

"Don?" I said.

Nothing.

"Don?"

I shook him, but he was out. I blew out an angry breath of air and shook my head. The last thing I wanted was to be some kind of baby-sitter. But there was nothing I could do at that point...

I turned the key in the ignition—

Badlo, badlo, badlo
Jo banna chahte ho
Badlo, badlo, badlo
Apne ko badlo

blasted from the radio and made me jump. I punched the off button.

"We are going to have to have a long talk when you wake up," I told the body next to me, and pulled out of the Albeiro parking lot.

I got onto the freeway without taking a single glance back.

Driving by myself was remarkably peaceful, despite all that had happened. The freeway was relatively flat with fields of cluttered cows on both sides. Eventually the fields started to turn into smoothly rolling hills as we entered the San Joaquin valley, and I had nearly forgotten about Don as I drove up and down the little humps, but that's exactly when he came to life again.

"Stop the car!"

"What?"

"Stop the car now!" His voice was so urgent that I did what he said, pulling onto the side of the road.

"Don't you see?"

"See what?"

"Look, Shay, look," Don said. "Look at the windmills."

There we were, somewhere in the San Joaquin Valley, close to Bakersfield I guessed, yellowish hills surrounding us like giant camel humps, and on top of these humps, yes, were these tall white windmills twisting into the sky.

"Yeah, so?"

"So? They look just like a place to sing!"

"What?"

"To sing. You know… to sing! Like in the movie. My

love song must reach across the country."

"But Don... I think those are like windmills for farming or something."

Don had gotten in a fight, acted about as stupid as I had ever seen anyone act, and now after about an hour's rest he was staring at these windmills and talking about singing. I didn't think so.

"Let's just go," I said, reaching for the ignition, but then realized that Don had somehow gotten the keys.

Holding them in his hand, he shoved open his door and got out. "Magnificent!" he exclaimed and began to run.

"Don! Don!" I called. "What are you doing? There must be a fence? You can't possibly get up..."

But he was gone.

There was nothing to do but follow.

I ascended the hill and looked down. Don was standing in a little valley. On one side was a small hill, on the other rising above him were the windmills spinning around. Behind Don was the breathtaking scenery of the valley, smooth tan hills stretching forever.

"Don!" I shouted.

Don turned to me, his arms spread wide, his head tilted back. "It's beautiful here!" he shouted. "Beautiful!"

"I don't think we should—" I shouted, but...

"DEVI!!!!"

Don's yell shut my mouth, and then the word bounced off the Valley, echoing back to us:

"Devi... Devi.... De... D."

"I'm coming, DEVI," Don yelled, and then, arms still wide he began spinning around in a circle, a look of total bliss crossing his face. Somewhere inside him, there was a swell of music, a large orchestral upsurge which was controlling his spin. This music overtook his body and suddenly he began to dance, hopping on one leg and then the other in a little jig of happiness.

As for me, all I heard was the wind and sound of nearby traffic.

His jig done, Don ran straight for me with the most

brilliant smile that I had ever seen and a speed that seemed destined to bowl me over. I got ready for the worst, but then he just grabbed my hands, looked deep into my eyes, and...

began to sing.

Pinwheel, pinwheel,
Windmills in the wind,
Carry this message to my love

He spun me around and, holding my hand, began to dance.

Oh my God, I thought, he really has gone crazy...

The song and dance continued:

My love is far
Far away
She is the jewel of my night
But we are coming to carry her away
Tell her, oh tell her,
Carry it on the wind,
We will carry the moon away

In my shock, I was amazed to note that Don's dance wasn't all that bad. Goofy, filled with little pantomime gestures, and fits of aerobic running and jumping in place, but not so bad. In fact, he'd obviously picked it up from the movies he'd been watching. He must have been practicing in front of the TV!

Pinwheel, pinwheel,
Windmills in the wind,
Carry my message to the moon,
She is far away, far, far away,
But send her this message on the wind,
We are coming to carry her away.

His song done, Don smiled at me, and shoved his hand into his pocket, fishing out my keys.

I stared at him, keeping my distance.

Don's father was right. He was mad. He really *had* gone crazy. What else could this windmill dance be but some form of insanity? What, I wondered, was I going to do? What on earth *could* I do about this?

"Come on, Shay. Let's go get Devi." He took my hand gently, to lead me off.

"Don…" I said hesitantly, "…could you, uh, give me my keys back?"

Step One: Get My Keys Back and Regain Control of the Car. That seemed reasonable enough.

But not to Don.

He looked at the keys dangling from his fingers thoughtfully, then closed his fist around them.

"No," he said, "from now on, I'm driving. Devi is my destiny, so I should be the one behind the wheel. That only makes sense, yah?"

No. Not to me.

"And one more thing, Shayla."

Don looked at me very seriously now.

Uh-oh…

"From now on, I do not want to be called Don…"

He lifted his chin proudly, his blonde hair covering up part of the valley view as it waved in the wind, his lips straight and serious. I glanced nervously at his fist, where I could see just a little glint of silver from my keys.

"Call me…" he said, "Rahul."

PART TWO

THE HINDI WORD FOR
LOVE IS "PYAR"

CHAPTER NINE
THE PASSENGER

WHAT DO YOU do when your best friend comes back from West Africa crazy? When he declares that he loves Indian movies and is suddenly talking in an Indian accent? When he wants to drive you across the country to meet an Indian girl he is madly in love with, and then, halfway across that country, in the middle of nowhere, he starts getting in fights, dancing and singing with windmills, and asking you to call him Rahul Ghosh?

When, in other words, he's gone totally, completely bonkers?

Well, if you're me, you don't do much of anything, precisely because he *is* your best friend, and you care about him, and you think that there might be a chance that you can help him.

And, also, there's the fact that he has the keys to your car...

So you go along for now. You just nod and head back across the valley with him without saying anything, and try not to look at his face, which is exuberant, whether from dancing, the idea that he will soon meet his Indian dream girl, or the fact that you bowed into him so quickly, you have no idea.

You feel like a complete loser as you pull your seatbelt on, and you are filled with all kinds of angry, murderous feelings when he says, with that stupid accent, "Only about two thousand miles to go!" and turns the ignition.

You turn away from him, and, with your forehead against your window, watching the camel hump hills go by, you mumble your only bit of resistance:

"I'm not calling you Rahul."

This doesn't make you feel any better, though, especially because he doesn't answer. In fact, he ignores you and turns on an Indian cassette.

Looking down at your feet, though, you do feel better, because there is your purse, and in your purse is your cell phone.

If you can just get some time alone, you realize, you can call someone. You can get help.

But who are you going to call? You don't want to call 911. After all, you don't want to get your friend locked up or anything, you want to help! You don't want to call his parents, or even your parents, because that's just embarrassing, not to mention treacherous. Plus you'd have to explain to your parents that you'd quit your temp job.

No, you don't want to call any of these people.

So… who do you call? Who could possibly understand a situation like this? Who could comprehend a condition as strange as your friend's?

You feel better when you think of the person, and then you just silently wait your chance… and try not to let the music in the tape deck drive you mad in the meantime.

CHAPTER TEN
THE ADVISER

"SHAYLA! I'M REALLY glad you called. When you left, I wasn't sure if I'd ever hear from you again!"

I could hear the dull throb of a computer laboring to be heard from below the pleasant voice on the other end of the line, and farther behind that, the light but frenzied tapping of fingers on keyboards. In short, everything I hadn't missed about misterbook.com.

"Well, here I am, Patel."

I took a quick look around to make sure I really knew where I was. The women's bathroom of the Burger Quarters Gas Stop was a spare but clean room, with three stalls, two sinks, and one trash can. In the corner were a decidedly unclean bucket and mop and a "Caution When Wet" sign written in Spanish. The floor, which I was now pacing back and forth on, was not wet at all.

"Nothing's really changed here since you left," Patel was saying.

No kidding. It had only been three days.

I watched myself pace in the mirror above the sinks, trying to think what to say, realizing that I didn't know all that much about Patel other than that he was the tech go-to guy at misterbook, that he'd occupied the cubicle next to mine, that he'd been nice, and most relevant to me now, that he was Indian…

But now that I was talking to him, how was I going to bring that up?

Looking at myself in the mirror, I realized that this conversation was going to be harder than I thought. I also realized that I looked stressed out and tired. There were big lavender bags under my eyes.

I investigated the bags as Patel chirped, "So what's going on with you? You never told me exactly why you were leaving, you know, what was up with your friend or whatever."

Patel really did seem happy to be talking to me.

I remembered suddenly the cake he'd given me as I left. No one else at the office had thought to give me a going away present. Only Patel had been so thoughtful.

I thought, too, of my stupid roommate and how, when I got up the next morning, she and her boyfriend had eaten the whole thing.

Ugh.

I'd better just get this over with.

I took a deep breath and said, "Patel, about that friend. I need some help."

I didn't know what to expect, but his response was surprisingly quick and unpremeditated. "What is it?" he said.

I thought that if somebody I had hardly known had called me like this, I would have been really cautious about offering anything in the way of help. But Patel seemed eager.

"Well," I said slowly, afraid that what I said next might be offensive. "You're Indian, right?"

It had been three hours since Don and his Wonderful Dance with the Windmills, an interminable amount of time of sitting in the passenger seat of my own car, not knowing whether my best friend had gone mad or was just on the far reaches of eccentricity, and not knowing whether I was a companion or a prisoner. But when we'd stopped at Burger

Quarters, a kind of gas station/restaurant/gift shop (we were both starving, of course, since Don had made us miss breakfast), I'd put on my most innocent voice to say "May I just use the bathroom for a second?" and Don's reply had been "Go ahead. I'll find us a seat."

In the bathroom, I'd pulled my cell phone out of my purse right away and made the call.

Patel was the easy choice. He was Indian and I'd already seen him watching a Rahul Ghosh video. Maybe he would have some insight on what Don was thinking.

Plus, his card had been lying conveniently wrinkled at the bottom of my purse, with his cubicle extension and everything.

I just hoped that he wouldn't think I was rude for asking about his ethnicity.

He didn't.

"Yeah, I'm Indian. I was born in Bangalore, but my parents moved here when I was only two. How come?"

I continued with a little more confidence. "Well, I'm in a really strange situation. My friend Don came back from the Peace Corps last week. He was in Africa for just a little over a year… and I didn't know this… but they show a lot of Indian movies over there…"

"Not surprising. Indian films and Hollywood films are neck and neck throughout a lot of the world."

I paused, not knowing how to get to the stranger part of the story.

"The thing is," I said, finally, "Don really got into Indian movies over there. I mean, I don't know, but I think he watched them every day or something…"

"Okay, so…" said Patel, and there was just a tinge of impatience in his voice. Oh no, I thought, maybe he thinks I want to borrow some videos from him!

"The problem is I think he loved Indian films too much," I said.

"What do you mean?"

"Well, now he's acting like he's one of the stars of these movies. I mean, he's really acting crazy, just like the way this guy acts in his films. This morning he started a fight with three truck drivers, and then he started dancing out in some big field full of windmills. I think he actually thinks he is this guy. That's what I'm saying."

I stopped. Everything had just gushed out of me.

I needed a breath, and I needed to hear what Patel was going to say.

He didn't say anything.

There was only silence on the phone and I wondered if maybe Patel had hung up.

Did he think I was the crazy one?

"I—"

"Which one?" he said softly.

"Huh?"

"Which Indian star does he think he is?" Patel's voice was calm and a little amused.

"He says he thinks he's an Indian actor named Rahul Ghosh."

"Rahul?" Patel laughed. "Yeah, I can see that. I mean, if you're gonna go mad, I guess Rahul isn't a bad choice."

"Well, I'm not sure if he's really crazy, or what, I'm just worried. I'm stuck in the middle of California on the way to Atlanta and I don't know what to do."

"Okay, okay, don't worry. I'm here to help. Tell me all about it."

I did.

I started by telling him all about Don, how he'd left for the Peace Corps, how he'd come back. I told him all of the events at the restaurant and at the windmills, but I made myself look a little better in the case of the windmill incident by pretending I protested more than I actually had. I told him how I'd said that I would never call Don "Rahul" and how I had been so surprised that he had let me go to the bathroom here at Burger Quarters.

Finally, I ended with this question:

"Well, what do you think?"

"I think that you're a really good friend."

"What?"

"Well, I think that it's really great that you're willing to pick up and go with Don. Now I understand why you left misterbook as quickly as you did."

"Oh, well, yeah, but… I mean, do you think I'm doing the right thing?"

"That depends. Do you think that Don is dangerous at all?"

I hadn't really thought about this too much so I had to pause before answering. "Well, no, I don't think that he's really dangerous, well, to anybody but himself. I don't think that he'd hurt me if you know what I mean."

"It didn't sound like that to me either. I have another question."

"Okay."

"Are you and Don just friends? I don't know how to put this delicately… Are you interested in him?"

This one gave me even more pause. I wondered if I should tell Patel everything, about the crush, about what happened after that. But that might have involved telling him about Brad, and there was something about Patel that made me not want to say anything about that.

"No, we're just friends."

"Okay, well, here's my suggestion. First, stay with Don. Go ahead and go on this trip with him, but watch him carefully. It sounds like he needs you now, and maybe this whole thing will die down once he actually meets Devi. Second, call me as much as you need to, but make sure that you call me every day. I'm here to help. Also, I'm going to call my younger sister today. To be honest, she knows a lot more about Indian movies than I do, so maybe she can tell me more about Rahul Ghosh's roles. How's that sound?"

"Good. Thanks so much, Patel."

"Of course. Anything for a friend."

I smiled. "Well, I'd better go. Don's waiting for me out there… I hope he hasn't done anything weird."

"All right," said Patel.

I took the phone from my ear and was just reaching for the disconnect button, thinking that Patel had really made me feel better, when I heard his voice again. I brought my phone back to my ear.

"Huh?"

"Listen, Shayla, like I said, I don't know a lot about Rahul Ghosh, but I have seen some of his bigger movies… and I do think it's worth warning you. I know you and Don are friends, but a lot of times in Indian movies, two friends realize they love each other. There's this movie called *Mere Dil Ko Kuch Chuhta Hai*, where Rahul Ghosh falls in love with his friend, and another one called *Saccha Aashik Apna Saathi Dhoondh Leta Hai*, where he travels across Europe with this girl and they end up falling in love."

My mind reeled, both at the long Hindi film titles and the message that I thought Patel was trying to get across.

"Um… What are you saying?"

"It's probably nothing to worry about, but… well… I'm just saying watch out. Don may be going to see this Devi, but, if he really is living out a Rahul Ghosh fantasy, if he's making his decisions based on what he's seen Rahul's characters do onscreen, well then, there's a chance he may end up falling in love with you."

I had no idea how to feel about that.

CHAPTER ELEVEN
THE LETDOWN

MY LEGS WERE shaking as I made my way back into the restaurant section of Burger Quarters, first passing through a lobby full of California keepsakes.

No, I thought. Impossible.

There was absolutely no way that Don would fall for me. Our past just didn't support that kind of thing.

I found him sitting in a booth by the window, looking out at the highway. On the table before him sat a huge hamburger and french fries. On my side of the table was a plate of fish and chips. Like a good friend, he'd remembered my favorite meal.

But could there be something more in his considerateness?

Could Patel be right?

"Hey," I said as I slid into my seat. "Thanks for ordering."

"It just came." Don turned from the window and reached out to touch my hand. "Listen, Shayla, I'm sorry about what happened earlier. I was wrong to act the way I did." Both of his hands now covered mine.

"It's okay," I said.

Now Don looked at me over his hamburger, and my fish, and gave my hands a soft reassuring squeeze. "No, no, I—I'm really sorry I took control of your car the way I did. That wasn't right."

That wasn't the only thing he'd done that "wasn't right," but I went with it, probably because of how warm and nice his hands felt on mine.

"Shay, the truth is this. It's very important that you are on this trip with me. We are going to Atlanta to meet Devi. I am in love with her and I need to tell her this, in person and to her face. I want you with me because you're my best friend, and I want your support."

I nodded. He was softly stroking my hands with his fingers.

Don, king of mixed messages.

"Thank you." Don removed his hands. "Thanks for trusting me."

I hadn't said that, exactly, but I realized this might be a window of opportunity. "Does this mean I can have my keys back?"

Without taking his eyes off me, Don reached one hand into his pocket and pulled out my car keys. He silently set them on the table between our plates.

"Shay, have I ever let you down before?"

I stared into his eyes, swallowed, and shook my head no.

"I won't let you down now. We'll get to Atlanta, we'll meet Devi, and everything will be okay." He nodded curtly. "Now," he said, and he wrapped the hands that had just covered mine around his burger, "I'm starving. Let's eat."

Actually, Don *had* let me down before.

It wasn't something that I was going to bring up over lunch, especially since Don seemed to be acting so normal all of a sudden. The last thing I wanted was to upset him into some kind of relapse.

But the fact remains: He had let me down in the past.

Twice.

I'd never tried to talk to Don about these let-downs before and now certainly didn't seem to be the time.

Actually, I'd never talked to anybody about what happened.

Well, except my psychologist, Dr. Ripples, that is.

And even he only knew about one of the times.

So I smiled at Don and dipped a piece of fish into the little bowl of tartar sauce on my plate...

But as we ate, my mind was back in the past, specifically on the Monday after the Seventh Grade Spring Dance, the dance where Don had stood up for me against Brad Newton and I had started to fall in love with Don...

and, I was about to find out, someone had started to fall in love with me...

SS

I wrote down the letters in green pen and then stole happy but critical glances at them, in between pretending to pay attention to Mr. Jerome who was talking about multiplying fractions, a subject I hadn't really gotten in the sixth grade, and still wasn't very interested in now.

SS—not perfect, I guessed. A little too much like the sound a snake makes, or kind of like the Nazi soldiers that Murakami had taught us about in World History, but still there was something nice about having two of the same letters make up your initials. Shayla Smith... Shayla SMITH... SHAY Smith... It had a nice ring to it, much better than Shayla Yost, and anyway, the initials *SY* seemed like I was bored or fed up or both...

"All right, folks, I'll see you tomorrow. And make sure you finish Exercise 5," said Mr. Jerome.

Exercise 5. *Sigh.* I'd missed everything Mr. Jerome was saying about fractions... again.

I closed my notebook quickly so that nobody could see what I'd been doing (I hadn't thought of marriage initials since Ben Xavier in the fifth grade and even the initials themselves had made me blush then!) and headed out the door with the rest of the class.

All of a sudden there was a noise behind me.

"Sssst!"

Somebody was hissing to get somebody's attention. It reminded me of *SS*, but I didn't think it was for me. I kept walking.

"Ssst!" came the sound again, "Hey… Hair!"

I turned around. Leaning on the wall right beside the door was Brad Newton. He had one knee bent up so that his foot was resting against the wall, and his head was cocked to the side, as if he were trying to pretend he wasn't the one who had made the noise, but when I said "Brad?" he looked at me right away.

"Hey," he said.

"Uh…" I couldn't think of anything else to say. Despite sharing metal shop with Don, Brad was actually one grade above us, and before the dance I had never talked to him before. But there he was. He had a reputation for being fierce, a bad boy, but the way he was looking at me now seemed very innocent.

"Sorry," he mumbled, looking down sheepishly.

"Huh?" I asked.

"Sorry. If I was a jerk Friday night. Sorry."

"Uh… it's okay?" I said, not liking how I added a question mark to what I was saying. But I was really confused.

"Cool," said Brad. He pushed himself away from the wall and stood on both legs. "You know, you're pretty cool. You know that?"

My eyes rolled around, trying to decide where to focus. Finally, I decided to look down. "Thanks," I said. I'm pretty sure I was blushing.

"Hey, you wanna hang out?"

Was he asking me to skip class with him? I knew that was something these stoner guys did sometimes.

"I've got a class," I said. "Mr. Murakami's giving a quiz

today and I really can't…"

"I mean after school. You know the trail off by the baseball field?"

"Yes."

I sure did. That was known as *The Stoner Trail*, where people like Brad went to smoke. I knew for a fact that they smoked cigarettes. I'd been told that they smoked marijuana too, but I wasn't sure.

"Come by after school. Me and some of my friends'll be there."

"I… I don't smoke."

"That's cool. Just come by and hang out for a while."

"Ummm…"

"Listen, Shayla," and this was the first time he'd used my name. "It'd be cool if you came. Anyways, that's where I'll be if you decide to. Later."

"Bye," I said to his retreating back.

Did Brad like me?

I wasn't sure how I felt about that idea, but it was exciting to think that someone was interested in me.

Don had never said that I was *cool* before. Nobody had.

But I like Don, right? I asked myself.

Yes, but he'd never said I was cool.

My whole face felt hot as I walked to Murakami's class.

My seat was still in front, but now Don had moved to sit right beside me. The whole room had rearranged itself subtly over the course of the year as people found their cliques. Jen Abrams had moved over with Erik Anderson and the jocks, and I was over here with Don.

Don gave me a smile as I sat down next to him, but there was no time to talk. Murakami started in about conjugating verbs right away. Don scribbled down a quick note to me on his notebook, and pushed it to the edge of the table. I leaned over to read it. I HAD FUN AT THE DANCE.

ME TOO, I wrote back.

ANY PLANS AFTER SCHOOL?

I considered. I couldn't tell Don about Brad because he

hated him. I wasn't sure whether I wanted to go to the trail or not, but still, I wrote back:

MY MOM WANTS ME TO GO SHOPPING WITH HER TODAY. CAN'T DO ANYTHING.

As I pushed the notebook toward Don, I was dazed. I couldn't believe I was lying to him. I still wasn't sure that I was going to go to the Trail, but I was intrigued.

"Hey," said Don after class. "There's a *Star Trek* convention next month."

"Another one?"

"Yeah. They're gonna have James Doohan."

"Who?"

"You know, Scottie from the original series. *I've given her all she's got captain, an' I canna give her no more. I canna change the laws of physics!* You wanna come with me?"

"Maybe," I said.

Maybe…

Maybe Don and I were just friends.

When I walked into the little copse of pine trees at the edge of the baseball field, I hardly knew what I was doing. Brad was standing there with three of his friends, two guys and one girl. Theresa Reisher looked at me with an open mouth: "Shayla Yost? *You* came?"

"Uh… yeah. I'm here."

Brad walked up to me. "Cool. I'm glad you came."

Brad turned out to actually be a nice guy. He made every effort to seem aloof, but really he wanted to spend time with me. That had never happened to me before, not like this. Don always wanted to do things, but he always wanted to do Don things. Brad wanted to know about me. That day, he walked me home, and from then on he always made an effort to be with me. He would be waiting at my locker after classes, or he would meet me as I walked to school. He was fascinated by how well I got along with my own family. His home situation was different. His mother and father had divorced when he was nine, and he and his three siblings called his mom "The Screamer."

I started to understand him, and even care for him, but

one day, when he asked me to kiss him, I said no. I wasn't ready yet, and in a way I thought I would be betraying Don.

Which is exactly what Don seemed to think a week later when he found out.

We were sitting on the couch in my family's den, watching an action video Don had brought over, but he didn't seem very interested. There was a bowl of tortilla chips between us, which I was eating and he hadn't touched. He was just sitting back on the couch staring at them and not at the movie.

"Are you okay?" I asked.

To my surprise, Don blurted out, "Are you dating Brad Newton?"

"Uh... well, we're hanging out a little."

"Why?" Don was incredulous.

"He's actually not so bad. I think you'd actually like him if you gave him a chance."

"Like him! That guy is a burn out."

"Look, he's not, okay. His family's a little bit weird and he has a hard time in classes, but he's actually trying hard."

"Look, just don't see him anymore, okay!"

I stared at Don, surprised, and a little cross.

Don stared back.

"Okay?" he demanded.

"No. That's not okay," I said.

Don's mouth hung open in surprise for a second. Then he closed it. "Fine," he said, and stood up. "You and Brad have fun together. I'm outta here."

"Fine," I said, really angry as he grabbed his bag and walked out.

The next day when I entered Murakami's classroom, Don was already there, a new *Star Trek* novel opened in front of him. He didn't look up when I came in and he didn't look at me at all as class got started. I wrote down a quick note and passed it to him: CAN'T I BE FRIENDS WITH BRAD AND STILL BE FRIENDS WITH YOU?

He glanced at the note, picked up his pencil and made a couple quick lines before handing it back.

NO, his note said.

For the last two weeks of school, Don disengaged himself from my life. He never called, he never spoke to me, and he went to the *Star Trek* convention with Brent Mellner. When I called him, his mother always told me that he was off studying at the library or helping his dad.

He didn't even sign my yearbook.

But Brad Newton did. And the next time that Brad asked me to kiss him, I did.

By the time Don finally came around, calling me on my birthday a week after classes ended, Brad and I had officially become girlfriend and boyfriend. Don never liked it, but he learned to tolerate it, and he managed to stay a good friend.

Those few weeks before we made up, though, were the first time Don let me down.

The second time…

Well, that's something I'd never even told Dr. Ripples…

After lunch, Don and I got back on the road.

My conversation with Patel had really made me feel better, and I was suddenly free—and ready—to enjoy myself, even if Don was acting wacky.

I decided to share my good mood with him. "Devi's a really lucky girl," I shouted to him over the sound of crunching gravel as we pulled out of the parking lot. In return, he flashed me a broad and, I think, appreciative, smile, but said nothing.

He was driving again. Even though he'd given me my keys back over lunch, he'd grabbed them back from the middle of the table just as we were leaving. I'd been surprised to discover that I didn't mind. Here I was, traveling cross-country (something I'd never done before) with my best friend (who might have been a madman) and Indian music blaring from the stereo (which I was actually getting to like, again to my surprise), and I was happy. More than that: I was ecstatic. I chalked my good mood up a little bit to the newness and oddness of the situation, but even more to the fact that, unlike Patel, I was no longer working at misterbook.com. Other than making me feel better about my situation, that phone call had also reminded me of what a soul-sapping job I had escaped when I agreed to go on this trip.

So whatever happened, I was going to enjoy myself. No matter what, nothing could possibly be worse than sitting in a cubicle answering email after email after email, for no real purpose other than to help customers who were too lazy to do their own Google searches.

Nope, I thought as I adjusted my seat back and looked up at the clear blue sky above, from here to Devi, I wasn't going to let anything bother me.

CHAPTER TWELVE
ON THE ROAD TO DESTINY

I WAS ABLE to enjoy nothing bothering me for just about an hour.

Then Don said, in an excited voice:

"Did you see that??"

I was back on the alert in an instant.

"What?"

I searched the landscape for windmills. None, thank God.

"That guy on the side of the road. It looked like he needed help."

He pulled my car onto the shoulder. I turned to look out the back window and could see, about two pool lengths behind us, a figure dressed all in black standing in front of a seventies-style gray car. The car had its hood up and a heavy cloud of thick gray-blue smoke was pouring out and curling around the man who was waving his arms wildly, sometimes to ward off the smoke and sometimes to get the attention of passing traffic.

Don was right. The man looked like he needed help.

He also looked, with his all-black wardrobe, like some

kind of Mafioso.

I couldn't see him all that well from this far away, but I could tell he was tall from the way he towered over the car, the top of his head about even with the lifted hood. His hair was semi-shrouded in smoke, but I could see that it was just as black as his clothes, yet very uneven, with bits and pieces sticking up in clumps, like a defective Chia Pet. From what I saw, I wasn't all that interested in helping him. I turned to tell this to Don...

and Don put the car in reverse.

"Don, we shouldn't do this."

We started moving swiftly backwards.

"Why not? He needs help," said Don.

"What if he's dangerous?"

I was starting to feel a little panicked. The closer we got, the more ominous this guy was looking. I could see now that he was black, over six feet tall, and that his jacket and pants were what seemed to be smooth black leather. He reminded me of Wesley Snipes in *Blade,* except his skin color was more Latte than Black Coffee.

"He doesn't look dangerous," said Don.

"He looks tough."

"He looks like a skeleton."

I took another look and sure enough, Don was right. The guy was incredibly skinny with a somewhat sunken-in face.

"Maybe he's in a gang."

I'd seen the movies about L.A. street gangs; I knew about Compton.

"He's wearing glasses."

Okay, that was true, too.

"I just don't feel right about this. He might have a gun."

Okay, the gang idea was pretty stupid. We were far from Compton now, just past Barstow, and everything was looking pretty much like desert. It could be the right scenario for a car hijacking, though. It looked like one of those teens-on-vacation/Death Valley horror settings.

Except there were too many cars on Highway 40 to be

very scary.

"Look, I'm going to help him."

Don stopped a little way in front of the other car, where the man had turned now to look at us, smoke wreathing his body from behind like an aura. Now I could see a blanket sticking out from under the hood. The blanket was baby blue—another indicator that this might not be the gangster/serial killer I had imagined—and had obviously been used to put out a fire. The car itself was square and long, a model that I vaguely remembered being a presence on the streets back when I was in grade school. It turned out, too, that the car was actually maroon, not gray. The front had just been *burned* gray.

"I'm leaving the keys right here," said Don. "If anything weird happens, you get out of here." He stepped out of the car, calling "Can I help you?" to the man.

Dang Don and his *Star Trek*/Rahul Ghosh ethics! Well, *Star Trek* at least; I still wasn't so sure what Rahul Ghosh ethics were like. Anyway, whoever Don was emulating, the bottom line was that he always had to help people, regardless of what they looked like. After all, as he'd always been fond of saying, the Klingons may have looked evil to Captain Kirk's crew at first, but by the time of Captain Picard, they were much better understood allies. This was Don's way of saying "Don't judge a book by its cover." Funny, then, how those same principles had never applied to Brad Newton and his friends...

Thinking these thoughts, I watched anxiously in the rear view mirror. Even if the man wasn't your stereotypical threat, he could still be bad.

Weren't serial killers often the nicest-looking people you could imagine?

The conversation seemed to be going well, though. Nothing dangerous seemed to be happening, which relieved me... until...

Don motioned to my car and the two of them both walked over. Don opened the driver's side.

"Shay, this is Michael." The man nodded at me. "He's

having car troubles."

"I think my car is dead," said the man. "I was afraid this would happen. I drove all the way out from New York, but my car is so old, you see…"

His voice was soft and, I have to admit, he didn't sound dangerous. Even his clothes didn't look tough anymore. They weren't even really leather, they were too shiny…

Oh my God, were they latex?

Latex?

"Can Michael use your cell phone?" Don asked. "He needs to get his car fixed."

This was not working out the way I had expected. *Any* way I had expected. I wanted to be mad at Don, but he was being so nice, asking me for my permission, and I couldn't be mad at Latex Michael because he was giving me this really shy, embarrassed smile that wasn't threatening at all. I decided to be mad at Patel. He had made this sound like it was going to be easy, a fun ride to Devi and it would all be over.

Dang it, Patel!

"Can I… talk to…. you… for a second?" I said to Don, trying to make my voice sound as bitchy as possible. I'm afraid I only sounded like a confused Captain Kirk.

"Sure." Don turned to explain to the man, but Michael had already figured out what was going on.

"It's okay. I'll be over by my car." Amazing. This stranger understood my mood better than my own best friend.

Don turned back to me.

"What are you doing?" I hissed.

"I'm helping."

"Well, I don't want to help. I don't want to give that man my cell phone."

"His name's Michael."

"I don't care. What if he's back there pulling a gun out of his car?" I didn't believe this anymore, but I wanted Don to realize how angry I was.

"Why would he be doing that? He seems nice."

"Don, I don't know what people are like in Africa… or even in some Indian movies… but here it's dangerous to help people."

"Oh, come on, Shay… Michael's just like me."

"What? How could he possibly be like you?" I suddenly had a terrifying image of both Don and Michael singing and dancing on the side of the road. I blocked it out.

"He's in love," said Don. "He's traveled all the way from New York to meet his boyfriend in L.A. and now his car's broken down. So… don't you see… we've got to help!"

"I don't want to," I said, without thinking, and then I thought a little bit and that irritated me because I felt like there was something important in our conversation that I should have noticed. Something Don had said that I'd missed.

"It's nothing big, Shay. He just needs to use your cell phone for one second so that he can call a tow truck."

"No."

"Come on, Shay. It's our obligation to help Michael. You don't know his story."

"Do you?" I snapped.

"Yes, I do." He gave me his best "I'm imploring you" look. "Please, Shay?"

I decided not to look at his eyes. I stared at the glove box.

I was right, I knew that. Stopping for strangers on the side of the road was a bad idea. Giving them your cell phone was even more dangerous.

But Don was right, too. Michael did seem to be okay.

"Fine! Here!" I handed him my cell phone. "But I think we should have a long talk once we're on our way again."

"Okay. Thank you, Shay!"

Ten minutes later we were somehow all sitting in my car, waiting for the tow truck to arrive. I was still trying to figure out whether I was a humanitarian, or just simply a pushover, when Michael began telling us his own very sad love story,

the one that had affected Don so much to say that Michael
was just like him...

CHAPTER THIRTEEN
MICHAEL'S STORY

"TERRY AND I met online in April," Michael said from the backseat.

"I've never met anybody online like that before, but it was obvious that Terry was somebody special right away.

"You see, I'm a teacher. I teach Communications at the Bruchner Institute in New York City. For Spring Quarter, I was teaching Interpersonal Relations, and part of that involved interview skills. I thought the best way to get started was by having my students go ahead and interview some real people, but I didn't want to make them go out and do this right away face-to-face. That might be too daunting.

"So I thought of Internet Chatting. I'd never tried it before myself, but it seemed like the perfect way for my students to get started. They could meet someone and ask questions without all the initial nervousness that comes with face to face interviews. Also, they could have a little fun and maybe make a new friend. So I gave my students this assignment where they were supposed to get online and have an Internet chat with another person, find out as much as they could about that person's goals, and then present a short piece of writing about who that person was…"

I looked at Michael in my vanity mirror. He seemed like an intellectual, with his wire rim glasses and his slow, careful way of talking. He looked kind, too, and, in a soft unassuming way, he was handsome, or rather "cute." I wondered if this was going to be a story about how he had been taken advantage of. Poor guy, had he gotten used and thrown away? Had this woman treated him badly?

"I didn't think it was fair for me to ask my students to do this Internet chatting if I didn't try it myself, so as I was planning the assignment I entered a chat room for the first time. I chatted to a couple of people, but nothing really seemed to go anywhere until this little winking smiley face icon popped up, saying HI, I'M TERRY, YOU SOUND INTERESTING.

"I replied, THANK YOU.

"I'M SORT OF A TEACHER, TOO, was the response. I'M A CHOREOGRAPHER FOR A LOCAL THEATER HERE IN WEST HOLLYWOOD. That's how the conversation got started, but it didn't stop there. Terry seemed like the perfect guy for me. He was kind, intelligent, inter—"

"What!?" I asked.

"I'm sorry, what did I say?" said Michael.

"Did you say that Terry's a guy?"

"Well, yes, of course. I'm gay. I thought you knew that."

"Um… no," I said, giving Don a glaring look.

"I told you," said Don with a shrug.

Oh my God, that's what I had missed!

"I hope that's not a problem." Michael was looking uncomfortable now.

"Well… no, it's not a problem," I said, thinking about Brad Newton and how he would have reacted if he'd known I was sitting in a car with a gay man. He probably would have broken something. "It's just… Never mind. I was just surprised, that's all."

Don reached out and held my hand. He knew what I

was thinking.

"I'm sorry, Michael," I said. "Keep going with your story. I'm really interested."

Please make this an interesting story, I thought. I don't want to think about Brad now. I don't want to think about what he did.

"Um... okay... well, as I was saying, Terry was just what I'd been looking for. The only problem... well, what I thought was the only problem... was that he lived in L.A. and I lived in New York. I didn't think that we would ever go further in our relationship because of this, but it was fun to talk to him so we kept talking.

"Over the next two weeks, we chatted every day, sometimes for five or six hours at a time. We had a great deal in common. We were both professionals, but more than that, we also both really liked the club scene. Every Friday or Saturday, me and my friends go out clubbing and we love techno, and I love to dance.

"We talked about everything under the sun, and it wasn't long before I started thinking about Terry all the time, when I woke up in the morning, when I was taking a shower, even in my classes. I found it really hard to get my work done. Grading seemed so unimportant next to chatting. You know, some people say that Internet chat is addictive, but I wasn't addicted to that... I was addicted to Terry. Every night I would come home and need to get my fix of Terry.

"I decided I had to meet him. I thought about how I could ask him, but before I could, one night out of the blue, he asked me! Of course I said yes. We considered meeting somewhere in the middle, between California and New York, but since my Spring Break was coming up, I thought what the hell, I'll come to L.A. I'd never been to Cali before, and I'd always wanted to visit Disneyland. Terry promised that he'd take me.

"Well, next thing you know, I was on a flight to LAX. It was perfect. Terry picked me up at the airport and when he saw me (of course, we had exchanged pics online) he ran up and hugged me and I think he even lifted me off the ground a little…"

"That's exactly what it will be like when I meet Devi!" interrupted Don. He was smiling broadly, swept up in the story.

"He sounds like a great guy," I said carefully.

Get out of my mind, Brad Newton.

"He is great. He really is," said Michael. "That first night he took me to this really fancy Tex-Mex place where everything tastes a little bit sweet and then we went to one of his favorite clubs, the Lights Out, and we danced and danced.

"Then he took me back to his apartment. He has a beautiful apartment in Marina Del Rey. It's got a kind of southwestern design with these big arching doorways and this stucco plaster that makes everything look like a Mexican restaurant on the outside. Inside everything is white and clean, and he's got two bedrooms and all this modern looking glass and silver furniture. It's elegant, but I was surprised that there wasn't anything in the way of artwork. The only picture in the whole apartment was a picture on his bedroom cabinet of a young, good-looking blonde lady. She was wearing this white blouse with big red dots and smiling this nice, happy smile. He said that this was his sister, Tara, and I didn't ask anymore.

"This is where we get to the strange thing about Terry. We could talk about anything at all, I felt free around him, I moved with liberty around his house. He was absolutely open about everything… Except one thing. He didn't want me to look in his closet. That's one of the first things he told me: 'I've got skeletons in my closet. Please don't look in there. It's really private.'

"Of course, I said I wouldn't. It was a little strange to me, but I respected his privacy, and I wasn't interested in the closet anyway. Still, once he said it, I could never get the closet out of my mind. What could be in there, I wondered, that was so terrible?

"I kept my word, though, and never looked… well, until the very last day. We'd had a wonderful week together, but every night when we lay in bed that closet just seemed to be looking at me. That closet door and I would stare at each other for what seemed like hours while Terry lay next to me snoring. (He's got this soft little snore like a cat's purr...)

"Anyway... Finally, the temptation was too much. That last night before I left, as Terry slept, I crept over to the closet and very gingerly pushed open the door, checking behind me to see that he was still asleep. Then I looked in.

"On one side of the closet were all his clothes, jeans and shirts and sweaters... but on the other side, all I could see was women's clothing... dresses... dress after dress, skirts, high heeled shoes, boots, scarves... blouses. I fingered my way through all of these odd neighbors... What were they doing here, I wondered. After all, Terry lived alone, and he'd never mentioned any woman friends. Why, then, would he have all these...?

"Then my eye caught upon one particular piece... a blouse... a white one with red dots... the same one his "sister" Tara had been wearing in the picture. I had no idea what was going on!

"All kinds of ideas went through my head. Some of them were good. Like maybe Terry's sister had left her clothes with him for some reason. That's what I wanted to think. Some of the ideas were worse than bad, though. What if that picture wasn't really Terry's sister, but his lover? What if Terry had a girlfriend, or even a wife? What if I was just something on the side, an experiment? That had happened to a friend of mine once, with this husband curious about gay sex who hadn't bothered to mention that he had a wife!

"No, I didn't want to believe that, but I just couldn't rule out the possibility. I almost shook Terry awake right then and there, but then I thought, if there's nothing wrong, he might get upset at me for doubting him.

"So I spent the night in his living room, watching Nick at Nite reruns, and thinking. By the morning, I had a plan. I was going to be subtle. I would just ask him some questions about his sister that would lead me to some answers. I would get him to tell me if it was her clothes in the closet.

"I had a long time to wait. It was after 11 when Terry

woke up. He came out of the bedroom, stretching his arms and grinning at me. 'Hey, how long have you been up?' he asked me. 'Just a little while,' I said. 'The sun woke me up.' 'Want breakfast?' he asked.

"He made scrambled eggs, toast and hash browns. He'd really been pampering me like this ever since I got there. We sat down at his glass dining room table and ate. At precisely halfway through my eggs, I asked my first question. It turned out to be the only planned question I could ask:

"'So, your sister Tara, what does she do?'

"He looked down at his eggs and dropped his fork. I couldn't tell if he was sad or if he was being deceitful. Then he looked back up at me. 'My sister's dead, Michael. She was in law school, studying to be a lawyer,' he said. 'But just before she was going to take her bar exam, she was driving to a party and got hit by a drunk driver. She died instantly.'

"'I'm sorry,' I stammered.

"'It's okay, Michael. I've gotten over it. I dedicate a lot of my professional choreography to her, and hope that she's proud of that.'

"I'd gotten an answer, but it wasn't the answer I wanted. Now I felt sorry for Terry, but the clothes in the closet were an even bigger mystery to me. If Tara was dead, why did Terry keep her clothes?

"'When did it happen?' I asked.

"'Oh, it's been a long time. Seven years.'

"I couldn't help now but think that this must be a lie. Nobody keeps a dead person's clothes for seven years. I was suspicious again.

"Another question came to my mind and I asked it: 'Did she leave anything for you?'

"'Well, she didn't write out a will or anything. She was only twenty-eight years old. What she did have ended up going to my mom and dad, and me and my brother, Bill. That couch in the living room, my breakfast set, some of my dishes… that's all that she left me. And her pictures. That's all I've got.'

"'Oh,' I said.

"'I really loved her,' Terry said. 'She was a great sister.'

"But here's what I was thinking. Terry had lied to me. He never mentioned the clothes. Even if they were Tara's, there's something freaky about a man who keeps his dead sister's clothes around after she's gone. All kinds of terrible thoughts were going through my head.

"I didn't even want him to walk me to my terminal, but he said he wanted to be with me up until the end. I couldn't wait to get on the plane and away from him. It seemed like I had made a terrible mistake. As I hugged him, the only thing I was thinking was that I would soon be three thousand miles away. On my way through the boarding gate, I looked back, and he was crying. His lips were quivering and he was making fists as if he were really trying to hold back his emotions. He really was sad to see me go. I don't think anybody has ever cried for me leaving like that before, but I hardened my heart and got on the plane. I wasn't going to think about Terry Blackburn any more.

'When I got back to New York, I immersed myself in my teaching and tried to forget about him. Sure, he would send me chirpy, happy e-mails, but I ignored them. At first, he didn't seem to get it, but then his messages changed. IS EVERYTHING OKAY, MICHAEL? he asked in one. ARE YOU THERE? he asked in another. I THOUGHT WE HAD A GOOD TIME. ARE YOU BREAKING UP WITH ME? he asked one day, and finally, DON'T I AT LEAST DESERVE AN EXPLANATION?

"He was right. I sent him an e-mail that simply said, I FOUND THE CLOTHES.

"YOU LOOKED IN MY CLOSET? he sent back the next day.

"YES, I LOOKED. I FOUND ALL THE CLOTHES, INCLUDING THE ONES TARA IS WEARING IN THE PICTURE ON YOUR MANTLE. I DON'T KNOW WHY THEY'RE THERE, BUT I DON'T THINK I CAN BE WITH SOMEBODY WHO HAS SECRETS.

"I CAN EXPLAIN.

"TOO LATE, I wrote back. And he didn't respond to

that. It seemed like it was over. Life went back to normal.

"But then, all of a sudden, just last week I got an e-mail from him. It was an invitation to something called The Eros Party. All Terry had written with the message was, PLEASE COME. EVERYTHING WILL BE EXPLAINED.

"I didn't answer that e-mail. At first I thought, How dare he expect me to give up everything and come down there? I've had enough of this. But then, I started to wonder. How would he explain himself? I was curious, and there was something more…"

Don was nodding vigorously. "You're in love with him."

Michael nodded slowly. "Yes, I'm in love with him. Other than the clothes in the closet, Terry is a wonderful person: fun, friendly, cute, good in bed…"

"Hey!" I interjected.

"What?"

"Uh… nothing. I just don't really think I need to know anything about that."

Don nodded. "Shay's right, Terry. You've got a great story, but those details are unnecessary. In Indian movies, the actors and actresses almost never kiss… That's offscreen stuff. Well, at least in Rahul Ghosh movies. He's more traditional. Younger actors these days, they don't mind kissing so much. But Rahul's style is the best. You've got to leave some mystery. Skimpy clothing and sliding your nose up someone's neck and cheek is about all we should see."

It wasn't exactly a non-sequitur, but it was so out of place that both Michael and I turned blank faces to Don. I had to smile a little bit to see that both he and I raised our eyebrows at the exact same moment.

"Yes, you're right," Michael said slowly. "I'm sorry about that." It was clear that he was dumbfounded by what Don had said, but he managed, with a will, to keep his story from getting derailed: "Anyway, to make a long story short, I couldn't ignore the invitation. I called around to get flights, but everything was too expensive since I'd waited so long. I only had four days to get here, so I borrowed my uncle's car... a real junker... and got on my way."

"Speaking of getting you on your way," said Don, looking at the rearview mirror. Michael and I turned to look at him. "I think your tow truck's here."

CHAPTER FOURTEEN
THE EROTIC EXOTIC BALL

"WELL, YOUR ENGINE caught fire and your transmission's shot to hell, I can tell you that. I'm happy to tow this away for you, but you ain't never going to be driving her again, that's for sure. This old gal is toast."

The sewn-on patch on the tow truck driver's grease stained blue shirt showed that his name was Johnny. He wore a blue LA baseball cap and sported a thin, uneven beard and mustache that didn't hide the fact he didn't have much of a chin. However, he did have a vast knowledge of cars, apparently, and he was able to speak with certainty when he told us that Michael's uncle's car had seen its last. This came as no surprise.

"What are you going to do now?" I asked Michael as Johnny pulled his truck back onto the highway with the dead body of the Impala trailing after it. Michael, Don, and I watched it go like a funeral party.

"I don't know," said Michael. "I can't call Terry. He doesn't even know I'm coming. If I can use your cell phone, I'll call a taxi to come get me."

Don shook his head vehemently. "Don't be ridiculous.

This Eros Party of yours starts at 9 o'clock, doesn't it? That's less than three hours away, yah? It's probably going to take at least that much time just to get to L.A. from here. There's no way you can get there in time if you have to wait for a taxi. No, we'll take you!"

"Really?" asked Michael.

"Really?" I said.

"Of course we will."

"Don, can I talk to you for a second?" I asked and pulled him aside. Michael waited patiently behind us.

"What?" Don asked.

"Look, Don? Are you sure this is what you want to do? I mean, I have nothing against helping Michael out, but we're already way past Bakersfield. L.A. is a long way south of here. What about Devi?"

"Devi will be fine. And anyway, how could I go and tell her I love her if I wouldn't even help out another person in love. Don't you see, it's like a karmic test. If we can get Michael and Terry together, then Devi and I can get together, too."

"If you say so, but… did you see that flyer?"

"Ah," Don smiled, "So that's what this is about?"

Michael had shown us the flyer invitation to the Eros Party that he'd printed out from Terry's message, and, if the truth be told, it sent shivers up my spine, and not the good kind.

The flyer read, in large gothic letters on a hot pink background,

The 2001 Eros Party…
(Hollywood's very own Erotic Exotic Ball!!!)

Cum 1
   Cum All
     Just Cum!

And as if that wasn't shocking enough, to the right side of this catchphrase was an illustration of a slender woman dressed in a devil costume, complete with horns and a winding tail, which swung out behind her and seemed to underline the last "Cum" in the announcement. The she-devil had a fully developed mustache and a sharply pointed goatee, but she was certainly a she. As if to prove this point, her naked breasts were sticking through twin holes in the top of her costume. Rounding out the bottom of her costume was a pair of high heel shoes, the heels of which seemed to be made of daggers. Even more alarming than her clothes was what she was carrying in her hand. Clasped in her pointy fingernails was a long, vicious looking, Indiana Jones-style bullwhip. "Down on your knees, slave!" read a speech bubble next to her face. Quite appropriately, a caption under the illustration read "**Bitch Goddess.**"

Below the announcement, there was actually a picture of a man—the Bitch Goddess' slave apparently—who was down on his hands and knees. He was wearing a metal-spiked dog collar and had his head bowed as if he were groveling to the she-devil.

Just in case there was any mistake about what kind of function this Eros Party was going to be, there was a list of activities in a smaller font at the bottom of the page:

Fetish Show
S&M Tables
Transvestites
Contortionists
Little Richard, the Thumbtack Man
Costume Play
The Bond Grrrl Band
Dancing
Door Prizes, and much, much more!

I had handed the sheet of paper back to Michael as if it had given me a Tabasco-laced paper cut.

"Well, yes, that is what this is about," I told Don now. "Have you ever been to one of these things before?"

"No, but who knows? It could be fun. Michael said

these things are just for people who like to dress up and show off their bodies. Sure, it's weird, and it's not something everybody does. But then not everybody should."

"Thank you, George Michael…"

"It's just like a hobby. It's not dangerous. Think of it as a cross-cultural experience. Anyway, don't you want to see how this story ends?"

What I was thinking was that, if we had to go, I might prefer just dropping Michael at the door and leaving. Still, despite myself, I was interested. Up to now the wildest thing I'd ever done, other I guess than actually dating Brad Newton for almost five years, was go to heavy metal concerts with him, where he always somehow ended up bleeding from slamming into someone in the mosh pit. This Eros Party would be a lot weirder, especially to look at, but from what Michael had said, probably nobody would end up bleeding, bullwhip-packing she-devils or not.

I nodded slowly. "Yeah," I said, "I want to see how the story ends."

Plus, I thought secretly, I wasn't in any rush to meet Devi Chakraborty. Let her wait. Like Don had said, she'd be fine. Just fine.

"Let's go," I said.

"There's the Hollywood sign. We're almost there!"

I looked up at the hillside where the famous white letters spelled out the name of the city. It was just after 8:30 and the sign seemed to glow against the black hills and night sky. "Wow," I said.

"Hollywood's not so impressive in the daytime, sweetheart," said Michael. "In fact, it's kind of slummy, but in the nighttime, Hollywood is *happening*!"

"Hollywood," Don sneered. "What's so great about Hollywood, yah? They can't even produce half the films as India. And even the ones that they do… no singing… no dancing…"

Don was sitting in the backseat with Michael. The two

men had really bonded since we'd started our journey. They both loved action movies. Michael was particularly fond of the *Die Hard* and *James Bond* movies and absolutely loved any adaptations from books by Michael Crichton and John Grisham, but he had learned all about Don's interest in Indian movies as we went. Well, maybe not all about Don's interest. He'd only heard Don *talk* about Indian movies, not seen him act like he was in one. But he had adapted to Don's crazy accent quickly enough, and he knew not to argue Don's point. Instead, he just laughed good-humoredly and said, "You are really going to like Terry. He loves singing and dancing, too."

But then we all became quiet right away, all thinking the same thing. Talking about movies had kept us occupied on the drive over, kept us from thinking about what was awaiting us at this Eros Party, what kind of explanation Terry would have, but now that his name had been mentioned, my car was suddenly a big question mark on rolling wheels.

Michael broke the silence. "Shayla, could you turn on the light?" As I did, I heard him unfold the frightening pink Eros Party flyer, looking for the little map he'd copied on the back. I glanced at him in the rearview mirror as he compared the map to the roads we were passing. He looked the same as when we'd met him, except he had replaced his glasses with contacts as soon as we entered L.A. It made him look younger, and quite a bit more attractive. I hoped that Terry would prove to be worth his trouble.

Michael looked from a street sign to his map excitedly. "Okay, was that Sunset Boulevard? Oh, yes, here's where you turn!"

I turned and found myself on a street full of used furniture stores, pawn shops, and Chinese restaurants.

"That's it!" said Michael. At the corner of the street, next to a tiny little Watch Repair business and across from a hot dog stand with a hot dog that looked frighteningly pornographic, was a large, non-descript square white building. It looked like it was an abandoned warehouse, the kind where you might find a rave. Adding to this impression was a line of people in front of the building, all dressed in different levels of nudeness and weirdness. Some looked like they belonged on Harleys, others looked like they belonged in a Dracula movie, and still others looked like they had Timewarped straight out of the *Rocky Horror Picture Show*.

"I don't know…" I said, looking at the people with trepidation.

"C'mon," said Don.

"Please," said Michael. "I'd really appreciate it if you guys were with me when I met Terry. I don't know what to expect."

"Okay," I said, hesitantly, but to be honest, I faked the hesitance. Weird or not, this looked like it could be really exciting. And as weird as these people looked, they were just dressing up for fun. They were letting off steam, unlike Don who seemed to believe he really was an action hero. Or maybe not. Don had been acting remarkably normal since we met Michael.

We paid five dollars to park across the street and made our way toward the line.

Halfway across the street, though, Michael stopped. He was beginning to be nervous. "Do you think I look all right?" he asked. "I'm not underdressed?"

I looked at him and then at Don, who, having nothing made of latex, leather, or silk in his bag, had decided to wear his blue boubou from Africa. "You look fine," I told Michael with certainty.

Actually, between the three of us, it was me I was worried about. Don's boubou might actually turn out to be the perfect costume for an "erotic exotic" party, and Michael's latex jacket was certainly a popular choice, as a quick look at the other participants showed, but my T-shirt and jeans combo just seemed way too normal. However, since the only alternative Michael had been able to suggest was going in wearing only my undies, I decided this was a time when I didn't mind being a misfit.

Michael, on the other hand, was desperate to look as

bizarre as possible. This club thing was, after all, his niche. "Could you sprinkle some of this in my hair?" he asked, producing a little vial of silver and blue glitter from his pocket and bowing his head.

"Sure," I said, taking a few pinches and sprinkling them over his funky hair. "Close your eyes. You don't want to get any on your contacts."

"Thanks."

We got to the line and I was surprised because Michael went straight for the door, passing by all the people waiting with cigarettes in their hands. "They're not waiting," he said. "They're hanging out."

In front of the door was a crew cut man with silver lipstick and black eyeliner. His pecs bulged under an aerated black tank top, and his arms popped out the side like two extra muscles. Michael and Don both reached for their wallets.

"Hey, you're Michael, right?" asked the Muscleman.

"Hey, yeah, how'd you know?"

The man moved away from the door. "You and your friends don't have to pay. Courtesy of the house. Go on in."

"Thank you," said Michael. When we were inside, he turned to the man. "Hey, can you tell me where I could find Terry, then?"

The man blinked. "Terry? Sorry, I don't know any Terry. Enjoy the show, though," he said, shutting the door in our faces.

A little dazed by the man's response, we turned to see where we were. Inside the warehouse it was dark, but obviously made up like a nightclub. At the front of the room was a stage where some kind of skit was going on. Three men and a woman in what looked like spacesuits were yelling and running after each other with SuperSoaker water guns; apparently this was funny because the crowd was roaring with laughter. Against the wall at the entrance, a haggard, cracked-out looking woman was sitting on a stool in front of a table full of plastic penises and chain/leather clothes. Before us and right in front of the stage was a dance area and to our right were chairs and tables. We headed toward the tables, walking past a fake Japanese schoolgirl (who I think was actually a man!), a woman in a bikini whose body had been completely painted so that she looked like a big green lioness, and a man whose hair had been fashioned to look like a parrot.

Looking around at all these strange and fascinating people, I bumped straight into somebody's shoulder. "Excuse me," I said, but he just kept going. I turned to see who I'd hit… but quickly turned right back. The man I'd hit was wearing bottomless red leather pants and his flat white butt was plain to see.

Sitting down was a welcome relief.

All of a sudden, a waitress was at my shoulder. She was wearing a sheer fishnet top and there was a black spider painted above one of her breasts, but other than that, hers was the most conservative costume there. Indeed, she wasn't even showing as much cleavage as the waitress Don had fought to protect that morning. "What would you like?" she asked.

"Beer?" Michael asked us. I looked over at Don, and was happy to see that this new cleavage didn't seem to draw his attention any more than the Albeiro waitress' had. He was staring at the stage where an announcer had replaced the water-gun fighters.

"I'll just have water," I said.

"Heineken," said Michael.

The waitress looked over at Don who was oblivious. The announcer was saying, "And now it is my great pleasure to introduce a lady who needs absolutely no introduction, a lady of class and distinction, a lady whose humor makes us laugh and whose beauty makes us cry…"

"Don?" I said.

Don turned. "Oh, uh, I don't know," he said, "What's your favorite?" he asked the waitress.

"Tequila. Straight up. With lime," she said without missing a beat.

"I'll take that," he said and turned back to the stage.

I know who's driving us to a hotel tonight, I thought.

"And without further ado," boomed the announcer, "Here she is, the Queen of Hearts and the Jack of Diamonds rolled all into one... Mademoiselle Lola!"

I watched the woman saunter onto stage in a long, satiny pink skirt and a red-dotted blouse. She was a heavyset woman and had long blonde hair and the longest, thickest, fakest eyelashes I'd ever seen. She reached out for the microphone. "Hello ladies and gentleman," I heard. "Excuse me if I'm not walking straight this evening. I'm not wearing any panties and I'm all hanging out." The audience laughed.

Ignoring the stage, I leaned toward Michael. "So, do you see..."

"Oh my God," Michael said, apparently not having heard me. He was staring at the stage with his mouth hanging open and his eyes wide.

"Michael?"

"No way," he said, "No no no way."

Now Don turned to look at him. Michael was shaking his head side to side with the blankest, most astonished look I'd ever seen.

"What is it?" Don asked.

"Don't you see? Can't you see it?" His eyes were locked on stage. Don and I followed his gaze.

"See what?" asked Don.

"The blouse? The red polka dots? You see?"

I felt my jaw drop now, too, as I realized what Michael was saying.

"See what?" asked Don, still not getting it.

"Up there, on the stage," I said. "Remember Michael's story..."

Michael lifted one slightly trembling finger and pointed at the stage.

"That's Terry!" he exclaimed.

CHAPTER FIFTEEN
SOMETIMES LOVE WEARS HEAVY MAKEUP

"BUT REALLY, FOLKS," the heavy man-woman with the red polka dots was saying, "It's not my job to make jokes. This is, of course, because I'm a diva. And a much more feminine one than Cher and Celine Dion... Well, fully-clothed, at least. I wouldn't want to be in a bikini contest with those two....

"No, but as a diva, it's my job to sing, to croon, to spread my beautiful melodies and harmonies to you, my adoring fans. Unfortunately, unlike all you lovely people in the audience, the Eros Party committee doesn't love divas as much as you do... even moi, you lovely, lovely audience. No, they've got a rule here... I can only sing one song. Just one tiny, solitary, little song... I said, 'One song! Who do you think you are? Even *Saturday Night Live* gives two songs!' and they said back, 'Sugar,' they said, 'Read your contract. You signed on for equal time with the Thumbtack Man and, diva or not, who can compare with a man who can poke five hundred thumbtacks into himself?' It's ridiculous, isn't it, but

I had to agree... Imagine, no matter how beautiful you are, a person who treats his body like a bulletin board is going to win out every time... He doesn't even have fashion sense; I mean, thumbtacks... I'd use post-its, of course...

"But anyway, sweeties, it's time for my song. This goes out to a man who is very special to me. He might even be here tonight." Terry put his hand over his eyebrows and scanned the crowd, but from the disappointed look on his face, I could tell he hadn't found Michael. This was very possibly because Michael was doing his best to hide behind me!

Terry shrugged and put his hand around the microphone. "Oh well... I don't see him, but if he's here now, hopefully he'll still be here after this song. Anyway, I dedicate this song to him. It's a song by Michael Learns to Rock... and Michael, I hope I did rock you... This is 'You Took My Heart Away'..."

And the man sang the song as a slow ballad, in a soft, slightly falsetto tone that sounded remarkably feminine. I glanced over at Michael and saw that his eyes were moist. Don was watching Terry, fascinated.

After one last high note, Terry stepped back from the microphone. "Thank you very much, darlings," said Terry, "Now, I must go backstage, but I will see you again soon."

He turned his back and strode off.

The announcer, who was a scrawny-looking man in a red bathrobe, came forward. "Thank you, Mademoiselle Lola. And now we give you... Thumbtack Man."

A heavy metal beat began, and a man wearing only cut-off black jeans stepped forward. He opened a brown paper bag in his hand and pulled out one thumbtack. He held it out for the audience to examine and then lifted it to his forehead... and stuck it straight into the middle of one of his eyebrows.

Don and I needed no more demonstration. We turned away at the same time as the Thumbtack Man reached into his bag for a second thumbtack.

Michael was already gone. I looked around the room

and saw him hurriedly making his way toward the stage.

"Come on," said Don, and we got up too, weaving our way through the crowd of half-naked people. We caught up with Michael just as he discovered the entrance to the backstage area. Together, we climbed a set of four stairs and stepped through the entrance, then blinked against the sudden, but dim, light, of backstage. There were several men and women walking about, and some at makeshift wooden tables applying makeup, but they all ignored us as we looked about the room, searching for a glimpse of Terry.

Don was the first to spot him. "Over there," he said, pointing excitedly.

Terry was sitting at a small dressing table, taking off his fake earrings in front of a vanity mirror. His blonde wig was already lying like a drugged Lhasa Apso on the table and his short dark blonde hair was gelled back over his head. He still wore his dress and makeup, but now he looked much more like a man. In fact, I was surprised to notice that he actually resembled my brother with his round cheeks and large Roman nose. However, he was quite a bit heftier than my brother.

"Terry," Michael said softly, his voice barely a whisper over the Thumbtack Man's heavy metal accompaniment washing back to us from the stage.

Terry shot his head around, as if startled, and then just stared at us, at Michael.

"Michael," he said, "You came. I wasn't sure if you would."

"I had to come," said Michael. "I didn't know what to expect. I didn't expect this…" He lifted both arms in a shrug that took in Terry, his wardrobe, and his mirror.

Terry looked up at him. "Are you angry?"

"No," said Michael. "No, I'm not. Why didn't you just tell me?"

"I was afraid," said Terry, simply. "I didn't know how you would react. Some guys don't like this, you know…"

There was a sudden quiet as the heavy metal music from the stage stopped abruptly. We all stood very quietly,

Don and I waiting to see what Michael would do next.

Michael opened his mouth to speak, but before he could, the announcer's voice was there, cutting him off: "Well, thank you, Thumbtack Man. You look really... sharp. Well, the stage show will be back in about half an hour, but for now, it's time for some dancing. We've got DJ Rom here from San Francisco and he's ready to give you some mixes!"

A new beat started up. "Hey, I like this. It's kind of Indian," said Don.

"Sshhhh!" I said, not wanting to interrupt Michael and Terry's moment. It did sound kind of Indian, though.

"Are you really okay with this?" Terry asked.

Michael took a step forward and just as he did, a man walked in from the stage and passed us. "'Scuse me, folks," he said. It was Thumbtack Man, covered from head to belly button in thumbtacks. I moved a little closer to Don as he walked by. Michael watched him go and then looked straight at Terry as he said:

"Are you kidding me? This... is nothing. If you had done that," he gestured after Thumbtack Man, "I would have had a problem!"

"Really, it's kind of a monument to my sister," Terry said. "I started doing this after she died. Honestly, I feel like I'm channeling her a little bit when I perform. But I've had a few people break up with me because of it. That's why I didn't want to tell you."

"Well, I'm here to stay," said Michael. "I really care about you, Terry."

"I really care about you too, Michael."

Terry stood from his chair, Michael moved forward, and they embraced as the beat of the song sped up and a high-pitched, nasal woman's voice appeared.

"Hey!" said Don. "This *is* an Indian song!"

"Ssshhh!" I said again, watching Terry and Michael hug.

Then Terry picked Michael up and spun him around in a way that amazingly matched the music. When he set him down, they looked into each other's eyes lovingly.

"Let's go, Don," I whispered, but Michael heard me

and turned.

"Wait guys, don't go yet," he said, disengaging himself from Terry. "Terry, these are my friends, Don and Shayla. They helped…"

But at that exact moment, we were hit by a swell of sound that was very familiar, the beginning of a new song… I couldn't quite put my finger on what song it was, but I knew that I had heard it recently…

Wait, could it be…?

Badlo, badlo, badlo
Jo banna chahte ho
Badlo, badlo…

Oh my God, it was! The Indian song Don had been playing in my car. One of *The Best of Rahul Ghosh*! What on earth was it doing *here*?

I turned to Don with dread.

What would he do?

The look on his face said it all. He had the same shiny-eyed, fanatical look that he'd had when he'd seen the windmills.

"Come on, Shayla, Terry, Michael, come on!" he yelled, his arms motioning with reckless energy. "We have got to dance!"

He spun and bolted out the entranceway toward the stage, leaving me, Michael, and Terry to stare after him. I turned apologetically. "He… uh… really likes Indian music," I said.

"Me, too," said Terry to my surprise. "These Indian remixes have really become hot in L.A. recently."

"Yeah," said Michael. "They're all over the clubs in New York, too."

"Really?" I said, feeling suddenly even more out of place at this Eros Party than I had before. It was like ever since we'd met Michael, we'd entered some Bizarro world where what Don did seemed to actually make sense.

It did to Terry at least. "Wanna dance?" he asked

Michael.

"Sure," said Michael. "Let's go."

They walked out, hand in hand.

I stood by myself for a minute, looking around the room, feeling remarkably disconnected from everything around me. Maybe I was the one who was going crazy...

Then I thought about Don lying on the floor of the Albeiro Truck Stop, his head haloed by this morning's breakfast...

That image got me moving for the stage. Whatever anybody else here might think of Don and Indian music, I knew a little bit more than they did. I'd seen him dance with the windmills, and I wasn't about to let him out of my sight, not even in a place as upside down as this!

Back out by the stage, things had transformed into a scene from Poe's "The Masque of the Red Death," a story Don and I had read way back in Mrs. Geddes' lit class. The stage itself was empty except for a lone microphone and the DJ booth, but the dance floor itself was now a pulsating mass of strange, shadowy costumes and spastic moving limbs. Everybody was moving and shaking and wobbling and twitching, and under the hypnotic flash of several disco strobe lights, it was all very disorienting.

And still it wasn't hard to find Don.

He was right in front of the stage, and, as I watched, he began lifting himself onto it, bringing one foot up to propel him all the way. About half the dancers—the ones in front—had turned to look at him, and they were staring at him in wonder as they continued to sway to the music. Terry and Michael were there, and they were doing the same.

Oh no...

I edged my way onto the dance floor, circumnavigating the gyrating bodies around me. "Don!" I yelled.

He was already on the stage.

He was heading for the microphone.

"Don!" I shouted again.

He picked up the microphone, cocked his head to listen to the song. It was in the middle of a musical interlude, no singing involved...

Don tapped his foot in time to the beat until the music swelled up and the vocals cut back in...

...and then so did Don.

He sang right along with the song, matching the beat, rhythm, inflection, and even notes. To my surprise, he sounded good, something that either had been missing, or that I had been too busy running after him to notice, in his morning "performance." Now, for the first time in a long time, I remembered that Don had stuck with choir all through junior high and high school, that he had even been one of the baritones in the *Jump! Singers* group which had put on special song and dance numbers during holiday assemblies at our high school. I guess I shouldn't have been surprised then that he was good... but I was.

I stood and just stared up at the stage, listening to Don and the Indian singer singing together in absolute synchronicity...

well, almost absolute synchronicity. It was clear that Don didn't know all the actual Hindi words. Instead, he made up a lot of his own.

So:

Rashtrapati banna hai to, badlo badlo badlo
Hero banna he to, badlo badlo badlo
Govinda ki tarah nachna hai to, badlo badlo badlo
Tez gaadi chalani hai to, badlo badlo badlo

Sang the Indian singer.
And Don sang:

Grab your partner and dance like so, badlo badlo badlo
Here is the place to go, badlo badlo badlo
Everything is beautiful, don't you think so?, badlo badlo badlo
Oh, it's really beautiful, no?, badlo badlo badlo

Luckily, he knew the main word, I thought.

Then, sensing movement, I looked about me. Everybody was still watching the stage, but their faces had changed from wonder to delight. Vampires and sex goddesses and men wearing nipple clips, all alike were smiling up at the stage. And they were moving, too, their heads bouncing to the beat of the song, accentuating each "Badlo."

Their enthusiasm was not lost on Don. He jumped up in the air, grabbed the microphone and holding it at a tilt... very Elvis, I thought... sang as if to the floor, these words, which at least had the same amount of syllables as the original song, if not the actual vocabulary:

> *Here I am up on this stage*
> *Feels like I'm in a cage*
> *I don't know what I'm going to do*
> *Maybe I'll do a stage dive for you.*

Yes, I'm absolutely certain those were not the original lyrics.

It didn't matter. The audience loved it. Don dropped the microphone and ran out into the crowd, flying off the stage into their ready arms. When they set him down, he continued to sing along with the stream of "Badlos" and he started up a little dance: a little spin and a clap, a spin back and another clap, then, holding one hand out as if he were the famous "Little Teapot" of our childhood, he pumped his chest out several times. This he followed by sticking both hands into the air and then swaying them from side to side in what vaguely resembled side-stretching exercises and, after several of these, he bobbed his head along with the beat. Then he did all that again, repeating every move exactly. On the third repeat, several people joined him, trying awkwardly to match his movement. More people joined in for the fourth repeat, and by the fifth time, he was leading an erotic exotic Indian line dance!

By that time, I was watching from off the dance floor,

but even my head was bobbing up and down, and I knew that I was smiling. Here was Don, who had once been forced to go to a junior high dance by his father, who I myself had taught to dance, and now he was leading a line dance himself. Here was Don, whose singing and dancing this morning had made me wonder if he had gone mad… and now that same singing and dancing was being applauded and aped by those around him.

I couldn't help it, but I felt…. well, *proud*.

"He sure is an interesting guy," boomed a voice at my shoulder.

I spun around, surprised. Michael stood there, with a huge amused grin. "Yeah, you can say that again…" I said. I had to shout to be heard above the music. I glanced at the dance floor where the line dance continued, with Don right in the center. Terry was there, too, a couple people away.

Michael nodded his head toward Don. "He's actually pretty good," he hollered.

"I think he's been practicing in front of the TV," I shouted back, still smiling.

"You know," said Michael, leaning in so that I could hear him better, "I wasn't sure about Don when I first met him, but he's got something there."

Somewhere inside of me there must have been some kind of sarcastic remark floating around, some refutation based on what I'd put up with all day, but standing there at the side of the stage watching Don dance, it wasn't coming to me.

"He's a really nice guy," Michael shouted.

I just nodded, most of my attention on the dance floor, responding to Michael's voice almost as if it were background noise.

"So… are you going to tell him?" he asked, as softly as he could shout and still be heard.

"Huh?" Suddenly, Michael wasn't just background. I spun around. "Tell him what?"

Michael came closer so that he could speak in his normal tone, and he continued now in a soft, calm voice—a whisper of a shout. "I've seen the way you look at him, Shayla."

The fear was automatic. There was no controlling it. I knitted my eyebrows and looked down, away from Michael's face. I may even have blushed.

"I don't know what…" I mumbled.

"You look at Don the same way I look at Terry," said Michael. My head jolted back up and I just stared at him, my eyes wide. "You're in love with him, aren't you?"

I could feel my glare coming on. Who was Michael that he could ask this question? I hadn't talked about my feelings for Don with anybody, although many had been interested. Don's father had always kept an eye on us, worried that we might start dating. My mother had always been excited about that possibility. Brad Newton had once, in a fit of rage, torn out all the pictures of Don from my yearbooks, feeling threatened by my friendship. But not one of them had ever asked me point blank whether I loved him or not. And here was Michael doing just that.

I wanted to be angry. I squinted my eyes and frowned at him. His almond eyes stared unwaveringly back. I tried, but I just couldn't get that anger to happen. He was just being too friendly for me to be mean… and anyway, I've never been very good at mean. Sarcastic yes, mean no. I thought about lying to him, but that thought just made me really tired. My shoulders slumped and I looked down at the floor.

Finally, all I could do was give him the truth:

"I don't know."

I said it slowly, letting all the air in my lungs come out with those words. Then I looked back up at Michael. He was still there, still looking like he wanted to help. And now that I'd started, I wanted to tell everything.

"It's complicated," I said.

Michael just nodded gently.

"Before he came back from the Peace Corps, I wanted to see him so bad. I thought maybe we could be good together. I thought maybe there was a chance that we…" I paused. I wanted to tell Michael about the last time I'd seen Don, the night before he'd left for the Peace Corps, what had happened between us... but I stopped just short.

"I'm not sure what I feel," I said instead. "And even if I was, I'm not sure that Don would feel the same way about me."

A strong memory of that night hit me: Don's arms, the electric heater, Worf looking down at us from the corner, his stern cardboard face judging me. The image was an unwelcome one, and I blocked it out.

"We've been friends for so long, and anyway, now there's this Devi thing. And Don's happy. I don't have any right to do anything."

Michael reached out with one hand and softly touched my shoulder. "Yes," he said. "Yes, you do."

I looked into Michael's eyes, and my lip trembled. "I've... never talked to anybody about this..."

It was true; not even my psychologist knew about this. He thought all my problems stemmed from Brad Newton.

Just starting to talk overwhelmed me. I felt like a shaken can of Pepsi; now that I had started to open up, everything needed to shoot out. I felt my eyes scrunch up. I was going to cry. Michael saw and stepped forward, wrapping his thin arms around me in a hug. I hugged back, hard.

"Shayla," he whispered in my ear, "I know it's confusing. I know that we've only just met, but I'm happy to listen. You and Don... you're good people... and I want to help if I can."

I raised one of my arms and wiped my eyes from over his shoulder.

"Thank you," I said. "I—"

"Hey, what's going on here?" boomed a voice behind me.

I spun around and out of Michael's hug. Don was striding toward us from the dance floor, followed by Terry, whose face was sweating. Don, miraculously after all his dancing, didn't appear to have sweated at all.

"We—" I started, and then realized I had no

explanation for why Michael and I would have been hugging.

It didn't matter, anyway. Don didn't care. "Why aren't you two dancing?" he said. "Terry and I were out there having a great time."

Terry nodded. "Yeah, but now we're tired. We need to sit down."

"Hey," said Don, looking at me a little harder now. "Are you all right? Your eyes look a little red."

I opened my mouth but nothing came out.

Michael saved me. "She got a little glitter in her eye," he said to Don, and then to me, "You'd better get yourself to the bathroom and wash that out."

"Oh… ah… okay," I said. "I'll be right back, then."

"We'll find a table," said Michael.

I started toward the bathrooms, but after a few steps, turned around. Michael was pointing Don and Terry toward an open table, but he must have sensed that I was looking at him. He looked back.

Thank you, I mouthed.

And, with a gentle smile, he mouthed back, *Let's talk*.

"Hey, good job, dude. That was cool."

It had been an hour since Don's dance and now, for what must have been the fiftieth time, somebody passing our table had noticed Don and stopped to congratulate him. This one was dressed up as Batman's sidekick, Robin, and he gave Don a friendly pat on the back before moving on.

"Thanks," said Don with a smile that could only be called glowing. He was feeling incredibly proud of himself now with all of this praise. Perhaps this is what he'd expected of me this morning. Well, anyway, I was happy for him.

Actually, I was just plain happy. Michael and Terry had worked everything out and Don and I didn't have to worry about doing any more driving or looking for a hotel that night; Terry had offered us his spare bedroom. And I knew, from the occasional looks that I shared with Michael over the table, I would have somebody to talk to about Don. As for Don, well, he was looking the most relaxed I'd seen him. In fact, his calmness had come back to him and, if I hadn't been with him in the morning, I never would have thought he was crazy, he looked so incredibly happy and normal.

And me… I felt amazing. For the first time in a long, long time, in fact for the first time since Don had left for the Peace Corps, I was actually feeling hopeful about the future. I kept breaking into uncontrollable smiles, and found myself giggling outrageously at certain points in our conversation.

Michael winked at me.

Maybe everything will work out, I thought. *Maybe I really should tell Don.*

It suddenly didn't seem so outrageous.

In fact, it seemed like the plot of an Indian movie. Woman and man go on trip, man thinks he's in love with somebody, but ends up falling in love with the woman he's traveling with…

Like that movie Patel was telling me about—

Uh-oh.

Patel!

I reached into my purse and pulled out my cell phone. 1:30! I'd forgotten all about my promise to call Patel that night.

"Excuse me," I said, picking up my purse. "I'll be right back."

"Don't be too long," said Terry. "This DJ's almost done, and the next act is the Bitch Goddess. You won't want to miss that."

"Okay," I said.

Hurrying to the bathroom, I wondered to myself, *Bitch Goddess?* It seemed to me I had heard about the Bitch Goddess, something about horns and chains… Ah yes, the devil-woman on the flyer, who was threatening slaves with a whip. Missing some of that didn't seem like much of a loss to me. Maybe it was actually the perfect time to call Patel.

But I didn't waste too much time on that thought. I was already dialing Patel's number as I pushed my way into the bathroom.

The Eros Ball bathroom was very different from the last bathroom I'd called Patel from—I'm always talking to Patel in bathrooms, I mused—; it was a small, dimly-lit room with only two toilet stalls, one occupied by a person with long silver boots, and a group of three women (or was one of them a man!?) in the corner by the sink chatting and taking long drags on cigarettes.

I only had a moment to register my surroundings, though, because Patel picked up in the middle of the very first ring. "Hello?" he demanded. He sounded irritated. Oh no, had I woken him up? I suddenly felt very silly for having called him, not just now but at all. Don seemed okay now; I'd jumped the gun. And now here I was calling the poor guy at 1:30 in the morning!

"Hey, Patel, I'm so sorry to call you so—"

"Shayla!" He didn't so much say the word as breathe it out in a powerful outpouring of breath. It sounded kind of like a roar, kind of like a sigh, kind of like he was channeling Darth Vader.

"Uh, I'm sorry if I woke you—"

Once again he interrupted in a shocked tone. "You didn't wake me up!" The cigarette smokers passed by me on their way out of the bathroom and I went to lean on the sink counter. "Are you kidding?" Patel's voice now seemed more outraged than shocked. "Shayla, I've been so worried about you!"

This made me giggle just a little bit. And there I was thinking he was going to be angry!

"What?" he demanded. "Why are you laughing?"

I stopped immediately. "I'm sorry. It's just… there's no reason to worry about me at all."

"Look, I know you're a strong lady, but if your friend Don is crazy, if he thinks he's Rahul Ghosh…"

He paused, waiting for some kind of response. I didn't give him one.

Had he really just said that he knew I was a strong lady? Wow, he really didn't know me…

"Shayla, I've been up all night and I've been—"

Now I was the one to interrupt. "Patel, listen. I think I was wrong. I think Don's all right… a little strange, but all right. Some interesting things have happened since I called you."

"Tell me," said Patel, tersely.

I gave him a brief run-down.

"So…" said Patel when I'd finished, "Don picked up a random guy on the street, took you to some kind of S&M club, and started some kind of Indian line dance…"

"Mmm…" I said. *I knew I should have left out some of the details!*

"…and you think he's okay?" Patel continued.

"It's not as bad as you think. If you'd have been here, you'd see. His dance was really, really good and people really enjoyed it. And it's an Eros Party, not S&M…" I paused. What a strange conversation to be having! What a strange place I was at! "Patel," I said, "the point is, I'm not so worried anymore. I mean, I think I can handle this."

Patel's response was short and immediate: "I don't think so."

"Huh?"

"Do you know what I've been doing all night?"

"Uh… waiting for me to call?" I guessed.

"My sister gave me some Rahul Ghosh videos and I've been watching them all night."

"Okay…" I said, hesitantly. I didn't know where this conversation was going, but it didn't sound good… and, to be honest, telling Patel about my day was already making me question my newfound belief in Don's sanity.

"The thing is… and I didn't know this before… Rahul is different from other Indian stars. Most Indian movie stars are always the hero—either they're fighting bad guys or falling in love. But Rahul… Well, Rahul is versatile."

"What do you mean?"

"He doesn't always play the good guy. Sometimes he's

the bad guy... and when I say bad, I mean really bad. Just tonight, in the movies I've watched, I've seen him throw a woman off a building, hang somebody, and shoot somebody to death. And in one movie he fell in love with some woman and he stalked her... She had a husband, they moved to Switzerland, he still followed them. And you know what, they thought he was totally normal too!"

"Are you saying that Don might be stalking Devi?"

"I don't know... but it could be. What do you know about this Devi?"

I knew nothing about her, really.

Except what Don had told me.

And like I said before, it hadn't seemed to me that there'd been any kind of romantic relationship in Don and Devi's past. Just friendship.

Which might mean that Devi was in for a big surprise when we showed up in a few days...

"I don't think Don's a stalker," I said, but now I was nervous.

"You need to find out. Ask him about her. Figure out what got him to want to see her. What made him travel cross-country for her."

"Uh... okay," I said. I wasn't sure I was happy that I'd called Patel. Just a few minutes ago, the toughest question I'd been planning to ask Don was if he liked me. Now it was back to asking about Devi... and maybe digging a little deeper, maybe asking about what exactly happened in Africa.

And Don had made it very clear that he didn't want to talk about Africa... very, *very* clear.

Patel was giving me a homework assignment I didn't want to take.

"And also," Patel said, "I think it would be a good idea to find out exactly which Rahul Ghosh movies Don has seen. That could help us figure out how he might act."

I felt numb. I nodded dumbly at the phone.

"I mean, maybe you're right," Patel said, "But I'm worried now that Don might be—"

Dangerous. That was the word that Patel said, I'm sure of

it. But at the time I didn't hear him because there was an abrupt earsplitting scream from out in the club. Even in the bathroom, away from the stage, it was loud enough to make me jump. All I could think was: *Don...?*

"What was that?" Patel asked, anxiously. He'd heard the scream.

"Uh... nothing. Just some act on the stage," I said. Who knows, maybe it was, but I didn't think so. "Listen, I've got to go. I'll call you in the morning."

I whipped the phone from my ear, hearing Patel's little voice desperately saying "Wait, I need you to keep your cell o—" but too late... I was already reaching for the off button and putting the phone in my purse. I was running out of the bathroom, back into the club, thinking: *Please let me be wrong. Please don't let this be Don.*

The image came to mind, unbidden and unwanted, as I ran toward our table.

I imagined Don up on the stage: completely cracked. This morning, he had seen the way the truckers had treated our waitress, and he couldn't let it happen. Now, I couldn't help thinking, faced with a stage show where a woman dressed as a devil was threatening half-naked, chained men with a bullwhip, he might not see any difference. Don, the protector, would have to act.

The picture in my mind, painted in urgent, worried psychology colors, was of Don standing on the stage, his legs apart, towering over a lady all in red who was on her butt on the stage floor, trying to crawl backwards and away from Don. What was terrifying was the look on Don's face: murderous, his eyes focused on her, his lips twisted up in disgust. Even more terrifying than that was what Don held in his hand: a long, vicious-looking blue bullwhip.

If I had had the time to think about it, the image would have been just as ridiculous as it was terrifying. As strong, heroic, and defiant as Don might look facing off against the Bitch Goddess, he would also look like an absolute buffoon.

His blonde hair would be matted down on his head from dancing, making him look a little like one of the Beatles with their moptop hair-dos. His face, of course, would be a wreck, with one eye bruised and blackened from the morning's adventure, and to add to the oddity of it all, he would still be wearing his African boubou.

This was the picture my mind conjured up, though, and it was so strong that I felt it must be real. I prepared myself for humiliation.

Reaching the main performance hall and looking at the stage, then, I was surprised that Don wasn't there. Instead there was the Bitch Goddess, looking almost exactly like I'd imagined her, except a bit chunkier, and she was dressed all in blue latex, rather than the Devil-red I had expected. The half-naked slaves were there, much as I'd envisioned, forming a semi-circle around the Bitch Goddess, tied up in unusual positions, and moaning as she wheeled from one to the other to threaten them.

But Don was not there.

"Shayla!"

The voice—Don's—called out from my right, sounding cheerful and unaffected by the violence on the stage. I whirled around.

There was our table, where Don, Michael, and Terry all sat, drinks in hand, smiling over at me.

"We're over here," said Don, with a relaxed smile.

I let out a long, deep breath, and walked over, feeling shaky. My body must have been awash with adrenaline, because I couldn't help but feel as if I were both turning to jelly and emerging from a daze at the same time. "I," I gasped, lowering myself delicately into my chair, "I thought…"

They all watched me, waiting.

"I heard a scream," I said. "I thought… Don, I thought you'd gone crazy again."

"Crazy?" Don asked, incredulously. "What do you mean? I'm not crazy."

"You know, like this morning. I thought you'd seen the

Bitch Goddess and decided to fight her, like the truckers at breakfast."

"Oh, that!" Don laughed, effortlessly. "Come on, Shay! That was totally different. Give me some credit. I know the difference between fantasy and reality." He paused, took a sip of his drink, shot a quick glance at the bizarre tableau on stage, then looked meaningfully back at me, seeming to put some serious thought into how he might convince me of his sanity. Finally: "I'm totally okay, okay? And anyway, there's no way I'd fight a woman, Shay, yah?"

I burst out laughing. I think it's the "yah" that did it. I didn't know if Don was really okay or not, but he hadn't been up on that stage, and that was a good thing. Maybe the best thing all day. I was so relieved that my laughter escaped in an unstoppable rush that felt like all the stress, anxiety, worry of the day—maybe even the last five years—was sputtering out like the air from an untied balloon. I laughed and laughed and then the table transformed and everybody, infected, began to laugh with me: Michael, Terry, and then finally Don.

When the chortles died down, I felt completely relaxed.

Things just might be okay after all.

I let that thought run through my brain and around my body, and felt all the tension completely wash out of me. And when the tension was gone, fatigue took its place. I was suddenly incredibly tired, as if stress had been the only thing keeping me going. My eyelids drooped, my head seemed to float like a buoy, light and empty and drifting above the ocean of my shoulders.

I yawned.

Things will be okay, I thought, and let my head nod onto Don's shoulder, my mind fogging into unconsciousness.

The last thing I saw was the blurry image of Don and the two lovers smiling at me, and then I let my head slide softly down Don's arm to the table, where I fell fast asleep.

CHAPTER SIXTEEN
THREE DAYS TO DECIDE

I AWOKE TO sunlight pushing its way through a thin white curtain and the sound and smell of eggs frying in the distance. The room I was in was bright and warm and the bed was comfortable, but I couldn't remember at all how I'd gotten there. I blinked against the light and rolled onto my stomach, trying to make sense of where I was. Slowly the events of the day before materialized in my mind and I remembered Michael, and Terry, and Don's dancing.

I smiled. This must be Terry's house.

There was a soft knock on the door and a head appeared: Michael's, with his glasses back on. I quickly looked down, afraid of what I might be revealing, but there was no need to worry. I was fully clothed.

"We didn't know what to do with you," Michael said softly. "You were hardly conscious when we got back here. We just dropped you on the bed and put some covers over you. I hope that was okay."

"Uh… yeah. Sure." I had a vague memory of stumbling toward a taxi and then later, stumbling again, this time up some stairs with my arms around somebody's shoulders…

Don's?

Which reminded me…

"Where's Don?"

"He's taking a shower. He was going to wake you up after, but I thought I'd go ahead and do it now. We never did have that talk we were going to have."

I looked up into Michael's almond eyes. "I don't know what to do," I said.

"It seems simple, honey." He sat down on the bed beside me. "You just need to figure out what you want."

"I know, but that's not so simple. Don and I've known each other since the seventh grade. We've been best friends that long. It's true I had a crush on him… I even thought for a long time that he might have a crush on me… but then all kinds of things happened and it just got all confused."

"What happened?"

"Oh, it's a long story. You know: I got a boyfriend… and then Don had girlfriends… well, he dated girls, at least, I don't know if any of them ever counted as a girlfriend… and then he went off to college, and the Peace Corps. And then, you know, that's when he went off the deep end."

"I think he's okay now, Shayla. I mean, he's still got that weird accent going, but he seems stable. He told me about what happened at the truck stop."

"He talked to you about *that*?"

"Yeah, and I'll tell you what. The impression I get is that he's dealing with something big right now. He knows he's off, and he's trying to make it better. He told me he was really sorry he put you through all that."

"Wow," I said.

I had to hand it to Michael. It was like he had some kind of power to make people talk to him about their deepest feelings, maybe even heal them. Suddenly, a nervous thought came to me.

"You didn't…"

"Say anything to him about you? Your feelings? No. Of course not."

I sighed in relief.

"Actually, he did most of the talking."

"Let me guess. Indian movies and Devi Chakraborty."

"Actually, no. All he talked about was you. How much he missed you while he was gone. All the crazy things you did in high school—"

My heart sank. "He told you about Brad…"

"Who?"

I kept my mouth closed. *He hadn't!* Could the disaster that was Brad Newton—the worst mistake of my life—have gone unspoken? Really?

"No, he didn't mention any Brad. He talked about a Brent Mellner, but no Brad."

Interesting…

"Anyway, the point is he obviously cares about you. He talked all about how he missed you, and how he wished he'd done things differently after high school. Shayla, he's absolutely over the moon that you took this trip with him. He said he couldn't do it without you."

Wow. I couldn't believe how sappy I was. I could feel my eyelids tensing up and my tear ducts puckering. I knew Don cared, but he never said so like that. I stared at my hands and willed my eyes to remain dry.

"Shayla…" Michael reached out and picked up my hand. "Don loves you."

Stay focused on the other hand! Stay focused on the other hand! You can keep it together!

"Yeah, I know, but *how* does he love me? As a friend? A sister? Maybe a sidekick? I just don't know what I am to him anymore." It was kind of a joke, mostly not a joke at all.

"I don't know, either, *maybe* something more. All I know is that he cares. And I think it would be okay to tell him your feelings, too."

"Yeah, right, as soon as I can figure them out for myself."

"Just talk to him, I guess. Get to know him again the way he is now. Then look back over your reasons for liking him in the first place. If you're just infatuated with the image of him as somebody you couldn't have before, drop it, but if you still honestly like him, if you really like him both as he was then and as he is now… well, then I'd tell him. I really would."

"I'll think about it."

"Okay," said Michael, "but don't think too much… Tell him before—"

I knew what he was going to say. He was going to say that I had to let Don know how I felt before we reached Devi's place in Atlanta.

He couldn't finish the thought, though.

Outside the room, we heard the bathroom door open and the sound of Don whistling an Indian tune, catching the rhythm, but not the exact notes. He could sing, but he certainly couldn't whistle, for some reason.

The whistle made its way toward my room and then Don pushed open my door. His hair was wet and slicked back so that it looked more brown than blonde and he was wearing a bright yellow t-shirt and tan shorts. "You're up," he said, not seeming at all surprised to see Michael there. "Great! Come on out. Terry's made us an awesome breakfast." He flashed us a smile and walked out, singing "Hum chal rahe hain, pyar ke raaste mein…"

"Guy really likes Indian movies," I said.

"Big deal," said Michael. "My boyfriend really likes to dress up as a woman. Go figure."

After a breakfast of eggs, bacon, and hash browns which was better than the day before, not just in quality but in the fact that we actually were able to eat it, Don and I said our farewells to Michael and Terry and with an exchange of phone numbers and hugs, we left.

Don, a backpack over his back, and his precious suitcase in hand, turned to me as we walked down the stairs, which I vaguely remembered from the night before. "Would you like to drive, or should I?" He looked handsome in his yellow T and beige shorts, and he smiled at me innocently.

"You drive," I said. "I've never seen the desert before.

I'd like to watch it go by."

"All right then." He turned and walked to the car, whistling the same tune from before, and in that moment, I decided to follow Michael's plan. I was going to figure out what my feelings were for Don exactly. But…

"Hey," I said as I pulled open my car door, "How long before we get there?"

Don broke his whistle, but in the same tune he sang, "Three days, maybe four, until we knock at Devi's door."

I didn't stop smiling, but I wanted to. Michael was right. There wasn't much time to figure my thoughts out… but there was one thing to do first. I had lied to Don just then; I hadn't asked him to drive so that I could see the desert. I had asked him to drive so that I could watch him. Before I figured myself out, I figured that I should figure him out, how far this Rahul Ghosh madness went, how infatuated he was with Devi, and how he felt about me.

Him first… then me… then us.

Three things to figure in three days…

That wasn't much time. Not much time at all.

But I'd have to do it.

I clicked on my seatbelt, turned to Don. "Let's go," I said.

It was nice to be the one saying that for once.

Don started the engine and we were on our way.

INTERMISSION

PART THREE

PAST AND PRESENT

CHAPTER SEVENTEEN
HIM

THE DESERT WASN'T nearly as interesting as I thought it would be.

If anything, looking at the ashy gray landscape with its sparse little patches of vegetation encouraged me to begin my investigation quickly.

"So, Don," I said, "is it nice to be back?"

He raised his eyebrows. "You mean in the States, yah?"

"Yah—I mean, yes."

"Sure, it's nice. There's a lot I missed."

"For instance?"

"For instance, you."

I hadn't expected that.

"Me?"

"Of course. You're my best friend, yah?"

I nodded, and tried not to let that comment sting.

"And I'll tell you something, Shay. I feel like you're finally coming back. I feel like I'm really seeing you now, yah?"

I gave him a long look. "What do you mean?"

"Well, the Shay I knew was always strong and always happy. Somehow you lost that for a while, but yesterday you were back. You were great with Michael and Terry."

Strong.

Once again, somebody was calling me strong. Had I missed a memo or something?

"It seems like I haven't had a chance to spend time with you for so long," Don said. "I'm so happy that you're here. It's kind of like that summer after seventh grade. Remember? We had that stupid fight over nothing? Then, it felt like there was this huge gap in my life until we got back together. And then suddenly it was like everything was better than ever. Do you remember that?"

I did. I'd just been thinking about it.

"Those were good times, weren't they?" Don asked.

"Yeah," I said, "they were."

My eyes wandered to the desert.

Barren and empty.

It was as if the jovial atmosphere inside the car and the landscape outside were mocking my past because I could see a direct parallel between the happy time before Brad and the emotional desert that came after him.

"Emotional desert" might not be the best term, actually.

"Bad times" and "Brad times" are not exactly the same thing.

For instance, the beginning of eighth grade was a wonderful time, in all respects.

First off, my friendship with Don was back and better than ever. After he called and apologized, things went pretty much back to normal between us. There were more action movies and tortilla chips in my parents' den and more long conversations about *Star Trek*. There were long walks at Shadlow Beach and frozen yogurt at TCBY and ferry rides and the occasional *Back to the Future* film (because I liked Michael J. Fox.)

All in all, we were back to having our general

camaraderie.

But there was more than that, too, because now Don became my confidante.

I had never had a boyfriend before and I needed somebody to discuss Brad with. Usually people talk to their girl friends about things like this, and I did a little, but since Don was my best friend, he ended up being the one I talked to the most. In a way, it seemed like a good idea to have a guy friend to discuss my relationship with. Brad and Don were both guys, so they might understand each other better.

On the other hand, as far as guys go, Brad and Don were polar opposites.

But this didn't stop me.

With Don, I shared Brad's interests, which were now partly my interests because I was dating him. So Don got earfuls of Ozzy Osbourne and Motley Crue, Brad's favorite bands. He watched Pink Floyd's *The Wall* with me because Brad had loaned me the tape. He even took a ferry across to Haricot Island with me and skipped stones with me in the beautiful make-out spot that Brad had found, although I never told Don what Brad and I did there.

The biggest thing that Don did, though, was be open to talking about Brad. I knew that Don didn't particularly like my boyfriend, but now that our dating had become official, he made an effort to listen to everything that was going on between us. And it must have been a monumental effort not to be judgmental.

Like when I told him about meeting Brad's mom for the first time.

"She works at the grocery store, and she always seems distracted. Brad can't stand her."

"Yeah."

"I mean I kind of understand her. She's got four kids and it must be hard—"

"She's got four kids?" Don, the only child, had his mouth agape. Four kids was an amazing number to him. To me, too. Even my one brother seemed like a lot!

"She's always running around after one or the other.

Brad's the oldest so he gets it the worst. She's always asking him to do something for her, like wash the dishes or feed the baby or mow. He's got it hard."

"Yeah." Don said. "I guess I should be nicer to him."

And Brad did have it hard. He and his mom lived in a cheap apartment, where Brad and his two younger brothers shared a room, while his mom and little sister shared the other. They apparently got child support from his dad, who lived in Idaho, but it was never enough, and they always felt poor.

What I'd had for dinner at Brad's house: SpaghettiOs and apple juice.

Now that we were dating, though, Don and Brad became civil. There was no more stealing of *Star Trek* novels. There were no statements of hate from Don. They weren't friends, and they didn't ever hang out together, but they tolerated each other for my sake.

In retrospect, this must have been hard for both of them, but especially for Don. Where I could say to Brad "Oh, Don's just my friend" and be done with it, Don, being the friend, was also the one who had to listen to long stories about Brad.

But he took it well, swallowing any irritation that he might have felt.

And if he hurt when I talked about Brad, either he hid it really well, or I was too in love to notice.

Unlike eighth grade, Don and I now didn't mention the name "Brad" at all. We passed the entire desert without one mention of him.

We didn't even stop for lunch. Instead, we made a double run for the border, stopping at a Taco Bell in a little town called Needles before crossing over into Arizona.

"I'm worried about Brad."

"What's up?"

Don and I and Worf were holding council in his room (with the door open as Dr. Smith always required... *as if anything was going to happen between Don and me!*)

It was January and Don had his thermostat dialed up to the "M" of *Comfort*. Still, I had wrapped myself up in one of his blankets.

Usually, I didn't talk about worries. I talked about how everything was fine. The only worry that had ever come up was the worry that Brad smoked pot, but Don had been okay when I told him I never smoked (which was true) and that Brad didn't do it around me. But something had changed over the Christmas break. Brad had gone to visit his dad in Idaho, and he had come back thinking of dropping out.

"Is that even possible?" asked Don. "I mean, isn't there a rule that kids have to finish school or something?"

"He'll be sixteen next month, and his dad told him there's no reason to be in school after sixteen, that he might as well get a job."

Don's expression was classically lost. At first, I thought he might be making the mental calculations on Brad's age (I'd never told him that Brad had been required to repeat the fourth grade, nor that he was a whole two years older than I was), but it turned out that Don had just never thought about the idea of leaving school.

"That's crazy," Don finally said. "What would he do?"

"I don't know. He says that he'd have lots of options. Apparently, his dad dropped out at sixteen and he turned out all right."

"Hm. What does his dad do?"

"He's a carpenter. Actually, he owns his own shop, and I guess he does pretty well. But I don't think that means Brad should follow in his footsteps."

Don shuddered, probably remembering Wood Shop, one of his least favorite classes ever. "I just don't get it. At all. What would he do?"

"Brad says he can get a job. He's thinking of going out to Idaho and working with his dad for a while. Just until he finds his own thing."

Don shook his head. His parents had so instilled the idea of graduating and going on from there that the very thought of not aiming for college floored him.

"Look, Shay," he said, and it was like the words were being forced out of him, like he had some inner demon pushing them out. "I'm not the biggest Brad fan in the world, but I know how important he is to you. And even if he wasn't your boyfriend, I'd say this. He'd be crazy to drop out. It's not that there's anything wrong with his idea of working with his dad, but he should look at all his options. Maybe there's something better for him, he just hasn't seen it yet. I don't know. But you should definitely talk him out of it."

"I've tried. His mom's tried. He just seems to talk about it more."

"Man," said Don, still shaking his head. "That sucks."

"Don, maybe there's something you could do."

"Me?" Don was shocked.

"Yeah, you don't know this, but Brad respects you."

"He does?"

"Maybe you could talk to him. If you told him to stay in, maybe he'd listen."

"Maybe he'd kill me, too."

"No, he wouldn't."

"I don't think—"

"Please."

"Shay—"

"Please. You know it means a lot to me."

Don gritted his teeth, looked at Worf. There was some kind of mental communication between him and the cardboard cutout.

"Okay, I will. I'll talk to him."

"Thank you," I said.

"Okay, then can we change the conversation? I'm hungry. Can we walk down to the drug store and get lunch?"

The hills in Arizona are kind of pink, jagged lines of rock

that stretch into the distance.

Don had been staring straight ahead at one particular hill for a while.

"What are you looking at?" I asked.

"See that hill there?"

I did.

"It looks like Devi."

"Huh?" I gave the hill another look. It did seem that there was a kind of face and woman's torso shape that could be made out on the side. "Yeah, I guess I see it."

"It definitely looks like Devi. It's a sign, Shay. It's dharma. I'm heading toward the right destiny."

Whatever. *Dharma*. It sounded like what I'd thought might happen when I sent Don to talk to Brad.

It did not go well.

Don was as true as his word. It took him a few days as he tried to figure out the best time to approach Brad, but ultimately he did it. He'd wanted to make sure that he caught him at a time when Brad was alone and hopefully in a good mood. This wasn't easy because Brad always had his group around him, including me, but finally there was a moment.

I was sitting with Brad and his posse in the cafeteria. Don was sitting a few tables away with a group of our mutual friends. I still thought of myself as friends with them, even though it was Brad I sat with these days. I also always noticed where Don was sitting, even if he was far away.

Brad was laughing and telling a story about his "old man" while the others listened, dutifully. Theresa Reisher, though, listened with a sour look on her face, because the fries Brad kept shoving in his face were hers.

Finally,

"Fuck, Brad! You've eaten half my fries. Can't you buy your own?"

"Hey, man. Chill, okay?" Brad bit the heads off the fries he was eating and dropped the others back onto Theresa's plate. "I'll buy my own." He looked around at his friends.

"Anybody got a dollar?"

Everybody groaned, but Larry Stumpel finally handed over three quarters and some dimes. Somehow Stumpel always had cash.

"I'll pay you back," said Brad, pocketing the coins.

"No, you won't, dickhead," said Stumpel.

"No, you're right, I probably won't." Brad stood up. As he walked toward the line, I looked over to Don. It was the perfect time. Don nodded slightly and stood up.

They reached the line at the same time, Brad in front, Don just behind.

Brad gave him a grumpy look and then a slight nod, which I guess was for my benefit as much as Don's. Brad was showing he could be well-behaved.

The lunchroom was loud and there was a table between me and the line, but I blocked out Theresa and Larry and Chris and Brian's talking and strained to hear what Don would say.

It started like this:

"Hey, Brad," said Don.

Brad was already turned in line, and he didn't even look back. "Yeah," he said, gruffly. He didn't want to talk. He just wanted to spend Larry Stumpel's money, pour some Thousand Island dressing on his fries, and get out of there. For him, I guess just not acknowledging Don was enough. That "Yeah" was supposed to end the conversation.

But Don was stubborn. He hadn't wanted to talk to Brad, but he'd said he would, and he was doing it for me.

"Brad, can we talk for a second?"

Brad turned half way to him and looked at him, gauging whether this would be a good idea or not. "Yeah, I guess. What's up?"

Don lowered his voice to keep it private, but I could still make it out, though I don't think anyone else in the lunchroom could. "Shayla told me about what you're thinking."

"Yeah?"

"I mean, about dropping out of school. She's worried

about you."

"Yeah, she said." His voice took on a harder edge.

"Brad," Don said, "I don't think it's a good idea."

"You don't, huh?" It was a threatening question. Brad sounded the way he did when his mom asked him where he'd been all afternoon. His least favorite question.

Don could tell that this wasn't going well, but he was committed. "Listen, I know that we're not exactly friends or anything, but I think staying in school would be better for you. I mean, you could have better opportunities."

"Who told you that, your mommy and daddy?" Brad leaned in. "Listen up, you're right, you and I are not friends, and this is none of your damn business. I don't know why you're all up in my girlfriend's shit, but I'm watching you. The only reason I'm not going to kick your ass right now is because she's watching, and another thing… I'll do what I fucking want, depend on it." He reached out and grabbed Don's shirt collar. "I've already got shit lined up, okay? I don't need some whiny little bitch trying to tell me what to do. So go back to your nerdy little table and be a whiny bitch there, because I don't need it."

So much for the idea that Brad had any respect for Don.

The two stared at each other, and Don held his gaze.

Brad talked right into his face. "Get out of here before I bust your big-ass schnozz."

Don, dignified, slowly pushed his hand away and, eyes locked on Brad, said, "I tried to help. I tried to help you."

It was Don that turned and walked away, very calmly, from Brad.

"I don't need your help, you little shit," spat Brad. "Who needs help from a little shit like you?"

But Don kept walking away, not even looking back, not saying a word.

Brad was seething, making the kids after him nervous. There was already a wide gap between him and the rest of the line because he'd stopped.

"Hey, said the lunch lady, "Can we get this line moving a little?"

"Fuck," hissed Brad. "Fuck, fuck, fuck, fuck, fuck!"

He strode to the door, and kicked it open.

"Fuck," he yelled again and there were a few more muffled "fucks" as he walked out of the cafeteria and the door closed behind him.

"There goes my dollar," said Larry Stumpel blandly.

Don and I stopped by a little brightly painted Native American store because, Don said, I'd love it.

I did. I was enamored with a necklace that had a Kokopelli emblem on it. "Kokopelli," its tag read, "The Flute Player, a fertility symbol."

"I'll get it for you if you like," said Don.

Shadlow Beach.

Brad held out the earrings like a peace offering.

"What are these for?"

"Just 'cause. C'mon, take 'em."

I let him drop them into my hands. I knew what they were for. They were an apology for the way he'd acted in the lunchroom. To Don. It was a nice thought, but...

"Whoah, these look expensive." I held them up to the sunlight where the clear jewels gleamed from their golden rings.

"Real diamonds," Brad said, blissfully.

I looked to him, askance. "Real diamonds?"

How could Brad afford real diamonds?

"Hell, yeah, baby," said Brad with a full smile on. He draped his arm over my shoulder.

This was the same Brad who had needed to borrow a dollar from Larry Stumpel.

"Only the best for my girl!"

This was the same Brad who was always broke. Whose family was always broke. Who I had to treat if we stopped by Baskin-Robbins for an ice cream. There was no way he could afford real diamonds…

"Brad, I can't take these."

He couldn't afford these. Honestly, I would have been surprised if he could afford *any* earrings, diamond or otherwise.

Where had he gotten them?

Brad's face hardened. "What?"

"I mean… how could you afford these? Real diamonds have got to be expensive."

"What? You think I stole 'em?"

"I didn't say that. I—"

"Look, I got a job, okay? I'm making money now."

"You got a job?"

It was the first I'd heard of it.

What kind of job could he have had in the two days since the lunchroom incident that would have already gotten him enough for diamond earrings?

"Yeah… Shit, if I'd known it would have been such a big deal, I wouldn't have gotten 'em for you…"

He was trying to sidetrack me. There really *was* something wrong.

"Brad… what job?"

"Fuck!" He was tense. He turned from me, fiercely. "Just a job, okay. Does it fucking matter?"

Brad never swore at me like this.

"You don't have to swear."

"Okay, but jeez, Shayl."

"I just wanted to know what kind of job it is?"

"It's nothing."

He didn't want to tell me.

"Fine, but just tell me."

"Can't you just leave it alone?"

"I'm just worried about…"

"Leave it." Under his breath.

"If you're making this much…"

"Leave it!" Lots of breath.

"Look, I…"

"Goddammit, will you stop being such a fucking cunt? I said I don't want to tell you, so quit fucking nagging the shit out of me!"

He glared at me with spittle hanging from the corner of his lips. I regarded him coolly. A seagull honked above us.

When the seagull passed, I turned and walked away across the pebbly beach.

He let me go. It was a two hour walk home and I did it alone, the whole way.

The woman behind the counter may or may not have been a real Indian. I mean, Native American. She had long, dark hair and tawny skin, but she seemed pretty white.

"That'll be fifteen bucks," she said, looking at the back of the Kokopelli necklace.

"Thank you," said Don, handing her a twenty. He clasped the necklace around my neck. "There you go, Shay. It looks nice."

The woman came back with change and then held it back. "Hey, what is your accent? You from Germany or something?"

"Germany!" Don was shocked.

"Well, you're from somewhere foreign, right? England?"

"England!!!"

"Yeah, I know. You sound like that leprechaun guy on the TV. You know, "Magically delicious." Where's that guy from? Scotland, right?"

"Ireland," I said.

"Yeah, you sound like him."

"I sound like the *Lucky Charms* leprechaun?"

"Well, a little. So, where *are* you from, hon?"

Don took his money and looked at her coldly for a second. Then he smiled and winked. "It doesn't matter where I'm from. The only thing that matters is where I'm going."

"Oh." The woman was bored with this now and there

were people behind us in line. "And where's that then?"

"Atlanta. I'm going for love—"

"Oh, yeah? Well, good luck with that then. Next!"

Back in the car, Don didn't turn the key right away.

"What was that all about?" he asked.

I told him the truth. "Your accent's slipping."

He turned the key. "Yeah, it does that."

Brad was slipping.

Badly.

"What's going on with him, Brian?" I asked.

The burly giant that I called Brian Wrczic, and everybody else called the Bear, shrugged. "Man, I'm not sure you want to know."

"Brian, it's me, Shayla. Brad won't talk to me, and I'm worried about him. Will you help me out?"

The Bear ducked his head, nervous and uncomfortable. "Okay, but you can't tell him I told you. He'd be super-pissed."

"I promise I won't say anything." There was an irony in the fact that this huge, frightening kid could be scared of my much smaller boyfriend, but he was. The Bear was a gentle giant, and he'd become a friend I could trust.

"Okay," he said, "but don't get mad. You know Chase?"

Chase. The guy who Brad and some of his friends got pot from. I'd been to his house once, and then I'd told Brad never again. It had been weird, this thirty-year old guy hanging out with junior high kids like good friends.

"Yeah, I know Chase."

"Well, he set Brad up."

"Set him up? What do you mean set him up?"

"Brad wanted money and Chase said he could make some."

"How?"

"You know... by working for him a little... selling stuff..."

"You mean Brad's selling pot for Chase?"

"Yeah," said Brian, "and stuff."

"What do you mean it does that?"

"Exactly that, Shay. My accent slips sometimes."

"Why?"

"Well, Dr. Acres said it was part of my PTSD…"

"Dr. Acres?" I sat straight up in my seat.

"Yeah, Shay. Didn't I tell you? Dr. Acres was my psychologist in D.C."

He hadn't told me anything.

"You didn't tell me anything, Don. All I knew was that one minute I thought you were in Africa, and the next minute you were home."

Don had seen a psychologist. Just like me. And he hadn't said a word. I was floored.

"Well, it wasn't quite like that," said Don. "The Peace Corps wanted me to stay in D.C. for a while for a little psychological help."

"How long?"

"Well, it was supposed to be ten weeks, but I only stayed three."

"So, what? You escaped from D.C. and came back home?"

"It's not like that either. Dr. Acres and I agreed that it was a good idea."

"She thought that you were okay."

"Well, not okay exactly. She couldn't lay her finger on it exactly. She said it was kind of a cross between post-traumatic stress disorder…"

"PTSD…"

"And dissociative identity disorder."

"Okay." I wasn't too familiar with the terms, but the message was clear. Something bad had happened to Don and that's why he'd started acting the way he did.

"She was fascinated by me. I think she wanted to write a case study on me, actually, I was such a strange case."

"But she let you go."

"She did. I don't think there was anything else she could do. I was acting pretty normal, and I wanted to go home. Really, I wanted to see Devi…"

Great.

"She just," said Don, "said I should watch out for certain things. In our sessions, it became pretty clear that I was alright most of the time, except certain things seemed to trigger certain behavior. Basically, I lost myself."

"Triggers?" I asked.

"Yes. She said as long as I avoided certain things, I should be fine. As far as she was concerned, being at home might be the best thing for me."

"And…"

"And I didn't agree," Don said. "I thought there was a better way to get over this. But I didn't tell her that because she probably wouldn't have let me go."

"So what did you do?"

"I played along and came home—and here I am with you."

"And you're alright?"

"Yes, as long as there are no other triggers. Sorry about the other day by the way…"

Triggers…

Something had triggered Brad Newton somehow. Ever since he'd talked to his dad about dropping out of school, he had been following a series of switchbacks that kept leading him further and further down the mountain of despair, and it seemed like nothing could stop him. Everything seemed to make him worse and worse.

Don talked to him about staying in school, Brad started selling drugs.

I talked to him again, he ignored me.

His mom tried to talk to him again, he disappeared for a week.

These   disappearances   and   mini-rebellions   kept

happening.

Then one night, I got a phone call. Brad was in Remann Hall, the local youth corrections agency, like a jail for young people. This was when my grandmother was in the hospital. "I knew you were hurting," he said. "I wanted to get you something nice." He'd broken into his neighbor's home, through a window he said was open, and stolen all their electrical items. He was caught red-handed trying to pawn them. "I didn't mean for anyone to be hurt," he said.

The upshot was that Brad's mom gave up.

"I don't know what to do with him anymore, Shayla." She was sitting with me in the waiting room at Remann Hall, waiting, like me, to see her son. "I can't handle him and the other three. He's a bad influence." She took a long drag on her cigarette, her face a neutral mask. "I've asked his father to take him."

"What do you mean?"

"I'm sending him to George's place in Idaho. His daddy's coming to pick him up when he gets out of here."

"But—"

"I'm sorry. I know you've tried to help him, but it's best for everybody."

"But what about his school?"

"His daddy promised me that he'd stay in school."

"But his dad—"

She cut me off. "I'm wore out, Shayla. Believe me, I'd keep him if I could, but I'm just plain wore out." She took another drag on her cigarette.

A week later, Brad Newton and I said our goodbyes and he was off to Pocatello, Idaho.

"I'll write to you," he said. "I promise."

"I'll write back," I said.

And just like that he was gone.

That's how Don ended up being the one to hold my hand when my grandmother died.

"So…" I said to Don, "What are the triggers?"

"I'm sure you've guessed."

"Um…" I thought. "You can't bear to see anybody in trouble." Don nodded. "You've always got to help. Especially if they're women, I think." Don shot me a quick glance. "Especially if they're being threatened by men."

I could tell from the way his fingers tightened on the wheel that I was right.

"If that happens, you go into full Rahul Ghosh mode."

He nodded.

"Also, when you think about Devi—"

Don didn't say anything.

"But if that's the case, is it really a good idea to see her?"

"Devi is not a trigger," Don said strongly. "Devi is the cure." He nodded to himself.

I stared at him. If Devi was the cure, that was great.

The problem was that Don's accent had returned full force when he talked about Devi—which couldn't be a good sign.

He looked at me earnestly. "Devi Chakraborty," he said. "Devi Chakraborty is the cure, yah?"

I nodded quickly. "Yah," I said. "Yah, yeah, whatever, okay, just keep your eyes on the road, Don!"

All of that craziness with Brad ended at the end of ninth grade. We had promised to keep in contact, and we did, but he was isolated far away in Idaho, and I was stuck in Yettikum.

However, luckily, I had Don.

But Don was making changes, too, and if my last year with Brad had been tough, Don was apparently going through his own tough times.

At first, I didn't understand what was going on. Although I had seen Don all summer, even as much as a few days before the beginning of school, when he showed up on the Tuesday after Labor Day, he had changed himself in many ways. He had a brand new, more in-crowd fashion, and he made every effort to talk to what we'd always called the "popular patrol," the kids who, like Erik Anderson and Jen Abrams, seemed to rule the school. It wasn't that he dissociated from me in any way. In fact, we were together more often now than we had been for a long time. We sat together at lunch, we sat next to each other in the three classes we shared, we spent almost every afternoon together. It was a bittersweet friendship, because as much as I enjoyed Don's company, I realized that I had so much of it because of Brad's absence. But anyway, we saw a lot of each other; it was just that he had now widened his spectrum to be able to make jokes with the popular kids.

That was September.

In October, there were even more changes. I started seeing less of Don because he started to join clubs and teams. For Fall, he was slated for Golf and Chess Club, and when he had time, he went to meetings of the French Club. He also tried out for the Winter Debate Team, and he began talking about being part of the Student Government for the Spring.

His complete transformation into Stepford Don, however, came the third week of October when he asked Katie Burke to go to the Homecoming Dance with him. Katie was a cheerleader, a petite girl who was full of pep, but she was nice, too—a kind of Midwestern nice. She wasn't full-blown popular and seemed to segue between all crowds, but she was still considered part of the popular patrol.

Don didn't even tell me he was thinking about asking her out.

"So…" I whispered to him one afternoon in Study Hall. "The word is that you asked out Katie Burke."

Don opened his mouth and then quickly shut it. He gave his history book a meaningful look, as if he needed to study it. This was pretense. Don did all of his studying at home between eight and ten, the two hours prescribed by his dad, and left his Study Hall time open to talk to me. We called it the "Shayla-Don Conversation Hour," but we always talked softly so that Miss Minton, who was always reading a crime novel, wouldn't separate us.

"So it's true!" I whispered.

"Yeah." He looked away.

"Hmmm… Katie Burke," I mused. "So what's up with that? I always thought you were more of a Savannah Terrell kind of guy…"

We both glanced over at Savvie Terrell, who was sitting on the other side of study hall with her friends. They were all reading fantasy novels. She was kind of cute.

Don looked both ways, and then leaned in to me. "I'm not anyone's type of guy," he said, confidentially.

I smiled wickedly. "But you asked Katie out… and you didn't tell me anything about it…"

Here's a strange thing… I knew I had Brad and his letters, but I was kind of hurt…

"There was no point," Don said. He was blushing.

"The point is you're going out with a nice girl."

"Yeah, Katie is nice," said Don, "but it's not serious. You know, I kinda *had* to ask her out."

"Had to? What are you talking about?"

"Listen, Shay—and I want you to keep this a secret, okay?"

"Uh… okay."

"My dad is kind of putting a lot of pressure on me to get a little more "involved." He wants me to hang out with the in-crowd, join a lot of clubs, be all college-material. Essentially, I've got to beef up my extra-curriculars so that I can get into a good school."

"So, what? Does this mean you're using Katie?" I actually liked Katie.

"Don't say it like that. That sounds bad. No, not really. Right now, we're just in it for fun—kind of casual dating. I like Katie. She's nice. And we're kind of more like friends than boyfriend-girlfriend. I think we'd both be fine if somebody else came along."

"So your dad is forcing you to be popular. Isn't that almost impossible?"

"I don't know. My dad says being popular is only based

on how much effort you put into it."

"Hmmm. But isn't there any girl that you actually like?"

Don looked at me funny. "I like you."

"Don't joke around. I mean anyone else."

"Oh, no, not really."

"Don," I said.

He had calmed down considerably. The air conditioner was blowing cool air at us.

"Mmm-hmmm?" He cocked his head.

"Uh… nothing."

I went back to my thoughts, but now something new had hit me.

Had Don been saying that he was interested in me that day, and I'd totally missed it?

We both stared out at Arizona. It hadn't seemed like a big state on the map, but it was taking forever to get through it.

It was about time to call it a day.

I'd considered dating Don, but through high school he was so busy. We hung out as much as we could, but often his clubs kept him away from me, although we did join Humanitarian Club together. To top this off, he ran for Treasurer of the Student Council, which ironically meant that a couple of times a month he would sit down with his old nemesis Erik Anderson, who had been voted President, to hash out plans of how the students could make Yettikum High a better place to be. His dad had wanted him to be President, but Don had stood up to him in the only way he knew how: meet his dad's desires halfway, but not all the way. He wouldn't be President, but he would be on the student council. Appeased. Somewhat. He wouldn't even think about the major sports—football, basketball—but chess, lacrosse, and tennis would have to do. Not ideal, but okay.

And he did all this as if it were just some kind of game.

"Look, Shay—being an active high school student is almost like dressing up for a *Star Trek* convention. You know you're not really a Borg—but you can make the movements and walk the walk."

And because he walked the walk his dad wanted him to, he was also able to dress up as that Borg and go to that *Star Trek* convention (yes, I caved, and went with him—just for the chance to spend a whole day together.)

It was my hope that Don would ask me to the Graduation Dance. He had stopped playing his dad's game when Katie Burke had ended up having bulimia and he'd needed to stick through the crisis with her like a good boyfriend. Ultimately, she was not just playing—the relationship *had* meant something to her, and Don had had to be very careful in the way he worked his way out of it. I think he ended up hinting to her that Cornelius Whitman on the football team had a crush on her, and then when she ended up dating Cornelius, he'd acted like it was all a big surprise to him. Still, from that point on, he never dated a single girl in our high school.

That had all taken the eleventh grade year and he was single again and proving completely resistant to the advances of his fellow Student Government rep, Secretary Danna Wilson.

I was just thinking that it was time to see if maybe Don and I should go a step further in our relationship, but I was shy about it...

And then something completely unexpected happened:

Brad Newton came back.

A calm dinner. Just Don and me at a little Mexican restaurant in Flagstaff. Everybody looked so young. Students on their break from Northern Arizona University. Our waitress reminded me a little of myself eight years before—polite, but distracted. She was probably waiting to get off, maybe to see her boyfriend.

It didn't matter. Don always left at least a 15% tip, even

if the service was awful.

I'm sorry to say that I was distracted, and that's why I let Don down the night he called.

I wouldn't have… but he called at the wrong time.

Absolutely the wrong time.

"Shayla, I can't handle it anymore. My Dad's going to kill me with this college stuff."

"Oh, yeah?" I said.

"He wants me to go to the UW!"

For the past year, Don and I had often talked about his father's sense of control and entitlement over his life, and I had always been the one to help, just like he had used to help me with Brad. We were always helping each other…

But tonight I could offer no help.

I rolled over on my bed and propped myself up on my elbow, cradling the phone with my chin.

Brad rolled over too and pressed his body against my back. He reached one arm around me and ran his finger across my chest.

"Well, then go. You'll be close to home!"

"What? Shay? Are you crazy?"

At the moment, I probably was. I knew that the last thing Don wanted was to go to college close to home, where his dad could spy on his progress, but…

Brad's hand was in my shirt, in my bra. He'd been back for a week, and we had slowly gotten back in this position. Our bodies were about to get reacquainted for the first time since ninth grade.

"Huh?" I asked. My breath quickened as Brad's fingers found my nipple.

"What's that noise?"

"N-nothing."

"Did you just giggle?"

"Uh… no… no, I don't think so."

"You did. You just giggled. I'm telling you I'm dying inside and you're…"

Brad's mouth, warm and deliciously wet, found my ear. "Get rid of him, baby," he breathed.

On the phone, Don's voice stopped. There was a tense silence during which Brad's mouth found the most sensitive spot on the side of my neck. I held in the moan and tried to stay in both worlds simultaneously...

"Was that Brad Newton?" Don said coldly.

Long pause.

But Don didn't even know Brad had come back.

I risked a lie.

"No."

I held my breath, tried not to giggle again. Brad was unbuckling my belt. The buckle tinkled across my button and fell audibly on the comforter. Dang it!

"No, why would you think..."

"Whatever." Don's voice was deep-frozen. "Listen, I'll see you in school, okay. Don't worry about me." And he hung up.

And I didn't worry about him. Because the truth was, Brad was there, and there was nothing I wanted more than to put the phone back in its cradle, turn my head, and find his lips.

Which is too bad, really, considering how everything turned out...

The one thing that could be relied on in this crazy cross-country trip was that every night Don would pull out his VCR for a little Hindi movie action.

The nightly showing in Flagstaff, Arizona, was a film called *Janm Ke Samay Badal Gaye (Switched at Birth)*, about two men who learned that they had grown up with the wrong families. Luckily, they had a shared enemy in the bad uncle who was trying to keep both of them down, and they united against him. As promised, it was an action movie this time.

I watched because that's something friends do for each other... share in their interests... even when those interests might be bizarre... *especially* when those interests might be bizarre… especially when there's still a chance to help…

I should have told Don about Brad's return.

Because I hadn't, he didn't want to listen at all.

And because he didn't want to listen, I couldn't ask him for help when I needed it.

And I needed it soon.

It didn't take me long to realize that Brad had changed for the worse since he'd been gone. He'd always been prone to mood swings. He would often say jerky things, but then he would feel sorry for days on end. People thought he was a bully, but I knew from experience that he was really a sensitive, tender person. It was something he showed me that he didn't show anybody else—but he wanted to be more like that. It was like he had a battle raging inside him between his good and bad self.

In Idaho, the bad self had gotten the upper hand.

I didn't notice at first. Several weeks passed that were absolutely great. It was nice to have Brad back, and I enjoyed being with him.

Then I saw the cracks.

I'd known that his dad wasn't a very nice person, full of hatred for others, but Brad had avoided that before. Now, though, it seemed as if his time with his dad had altered his view of the world, made him look at people with derision.

Whereas before he'd seemed to have a grudging respect for people like Don yet still called them "nerds," now he had no respect for anyone different from him. Blacks were now "niggers," Asians were now "gooks," everybody was a "faggot" unless he liked them. He'd used to at least tolerate my mentioning of my friend Don, but now I had to make sure not to say his name, because it was a certainty that Brad would make some comment like, "That gayboy? I don't know why you'd hang out with some cocksmoker like that. What is it, he shares his panties with you?"

And believe it or not, that was Brad being restrained.

If he really saw a gay person, watch out. He claimed his

dad had once beaten up a gay guy in a bar, and I believed it. Brad's dad had certainly indoctrinated him. One day with Brad—I'd already been thinking of calling it quits at this time—we were at the Tacoma Mall and saw two guys holding hands. Brad lost it. He let go of my hand and rounded on them. "What the fuck do you homos think you're doing? Holding hands in public? You want us all to know you suck each other's cocks? You like getting poked, huh? How about I give you a poke with this?" He opened his jacket to reveal a switchblade. The two men looked at each other in astonishment. They had stopped holding hands. They backed away. Brad closed his jacket with a sneer. "No, I know—You pussies like the feel of man spit, right? Well, feel this!" And he spit in their faces.

I don't know how we got out of there before security came.

All I do know is that was all I could take. I called him that night—my mother held my hand while I did it—and told him I couldn't see him again, that his behavior was too bad.

He had a three word response for me:

"Fuck you, bitch."

If only those had been the last words we shared…

Amazingly, Don fell asleep in the middle of *Switched at Birth*, right when it was getting exciting. The bad uncle had just cornered the two men in a dead alley and he had a jeep and five goons with him. How would they escape?

But Don was snoring.

I gently got up and turned off the TV.

I looked at Don on the twin bed next to me. His head was turned to the side, but I could just see a little of his black eye, more of a yellow-green now. Pretty soon it would be gone, maybe even by the time we saw Devi.

It wasn't the first black eye I had seen on his face…

***

On March 2nd, two months after I broke up with Brad, Don was sitting in a Denny's with his fellow student council members. He, Erik Anderson, Trisha Nguyen, and Danna Wilson were trying to hash out a plan in which Student Skip Day would actually be sanctioned by the school itself, with fun activities on campus, so that people would actually want to stay at school rather than going to play volleyball at the local beach like they usually did. By Don's account, Trisha had come up with a brilliant proposal to present to our principal, Mr. Johnson, and they were all celebrating with a milkshake.

That's when Brad Newton walked in.

How he'd known Don was there nobody knows. Maybe he'd been trailing him for a while. Maybe it was just a cruel stroke of luck that he happened to walk into that Denny's at that exact moment.

Whatever it was, he spotted Don right away.

"So do you think this will work?" Don was asking.

"Are you kidding? This will be kickass," Erik said.

"Yeah, Trisha, I really like this plan," said Danna.

Trisha Nguyen was blushing and smiling widely as Brad Newton strode over to the table. When Brad kept coming, straight for the back of Don's chair, her smile faltered, and Erik, in the middle of a long suck of milkshake, stared challengingly up at the new arrival.

Neither Don, nor Danna sitting next to him, had a chance to interpret their fellow council member's expressions. Brad clamped a hand on Don's shoulder and both of them jumped.

"I need to talk to you," Brad said. His breath came at Don, rancid, smelling of beer, yet his face was tough and stern, a mask that Don couldn't quite read.

"Okay," Don said, but he indicated the others at the table with his head. Maybe, his head was telling Brad, this could wait for later, when they'd finished discussing Student Skip Day.

"Now," said Brad.

"Okay," said Don with a shrug. "Sorry, guys." He stood

and took his jacket.

Who knows what Don thought Brad wanted to talk about. We'd broken up two months before. Maybe he thought Brad wanted to get me back, wanted to talk to Don about how that might happen. Maybe he thought Brad was finally going to give back his *Star Trek* book.

He had no idea what the real reason was.

Erik seemed to have a clue, though. Perhaps he'd seen Brad in a fight before. Perhaps he'd *been* in a fight with Brad before. Who knows—but the point is he saw something in Brad's face that gave him the idea this wasn't a social visit. He moved to stand up, placing his hands on the table.

"Not you, Jock-Itch," Brad said and Erik froze. "This is between him and me."

How did Don not see it coming? Maybe because he didn't hear those words from Brad to Erik as he was already at the door. He was holding it open for Brad. He was actually being courteous.

"You first," said Brad.

"All right." Don went through the lobby and out the door, then turned to Brad. "What—"

Brad decked him in the face and Don stumbled.

"You *fuck*," said Brad, and hit him again in the gut.

Don lifted his hands to protect himself, but he didn't have a chance. He hadn't seen it coming and now the onslaught was too fast. Kicks, punches, Brad yelling, "I *know*, I *know*, I *know*," Don managing to stand through it, but just barely, Brad slamming him into the glass Denny's door.

I hate to think about what might have happened if Erik Anderson hadn't come out when he did. Brad didn't want to fight two; he took off as soon as Erik opened the door, leaving Don gasping and leaning on the Denny's wall.

"Holy shit," said Erik when he saw him. It had only been about two minutes, but Brad had really done a number on Don.

When Erik grabbed Don's arm to help him up, Don clenched his teeth.

"Sorry, man. Listen, Danna's calling the police. They'll

get Newton, but I think we'd better get some help for you. C'mon, I'll get you home."

Don remembers the taste of blood as much as he remembers Trisha standing at the door staring at him in shock.

What Don remembers most of all is the faces at the windows. Everybody at Denny's, it seemed, was rubbernecking. Only Erik had come out to help.

"I think he needs to go to the hospital," said Trisha.

"No," said Don, and a stream of blood trickled from his mouth. "I need you to take me somewhere else."

"I can't talk," I told Patel. "Don's doing fine. I just... I'm tired, that's all."

"SHAYLA!!!"

My mom's voice was high and piercing—a scream.

It would have taken a lot for me to get off my bed at that moment. I was curled into a ball with the pillow over my head. I was someplace else.

But the urgency of her voice made me spring into action. I ran down the hallway where I found Don sitting at our dining room table, his cheeks bruised, one eye puffed up and blood running down his face. One arm hung awkwardly at his side while he clung to his stomach with the other. His nose looked swollen and misplaced on his face, as if somebody had played Mr. Potato-Head with him and messed up.

"Hey, Shay," he said, and tried to smile. One of his front teeth was missing.

My mother hustled into the room with a wet paper towel and began dabbing at Don's lip, which was swelling as we spoke.

"What happened to you?!" I asked.

"Brad beat me up," he said.

My mother froze mid-dab. We exchanged an anxious

look.

"Well, we'd better get some help for you, Don," my mother said. "I'll call your parents."

With my mother gone from the room, Don and I looked at each other, him through the slit of his one eye. He looked like Popeye if Popeye hadn't been strong to the finich.

"I had to come," he said. "I was worried about you. I thought he might come to hurt you, too."

Thank you, I wanted to say. *I love you. I'm sorry.*

But not one of these things sounded even remotely appropriate at the moment.

In the kitchen, my mother was speaking on the phone. "No, no, Mrs. Smith… he's okay, just battered up. I think his arm might be broken. Apparently, the other boy just attacked him out of nowhere."

"How did you get here?" I asked.

"Erik Anderson," he said. "He's waiting outside in his car right now. We'd better tell him I'm taken care of…"

"I will," I said. I touched Don's shoulder as lightly as I could and then headed for my front door.

"It turns out," said Don, and I turned to see his distorted, bloodied smile, "Erik wasn't such a *ha'DIbah* after all."

CHAPTER EIGHTEEN
ME

FOR ALMOST FIVE years after graduation, I visited my psychologist Dr. Ripples because of what happened that night.

I sat across from him and his Bobble-head Mariners Ken Griffey, Jr., and told almost everything: about my relationship with Brad Newton, about how much he'd changed when he came back from Idaho, about my friendship with Don, and all about that terrible night.

The only thing I left out was my feelings for Don.

This is, I guess, because I saw Dr. Ripples and Ken Griffey, Jr.—the head shrinker and the shrunken head—as a duo of exorcists. I wanted to tell them all about Brad so they could excise him and all of my bad feelings from my life.

Don, however, was hope. He was a man I could rely on, a man I could love, a man who just might save me in the end. And I didn't want them to take that away from me.

So I never mentioned those feelings.

However, there's one thing I told Dr. Ripples that I didn't tell anyone else. Not Don, not my mom, not my dad, not Jack.

Driving across country with Don, five years after it had all gone wrong, this was still my biggest secret.

Because the night that Brad went crazy...

That night, I was pregnant.

I had known for about a week before.

There were signs. First off, my breasts had gotten bigger, but that by itself wasn't a big deal. That happened with my periods. But I wasn't having a period! And I was having sudden cravings for different foods, which was new, and when I woke up one morning and immediately had to throw up, I knew something was wrong.

A pregnancy test proved it.

Up until that point in my life, I don't think that there had been anything more embarrassing than the feeling of going to the store to buy a pregnancy test. I'd made sure to go to the store I and my parents didn't ever shop at, the one where Brad Newton's mom didn't work, and I checked all the aisles carefully to make sure that nobody I knew was there—but still I was full of shame as I handed my money to the cashier, the oldest, nicest looking lady I could find. I think I was holding out hope that her memory would be so spotty she'd forget me as soon as I left.

The embarrassment of buying the test soon gave way to the embarrassment of taking it, and then, three minutes later, to the mortification of seeing two lines when I had only wanted one.

I was pregnant, and there was only one possibility for a father.

I had no idea what I was going to do. The only thing I knew was that I had to tell Brad.

"What?! You gotta be fuckin' kiddin' me!"

Brad had been sitting next to me on the bed, running his fingers through my hair and looking loving. He'd thought I'd called because I wanted him back. He'd thought—

because my mother and brother were out at the grocery store—that I wanted to be alone with him so we could have sex. He'd been *waiting* for this.

Now he jumped off the bed and away from me like we were two magnets. He was repelled. He just stood and stared straight at me with his eyes squinted, measuring me the way he might measure a piece of shit he'd narrowly avoided stepping in.

"No," I said, "it's true. I took the test… twice… and—"

"It ain't mine."

His voice was sure, a little bit angry. He'd made up his mind.

But he was wrong.

He was the only person I'd ever been with.

"Brad…"

"No!"

The anger took control. He swept his arm across the top of my dresser, knocking to the floor perfume bottles, a stuffed animal, and the little glass Enterprise that Don had given me—as a joke—the Christmas before.

"I used condoms! The fucking thing ain't mine!"

He was right about the condoms, at least. He *had* used them, which either meant we were the unlucky 2%, or, more likely, in our excitement to be together, we had been a little careless with how we had put it on.

But he was definitely the father… and I needed to talk to him about what we were going to do… because I had no clue…

"Brad—"

I stood up with one hand held out.

"NO!" He was seething. He knocked my hand aside, and then with just a millisecond of looking at my face with his teeth gritted in disgust, he raised his own hand and slapped me across the cheek with such force that I flew into the dresser. I bounced off, then fell face down on the floor.

"Get up," he said.

I stared at his boots.

He'd never hit me before...

"I said get the fuck up!" he said. He leaned forward and grabbed me by the shoulders and pulled me to a sitting position. I stared at him cautiously, my ear ringing and my cheek stinging as if a thousand little Riverdancers were dancing on the skin.

He grabbed both cheeks between his hands and leaned his face in close, so close that when he spoke, I felt little flecks of spit land on my mouth. "I thought you were good, Shayla, but really you're just a little whore, aren't you? So who is it? Who've you been fucking other than me?"

"Brad, I swear, it's yours."

"Bullshit!" He slapped me again. "I only just been back. It's not mine."

He'd been back two months, and we'd been together at least ten times before I broke up with him, but I was afraid to say it.

"Who is it?" he screamed, his voice angry, his eyes rolling around the room—and in that moment, he spotted the little glass Enterprise...

I saw the thought take form on his face, his jaw tightening, his lip curling, his nostrils widening, his breath coming out in one evil roar, like the sound of a crowd at a stadium with the volume turned down.

"It was that little faggot, Smith, wasn't it?" He picked up the Enterprise and shoved it in my face. "Wasn't it—!?"

I tried to shake my head, but he was still grabbing my other cheek. "Don—" I said.

I meant to say "Don and I are just friends," but Brad didn't let me. In fact, he seemed to take that one word as confirmation.

"Don!" he sneered. "I knew that little queer was hot for you, but I never thought you'd fall for that shit. FUCK!" He threw the Enterprise across the room, where it shattered against the wall.

"Brad—" I tried again.

But I shut up right away when he pointed his finger at me. He stood looking down at me, his chest rising and falling as he breathed heavily, that finger pointing the whole time. The moment seemed to go on and on, but then he finally put down his arm.

"Fuck you, bitch!" he said and gave my bookshelf a kick that knocked books to the floor.

Then he stormed out. I heard him stamp down the hall and then open the door, I heard my mom's voice from outside—"Hi, Brad... Brad?"—as she and Jack came in with the groceries, heard the sound of Brad's car starting up, the soft, but urgent footfalls of my mother coming down the hall.

"Shay?" she asked, gently pushing open my door. "I just saw Brad. Honey, is everything...?"

She took in the scene—the fallen books and perfumes, the shattered glass, the daughter with her back against the dresser holding her stomach and fighting back tears.

"Are you all right?" she asked.

I was just glad that the cheek Brad had hit was facing away from her. I didn't want my mom to see the slap mark that I knew would be there. I drew in a breath that felt like a sob—but held the tears back.

"I'm all right," I said. "Mom, can I just be alone for a little while?"

"Shay, are you sure...?"

"I need to be alone," I told my mom, more forcefully than I needed to. Instantly sorry, I said, "Please, Mom... I'll be all right, I just want to be by myself for a while."

"Okay, honey, if that's what you want... I'm here to talk if you need me, you know that." She gave me one last worried look and then gently shut the door. As worried as she was, at least she got to go back to Jack and unloading groceries.

I had to deal with this alone.

I pushed myself up from the floor and reeled to the bed.

Why did my stomach hurt so much? Like a knife were twisting around inside me...?

I curled up on the bed and began to cry.

That's where I was two hours later—just all cried out— when Don came to my door, bruised and battered and in pain, but more concerned about me.

In a way, that was my fault.

I lost the baby.

That was my fault, too.

I should have known better than to invite Brad over when I was all alone, when he had been acting so unpredictably.

But I had thought he needed to know. And I certainly hadn't expected him to hit me.

I'd been confused and frantic. I was pregnant, and I had no idea what I was going to do.

I remembered a girl named Tanya Windham, who'd graduated the year before, how she had been eight months pregnant when she walked across the graduation stage. I'd been sitting in the audience, and I heard all the whispers as she crossed. I hadn't wanted to end up like Tanya. The thought absolutely terrified me.

But I also hadn't wanted this. To lose my pregnancy this way seemed so wrong.

I didn't tell anybody. Not Don, not my mom, not a soul.

Brad knew, of course, but he never said a word about the baby. The last time I saw him was in the court room, and he didn't look at me once. He didn't say a word, didn't take the stand, just pled guilty for assault and let them lead him away.

The doctor who saw me the day after knew, but he was never going to tell anybody.

The only other person who ever knew wouldn't hear about it until a year later. Even then, it was difficult. Dr. Ripples was my psychologist, the person who was supposed to listen to things like this, but I had to force myself to tell him. Every day for two months, I promised myself I would bring it up, but in session, I couldn't do it. Finally, one day, I had just told him that there was something I needed to say, but I couldn't get it out. He spent three sessions asking questions, making guesses, coaxing it out of me, but when he finally did, I didn't feel much better.

Dr. Ripples told me why. "It's not enough even for you to tell me, I think, Shayla," he said as the Ken Griffey, Jr., head bobbled. "Eventually, you're going to need to tell this to somebody else, somebody who you care about, who cares about you, who can help you move forward."

Someday, I'd thought, I could tell Don.

Someday.

But at that point, five years in the past, in the aftermath of the Brad Newton incident, I didn't think about telling Don at all.

I was just happy he was still my friend.

CHAPTER NINETEEN
US

ANOTHER BATHROOM, ANOTHER mirror, this one in Amarillo, Texas.

It was Wednesday night. I'd just made my nightly report to Patel, and was getting ready for bed.

Patel had been happy to hear that Don was still doing okay, but he'd been quick to point out that we weren't out of the woods yet. Unlike Don, Patel thought that Devi just might be the trigger, and not the cure.

Devi.

We were closing in on her now. Only two days to go.

Don had stopped in Amarillo to rest and gain some energy, but he was committed to arriving on Friday evening.

"Why?" I'd asked when he'd told me that afternoon. "What's so special about Friday? I'm sure Devi won't mind if you show up on Saturday."

"It has to be Friday because Saturday's her birthday. I want to be there with her when she brings in her new year. Anyway, she's expecting us for Friday night."

"You never told me we were coming for her birthday," I protested.

"I didn't?" Don asked innocently. "I could have sworn I told you…"

He shrugged, blowing it off.

I glared at him a while, but then I let it go, too. It was frustrating that he would wait until now to tell me something like this, but among all the other frustrations Don had given me in the last few days, this was pretty small-fry.

After all, birthday or not, it didn't really have any impact on the big decision I had to make—other than that it made it more urgent that I make it soon.

We'd make a big push the next day, Don had said, and get to Memphis, and then on Friday, we'd have a nice, leisurely drive for the rest of the way to Atlanta.

Which didn't give me much time at all…

I twisted on the water in the hotel sink, plunging my hand under its stream to check the temperature.

So far, Don's behavior had gotten better and better. The accent was almost completely gone, and the "yahs" were only very occasional. The only crazy thing he kept up was his dedication to Devi, and I was beginning to think this wasn't so crazy after all, that it might actually come from some real feelings and mutual care.

I had listened to everything Don had on Devi, how they had met in a class, how she had basically been his superior, an upperclassman, but how they had somehow ended up sitting next to each other and liking each other's company. They had gone out together many times, but they were more colleagues than anything else. Romance had never bloomed for Don and Devi, but reading her letters to him in Africa, he had seen how it could have. Devi was the one for Don; he was sure of it.

But was Don the one for me? That was the big question.

I had waited for Don a long time, thinking he was. I just knew that he could make my life better, that we could work.

At the beginning of this trip, it had been almost impossible to think of us ending up together with the way he was acting, but now, two days beyond Michael, I was back to my original thoughts. I loved Don and wanted him to love me. The only thing stopping me from telling him was Devi.

If he loved her so much, did I have the right to stand in his way?

I just didn't know...

The water was just about right now. I gave myself a quick glance in the mirror. I looked tired, which was exactly how I felt.

I splashed some water on my face, but of course that didn't make me feel any better.

I had planned on telling Don, but the right moment had never come up.

Brad's attack had come in March, and with the school year coming to a close and Don heading off to college all the way in Georgia, I knew I wouldn't see him much, so I decided not to say anything. It wasn't exactly a conscious thought, but somewhere in me, I imagined he would come back to be with me.

I wandered through graduation feeling half-dead, with Don standing beside me, excited and hopeful, but I'm sure worried about what was to come in his future as a doctor.

Don had decided to go to Emory University in Georgia as a kind of compromise with his father. Basically, Don would study medicine like his dad wanted, but with the condition that he would do it far away. Emory was a good medical school, and his dad hadn't had any problem with it, but I still couldn't help feeling that Don was fooling himself. Just because he would be far away didn't stop the fact that he had lost the battle over what he would do with his life.

Most of all, though, I didn't want him to go. But he promised holidays and summers, and I thought I could live with that. Anyway, I had my own therapy to get through. I wanted to be able to tell Don the whole story of what happened that night. I didn't want anything to be a secret between us. If I could do that, I thought, then I deserved to be with him.

The staying-at-home thing happened slowly. At first, my parents thought it would only be temporary, and so did I. I'd decided not to start college right away, to take a year off and get things together, but I had a much harder time than I thought. I'd started sessions with Dr. Ripples in the summer, and my parents had been happy to pay for them, but it seemed like the more I talked, the worse my problems became.

The sessions continued, and I continued to wait for Don to come back. This didn't happen the way I wanted, either. Don came back for Christmas for two weeks, but we didn't spend as much time together as I thought we would. He argued with his dad about the classes he had signed up for in the spring; he wanted to unwind with an art and lit class, but Dr. Smith saw both of these as unnecessary, as of course he did the Science Fiction/Fantasy Club that Don had helped spearhead at Emory. Don was miserable for almost the whole time he was home, which made me more miserable after he was gone.

The following summer and other breaks were similar. I had fun with Don while he was around, but he couldn't stand talking to his father. By his junior year, he stayed in Atlanta all year long, and we kept up through letters and emails. "Dear Shay," he said in one email I kept for over a year, "I wish I could see you. I'm just trying to figure some things out right now about my future. I'll let you know everything as soon as I know."

He came back one last time for Christmas Break of his senior year. He'd figured it all out. He needed some time away before medical school; in fact, he might never go back. He'd already applied and been accepted into the Peace Corps, without a word to either his parents or me, and he would be heading out to Biribiri, West Africa, the next June, straight from college. He'd come home to tell us.

My world came crashing down. Somehow, in my mind, I'd figured Don would finish college and come back to Washington and everything would be okay, that his being close would help me figure myself out. Now I didn't know what I'd do.

My parents were already putting out feelers that said they were hoping I'd get things together. Jack was going to be graduating in the spring and he planned on doing two years at a community college and then transferring to Western Washington or somewhere. Didn't I feel like now was the time for me to think about my future a little more?

They weren't pushing me out at all—in fact, they'd be happy if I stayed, they said—they just wanted me to think about it. And I just wasn't ready.

I felt betrayed. Don's senior year was supposed to be a great time, a time when he came back, a time when I told him how I felt, a time when I finally got over the demons of my past and started moving forward.

Instead, it was turning into the worst year of my life.

It was the night that he left that I really wanted to tell him.

His bags were all packed.

Worf was still in the corner.

His parents were upstairs, where we could hear their footsteps once in a while. There was little chance of an interruption. Don and his father had hardly talked since Don revealed his plan.

We sat on bean bags, looking at the glow-in-the-dark stars on Don's bedroom ceiling, thinking our own thoughts.

My thoughts? When I finally left that night, it would be another two years until I saw Don. It was getting late, but I didn't want to leave. My heart was breaking, and I couldn't even tell my best friend.

"I'm going to miss you, Shay," Don said.

I turned to him on my bean bag. "Don't go," I said.

He looked over at me, his blue eyes piercing. "It won't be so bad. It's only a couple years."

That's what you said about college.

I felt my eyes water up. I couldn't believe he was going.

Don reached out and touched my shoulder.

"Don," I said.

I'd so wanted to tell him.

Now, he looked into my eyes with compassion.

I felt like crying.

Instead, I leaned forward and kissed him.

His eyes widened; I kept kissing.

There was no thought. I wasn't doing this to try to get him to stay or anything. It was completely impulsive, and I didn't want to stop. I closed my eyes and pressed my lips to him...

I thought he kissed back...

But when I reached forward with my arms to hold him...

He pushed me gently away.

"Shayla," he said.

"I'm sorry." I turned away.

Worf stared at me.

"It's just..." Don struggled for words. "I'm leaving. Tomorrow. And."

"It's okay."

"Let's always be friends."

"Of course."

I couldn't look at him. I still felt his warmth on my lips, tasted him, all candy canes and egg nog...

I felt like a fool. An absolute fool.

But I felt even worse the next day.

Because the next day, Don was gone. And I was alone.

"Don?" I said.

"Mmmm?"

There was a constant thump-thump-thump as we drove down the highway. It had been with us ever since we had entered Oklahoma. The roads somehow were set up this way because, apparently, Oklahoma was seriously against falling asleep at the wheel. I could see from the landscape why this was such a concern.

"Do you remember the night you left for the Peace Corps?"

I'd decided to make one last effort. We'd talked about everything else we shared, but never this. That night had gone unspoken since it happened. If we could talk about it now, maybe we could talk about other things. If not...

"Sure. I had dinner with Devi and a couple friends, and then the next morning I took a taxi to the airport."

"No, I don't mean that. Not the night you really left. The night you left Washington. The last time you saw me before you went."

He considered.

"No, not really. All of that is kind of blurry for me. I remember that big argument with my dad, and rushing to the airport in a hurry, but that's about it."

"Your dad wasn't talking to you at all when I saw you that night, Don. Don't you remember? We sat in your room and talked. We turned off the lights and just looked up at those little glow-in-the-dark-stars you had glued all over your ceiling."

"I forgot all about those stars!" Don laughed.

"You said you'd miss me..."

Don squeezed his chin, furrowed his brow. He tried to remember.

"I said 'Don't go' and you said it would only be two years...?"

"I'm sorry." Don shook his head. "I just can't remember at all. There was so much going on."

"Oh..."

"Why?"

"Oh... I just wondered... I just wondered if you remembered."

How could he not remember that night?

I'd thought about that night so many times since he left! It was inconceivable that he could have forgotten...

Or maybe he'd just blocked it out of his mind. Maybe he hadn't stopped me kissing him that night because he had to go, but because he didn't like me...

But I had been sure I'd felt him kiss back!

But it didn't matter. The point was he didn't remember. His feelings for me just weren't the same as mine were for him.

I was being selfish, and not a very good friend at all, and it was time for me to stop.

From now on, however much it hurt, I would put thoughts of Don and me aside. It was Devi that he wanted, that was obvious, and I needed to support him.

It was time for me to be a good friend.

I'd let him have Devi.

Even if it meant I had to be alone.

CHAPTER TWENTY
LAST CHANCE

IT WAS THE day before Devi's birthday.

Don had practically been jumping from foot to foot in anticipation by the time we stopped at a hotel in Memphis the night before, but that hadn't stopped him from thinking about me.

"Have you ever seen Graceland?" he'd asked.

"No," I said, but Don knew I had always loved Paul Simon's *Graceland* album. In fact, in between thinking about Don and Devi and me, I had been aware of the fact that we were getting closer and closer to Elvis' home, and Simon's song had played in my head many times already.

"Well, we're going to Graceland, Shay," he said. "Tomorrow morning!"

And he began to sing, but not an Indian song this time. It was the lyrics from "Graceland."

Maybe Devi really was curing him!

I joined in, singing.

We were going to Memphis.

I was finally going to see Graceland!

***

Don was *still* practically jumping from foot to foot as we toured Elvis' old house.

I was happy to be there, but Don's eagerness was wearing off on me. We were only six hours away from the end of this trip, and now that I had decided to let Don have Devi; I just wanted to see how everything worked out.

At least that's what I kept telling myself.

Mostly, I just wanted this trip to be over.

Now that I was here, I couldn't have cared less about Graceland.

I told Don this as we stopped to peer into the Jungle Room, the incredibly gaudy area that Elvis had furnished, apparently to irritate his dad, with thick green carpeting on both floor and ceiling, wood paneled walls, and all kinds of animal images, from monkey statuettes, to dragons carved into the couch arms, to a worn stuffed panda next to a guitar on a chair. "I'm ready to go meet Devi," I said.

Don was ecstatic.

"You are great, Shay!" he shouted and threw his arms around me.

As testament to the fact that he really was better, he didn't start singing this time. He just said "Let's go" and started on his way out past all the Elvis tourists.

This left me to fill in Don's—and Rahul's—signature line:

"Yah, yah, yah, yes I am great," I sang softly, bitterly, to myself as I followed after my friend.

Mississippi, Alabama, Georgia…

Almost there…

When we passed Six Flags Over Atlanta, basically a giant amusement park, where we could intermittently see a roller coaster snaking around behind some trees, Don handed me a piece of paper.

"Could you read these directions for me?" he asked.

We must almost be at Devi's. It was only 5 p.m.

"You're going to want to take Exit 13," I said.

We did, and I gave Don directions, eagerly waiting to see where Don's "goddess" might live.

I was surprised, then, when the address on the piece of paper ended up not being a residence at all, but a shopping center.

"What's this?" I asked, looking up at a little store that said *Raja Boutique*.

"I just wanted to make one stop," said Don. "You know, I want to look my best for Devi for her birthday."

"You're buying clothes?"

"Of course. Is there a problem with that?"

"Not really…"

We walked into the store, where we were greeted by racks of Indian clothing, the heavy smell of incense, and a burly bearded Indian man in a turban. "Good afternoon. How may I help you?" he asked.

It had been the first time in a couple days that I had heard such a thick Indian accent, since Don's had been fading, and I shot a quick look at Don. This had better not cause a relapse.

"I'm picking up an order for Don Smith," Don said in his normal accent. I let out my breath.

But wait a minute… did he say "order?" He'd ordered ahead?

"Ah, yes," said the man. "You are the one that wanted a sherwani. Hold on. I will get it for you."

As the man disappeared into a back room, I raised an eyebrow. "Sherwani?"

"It's an Indian traditional costume, something they wear for special occasions."

"Like birthdays?"

"Yeah," said Don, "you know, like Rahul wore last night in *Saccha Aashik Apna Saathi Dhoondh Leta Hai*."

I ignored the incomprehensible stream of Hindi words and just thought back to last night's movie. There had been only one scene where Rahul Ghosh hadn't been sporting jeans and a T-shirt…

It had been a *wedding*…

"Do you really think you'll need traditional clothing?" I

asked. "I mean, it's not like we're going to a party or anything."

"Who knows? Maybe not," Don said amiably. "This is just in case."

Just in case what?

The Indian man was back, holding in his arms an outfit on a hanger with a protective plastic cover. He began to take out individual pieces and set them on the counter before Don. "This is the sherwani," he said, indicating the main piece of clothing, a long, shiny white Indian top with intricate gold and red designs embroidered down the middle and along the neck, cuff, and bottom. It was as long as a dress, and I could see that it would cover Don's body from immediately below his chin to just below his knees.

And there was more.

One by one, the man showed off the other items that would finish off Don's outfit: a pair of kurta pajama pants to be worn under the sherwani, a thin scarf to wrap around his shoulders, and a pair of pointy shoes called mojaris.

"Wow," I said, and in my mind I thought that Devi would have to be impressed if Don actually had a chance to put these on.

If he put them on at the right time.

Otherwise, she'd just think he'd gone mad.

"Great," said Don, running his eyes over the clothes.

The man got down to business. "That will be $650," he said.

Don pulled out his wallet without any sense of surprise, and paid the man.

$650, I thought as we walked back to the car. *That's one heck of a "just in case."*

"Hey, look, the mountain's out," said Don with a big smile.

"Huh?" I said.

Ahead of us, through the windshield, was what looked like a big rock.

"That's Stone Mountain, the biggest piece of granite in

the world," said Don.

I thought about the imperial, snow-capped mountains of home: Rainier, St. Helens, Hood, Shasta.

"That's not a mountain," I said.

"Anyway," said Don, "what matters is that seeing it means that we're almost at Devi's."

Which meant that I had to steel myself.

I may have decided not to get in the way of Don and Devi, but that didn't mean it would be easy.

I'd be letting go of the man I loved…

Fifteen minutes later, Don pulled into a parking space at the Peachtree Point Apartment Complex, a well-looked-after property with neat paint and landscaping.

"Everything around here is called Peachtree," I joked, unsnapping my seat belt to get out.

Don didn't move.

"Uh, is everything all right?" I asked, with my hand still on the door handle.

Don looked straight ahead at the steering wheel. "I'm afraid there's something I need to tell you," he said.

Uh-oh…

"I wasn't completely honest with you before."

What?

"About what?" I asked… feeling a shiver run up my spine.

"You asked me if I remembered the night before I left for the Peace Corps."

I can't believe you're talking about this now…

I squeezed the seatbelt between my fingers.

"Let's not talk about it," I said.

"No, I think I have to. I think I need to tell you the truth about what happened. I don't want anything hanging over our time here. Over what happens with Devi."

"Listen, I kissed you. I'm sorry. It was just a bad idea."

Please stop talking…

"No, Shay. No, it wasn't. That's what I wanted to tell

you. I wanted to kiss you back. I wanted the same thing you wanted. I can't tell you how many times I wished that I'd been able to turn back the clock and change that. I loved you. You were my best friend, and I loved you. I didn't know it until Brad took you away from me, but I felt the same thing for you. I just didn't want to show it. I didn't want to hurt you. I knew that it wouldn't have worked out."

Do something, I willed myself. *This is your chance.*

"I just wanted you to know."

I was dumbfounded. Why was he telling me this now? When I had pretty much decided to let it go?

He'd felt the same way I did?

I felt him take my fingers in his hand and give them a squeeze. "Missed opportunities, though, right?" he said with a nostalgic little smile. "All in all, I guess it's better things turned out the way they did."

You do?

He patted my hand lightly. "Let's always be friends," he said.

Oh no…

No no no…

Not again…

That's exactly what he'd said that night. It was all happening the same way!

And I could have changed things then if I'd just said something…!

"You ready?"

I nodded, dumbly.

Do something, girl!!!!!

He opened the door and stepped out. I did the same, feeling numb.

We walked to the apartments and up the stairs.

Tell him, tell him!

This is your only chance!!!

I think my mouth was broken. It wouldn't open.

I was just mutely following behind as if I didn't have a thought in my head.

If he knows how you feel…

I was suddenly sure that it could work. He had been acting more and more normal since we'd left. Everything was going to be okay. Everything was going to be okay... if only I could part my lips and speak...

Don raised his hand to knock. His knuckles moved toward the door. Any second he would be knocking...

Should I?

Should I do it?

Did I dare?

"Don," I said, a whisper barely.

He knocked, looked back at me with a quizzical smile.

I could hear footsteps rushing from within. This really was my last chance.

"I think..."

A hand on the doorknob. Doorknob turning.

"I think I love you."

Don's face fell exactly as the door swung open. He stared at me. I stared at him.

"Don!"

Devi was there in the doorway, still in her hospital scrubs, a green T-shirt just peeping out from beneath.

"You made it. I'm so happy to see you." Her arms were spread wide. She wanted to hug him.

She hadn't even noticed the atmosphere here at her doorstep.

Slowly, mechanically, Don's head turned to her. "Devi," he said... *uncertainly?*... and moved into her arms.

He didn't lift her, didn't twirl her around in the air like he'd said he would. He hugged her tight, as if he were afraid he might lose her. "I'm so glad to be here."

She laughed, a happy sound that seemed completely out of place at that moment, and untangled herself.

"I guess you are," she said. "Why don't you come in?"

She moved to the side and he stumbled in, staring at me over his shoulder, and the hurt was there... the hurt that I didn't want to cause... *But was there something more?*

"And you must be Shayla?"

I nodded.

"Don't just stand there. Come on in. Don has told me so much about you. Come in."

She reached for my hand...

And crushed my heart.

PART FOUR

THE NAME "DEVI" MEANS "GODDESS"

PART FOUR

CHAPTER TWENTY-ONE
WHEN A DOOR OPENS, SOMEWHERE A WINDOW'S BEEN SHUT

I MOVED PAST Devi in a daze and went to stand in the hallway beside Don, who was facing away, looking into her apartment, and away from both of us, unreadable.

I looked at Devi, who was pushing the door closed. As she did, she turned her head and winked at me over her shoulder, giving a cute little shrug. That cuteness was *not* what I needed right now.

She smiled at me, an honest, open smile, which I hated her for, and I took the time to appraise her. She had white, white teeth and her hair, up in a bun, seemed black and shiny and alive. She moved with a true confidence that seemed straightforward and sexy at the same time. In fact, she exuded self-confidence and self-belief.

She was just a little bit darker than I had imagined, and her nose was just a little bit bigger, but otherwise, she was exactly the girl in Don's picture. In fact, she was even more beautiful.

Which meant she was more beautiful than me.

To say that I felt terrible would be an understatement.

There was no way I could have returned that gorgeous smile. In fact, I was lucky that I was only exposed to it for a second, because I was just fantasizing what it would look like if I pulled out one of her front teeth.

With the door closed and latched, she turned fully and focused on Don, or rather Don's back, since he hadn't turned around yet. I saw him from the side, though, and he was not looking good. He had his hands shoved in his pockets, and his eyes darted around as if they didn't want to look at any one thing too long, or as if they were trying to escape being looked at. He looked shy and uncomfortable, and as if he were in pain.

"Let me see you, then," Devi cooed.

Don shyly lifted his head up, spun around to look at her. By some amazing power of will, he transformed himself enough to give a broad smile and keep his eyes focused. He almost succeeded in looking genuine, but his pocketed hands and the slight slump in his shoulders showed otherwise. This was not the devil-may-care Don I knew.

None of this registered on Devi. She stepped up to him and looked him up and down, then "Oh, wow," she said, and placed her hand on his upper arm. "It looks like they beefed you up over there in Africa. What are these muscles?" She had that school-teacher way of talking that I guess some men like, all building up the ego, and the touching thing couldn't hurt. Her super-niceness was really starting to irritate me.

But the fact is that, deep down, even I liked Devi. She seemed nice, and the way she talked was friendly, and the big thing was it appeared to be completely unaffected. She was genuinely nice and friendly.

Actually, I wished I could have had somebody to talk to me and touch me like she did to Don.

It was just that *watching* her talking to and touching Don made me want to scream.

"Oh, let me hug you again. Come on." Devi grabbed

him and embraced him in another bear hug…

…and inside of me, a little Edward Munch was absolutely howling.

Through all that internal noise, though, I noticed that Don, wrapped in that bear hug, was not focused on Devi, but on me. He stared straight at me, with his mouth a stiff, solid line and his blue eyes clear and focused. I felt my own eyes widen. What did the stare mean? Was he angry? Was he shocked? Had I ruined his moment, was that why? I played nervously with my hands and grimaced back at him, hunching my shoulders self-consciously.

"Actually, Devi," Don said, straight into her ear, never once taking his eyes off me. "Could you give Shay and me a minute? We were… discussing… something, and I think we'd better finish."

"Oh… uh…" Devi stepped back, looking from Don to me. "Sure. I guess I had better go and get changed. I mean, I didn't even realize I was still wearing my hospital…" Her brown eyes honed in on his set expression. "I hope everything is okay… I don't…"

She was rambling.

"Devi," Don said, softly.

That one word brought her back.

She looked at Don, her head tilted to the side questioningly.

Dang it, even her questioning look was attractive!

Don had his gravest look on.

Devi waited.

And he broke into the biggest, goofiest grin possible. His body uncoiled and he puffed back up like a sponge in water.

"Hey! Just joking, yah? Everything's great!" He spread out his arms. "Come on. We're so happy to be here!" And he did exactly what he had meant to do in the beginning. He gave her a huge embrace and spun her around in a circle…

…two circles…

…three circles…

Her green hospital top swung out behind her like a sari,

and halfway through the second circle something snapped in her, and she broke into a delighted—and delight*ful*—laugh. Her smile was humongous.

When Don set her down, she gave him a soft protesting slap on the shoulder, but it was clear that she was thrilled. "Oh wow! Same old Don, huh? Crazy as ever!"

"Dil…" said Don, "…deewana hai."

"Huh?"

"The heart is crazy."

"What? You're speaking Hindi now?" Devi sounded astounded… and still delighted.

"A little."

"Wow. What is going on with this guy?" Devi gave me a conspiratorial wink and pointed at him as if I were sharing in this joke. "Who is he? Do I still know him?"

I'm sorry to say that my smile probably looked more like she'd been pointing to a turd than to my best friend. "Probably not," I said, then realizing that I had said this about as positively as an electron, I rounded it off with what was supposed to be a joke: "He really is crazy, too." My timing was off, though, and my tone, too, so this ended up sounding pretty bad, also.

"Hey, all right," said Don, saving the mood. "Devi, why don't you go ahead and change. We're going to take you out to dinner."

"Really? Right now? You don't want to come in and chat first?"

"Nope. Dinner first and then chat. We've got reservations in…" He looked at his watch… "forty minutes."

"Really?" said Devi.

"Really?" I said at the exact same time.

"Hey, it's your birthday. I come prepared. And you'd better dress nice. We're going to the Continental."

The name of the restaurant spurred a gasp and another delighted hug from Devi. "The Continental! Oh, wow. I *do* need to change. I'll be right back! I'm going to put on my *fancy* clothes!"

Devi Chakraborty pranced lightly from the room.

The lightness went with her.

My plan was to turn to Don and say something cutting about how he hadn't told me anything about our going to a fancy restaurant... in fact, I hadn't brought anything all that nice to wear, come to think of it... but the look on his face stopped these thoughts in their tracks.

Don stepped to me with all the gravitas of somebody at a wake, and I was the body in the coffin. He touched my cheek.

"Shay, I'm really sorry... I had no idea you..."

His fingers on my cheek felt so warm and comfortable. I closed my eyes and leaned into them.

At that moment, I wanted to tell him to drop Devi.

I wanted to tell him that I loved him.

I wanted to tell him that I would watch every Rahul Ghosh movie out, learn to dance like a Bollywood star, tan myself Southeast Asian...

But then, instead of saying any of these things, I took a deep breath, and decided to play against type. It was time to withdraw from the race.

"She's beautiful, Don."

He stared at me, his hand on my cheek.

"She's beautiful... and nice... and she obviously cares about you. Maybe she's what you need."

Don turned his face from mine.

"I mean she's..."

His shoulders shook.

"Are you crying?"

He was, his eyes moist and big streams of tears rolling down his cheeks. He was sniffling, too.

"Stop that," I said, totally embarrassed. "It's okay."

"Okay?" he said. "Okay? It's not okay." Through all the tears, a sudden beaming smile broke out. "I've got the best friend in the universe, and you say it's okay? It's better than okay. It's great! Thank you, thank you, thank you, Shay!"

And he hugged me and spun me around in the air. I shook like a rag doll, not nearly as elegant as Devi.

I was a little dizzy when he set me down, his hands on my shoulders, his wet eyes wide with wonder and glee.

"I love you, Shay!" he said and gave me a big hug.

I love you too, Don...

I pressed my fingertips into his back, knowing that when this hug ended, it would be over.

I didn't want it to be over...

Then, suddenly, it was.

Don gave me one last squeeze and let me go.

"Now..." he said. "When do you think I should tell Devi I love *her*?"

Ugh.

CHAPTER TWENTY-TWO
AN ENCHANTED EVENING

"I SWEAR TO God, it's like he's totally better."

Patel listened patiently as I told him everything that had happened at dinner, which was essentially nothing, other than that Don had acted like a total gentleman.

We'd gone to the fanciest restaurant Don could have thought of. The Continental was a high-class restaurant with an elegant décor, charming service, and a clientele that looked like the cream of the Atlanta crop; everybody was dressed to the nines in fancy suits and evening dresses.

And so were we.

As Devi was getting ready, and as I reeled from that last hug, and as Don made the executive decision that tomorrow would be the best day to express his love for Devi, it being her birthday and all, a question had formed in my mind.

"Wait a minute. This sounds like a pretty elegant restaurant. What are we supposed to wear?"

"Ah-ha," said Don, and he knelt and opened his suitcase. Like a magician, he extracted a full suit with a pink bowtie for himself and, for me, a beautiful blue silk dress that ended up fitting perfectly.

"Wow," I said.

How he'd managed to keep these clothes so pristine with his particular packing style, I'll never know. I was just glad that we would both look presentable.

I was also glad that the dress was so easy to get into.

I was all ready and putting the finishing touches on my makeup when Devi emerged from her bedroom in a sleek black dress that showed off just a hint of cleavage, but I was quietly thrilled when I noted that, in my new dress, I matched her on the fashion front.

Don emerged from a guest bedroom in his suit, and we headed out, all three of us looking fabulous.

Don was amazing. If I were Devi, I would say he was scoring points across the board, and he just kept scoring at dinner.

At the restaurant, Don was the soul of wit. He recounted funny—but notably not crazy—stories of our trip to Atlanta, like our encounter with Michael and Terry, and he even trusted Devi with some stories from Africa that he hadn't shared with me. In fact, they were the only stories about Africa I'd heard at all.

He told about the man who had come to his house to sell a monkey, and when denied the sale, repitched the monkey with an added bonus: the monkey could smoke!

He told another story about how, out of boredom, he had created a full-scale Monopoly board game in the dust and dirt outside of his hut and taught all of the village children to play, using cut-out drawings of goats and boubous and mangoes as playing pieces instead of dogs and top hats and thimbles.

He told—and we laughed—about the night that two mangoes had fallen onto the thatch roof of his hut, and, thinking he was under attack, he'd stood at the door with the only weapon he could think of: one of his Tevas sandals.

But the night wasn't all about Don. Devi and Don reminisced about old professors and old friends at Emory, Devi talked about her new life as a resident and some of the frustrations that came with it, and even I joined in with stories about my last few months at misterbook and some of the silly things that clients would ask, such as the lady that had called in wondering who had written the *Autobiography of Benjamin Franklin.*

And of course, we all raised a glass to Devi's birthday.

All in all, it was a great, fun evening, only marred by the fact that I was giving Don up to Devi.

But I comforted myself in the fact that I was doing the right thing, even though it hurt my heart.

And it did seem to be the right thing. A large part of what made the evening wonderful was the fact that Don seemed like he was back to his normal self. He never once mentioned Rahul Ghosh or Hindi movies or anything like that, and his accent didn't make an appearance once the whole night. Even the "yah" had disappeared. It was like being with Devi had cured him completely.

I was a little resentful. After all, here was Devi getting the real Don whereas, for the last week, I had endured his music and fake accent and craziness, but whenever I thought this, I'd push my wine glass Don's way and let him fill it up.

If he and Devi could be happy, who was I to ruin that?

And if the wine could help me get over what otherwise would have been an awkward meal, I was happy to keep drinking…

There was only one uncomfortable moment. That was when, during dessert, Devi turned to Don in the middle of spooning a scoop of vanilla ice cream, and asked, "So how long are you here?"

"As long as you'll have me," Don said with a smooth smile.

"No, no, I mean how long are you here in the states?"

I leaned forward.

She didn't know, I thought.

But then with a shock I realized that I didn't, either.

I had just assumed that Don was back for good, or that he'd been kicked out or something for being nuts. But he'd never actually said that. He'd been so vehement in saying that he didn't want to discuss Africa that I had not asked anything.

And I didn't know…

Don took a sip of his wine. "That depends," he said.

"Depends?" asked Devi.

"On what?" I asked.

"On whether I leave or not."

Devi gave him a playful swat on the arm. "Don't be mysterious. I thought the Peace Corps was two years. You've got to know when you're going back."

"I know only one thing…" Don tilted his glass and watched the restaurant lights glint off the wine inside.

"What's that?" said Devi.

"That's that…" he turned to her lazily, and as if he were changing the subject, "you look stunning in that dress!"

She laughed delightedly.

"Same old Don!" she said.

I poured myself more wine.

"It sounds like he's going to be all right," said Patel. "Maybe you don't have to worry about anything anymore."

"Ya think?" I twirled the phone cord in my hand and stared up at the ceiling. It seemed to move. I was pretty drunk.

"Seems like it. Maybe this Devi's good for him."

"Do you think so?"

"Why? What do you think?"

"I think she's…." *Too good to be believed.* I paused, controlled myself. "She's nice. She's perfect, really. She's beautiful. Smart. I wasn't sure what she'd be like, but she's pretty cool. Cooler than me."

"That I doubt," said Patel. "You're pretty cool."

"Don't mess with me."

"I'm not! Anyway, the important thing is that things are working out. You're happy for them, aren't you?"

Was that the ceiling or me that was lopsided? I couldn't tell.

"Yeah… I guess so."

"Good."

"Patel...?"

"Yup?"

"Thanks for talking to me. I'm going to go brush my teeth."

There was a light down the hall in the living room, but the hallway itself was dark. I made my way carefully from the room Devi'd given me to the bathroom, feeling my way with one hand, and holding my toothbrush and toothpaste in the other.

They were in the living room. I could hear their voices, Don's soft and vibrant, Devi's low and smooth and pleasant. I had no idea what they were saying. I didn't think Don had told her his feelings yet. He'd said he would wait for tomorrow. A beautiful birthday surprise...

I shuffled toward the voices, thinking I'd better say good night.

But at the end of the hall, I was confused. Surely, I should have seen them by now. The kitchen had been in full view to the right, but it was dark, so I knew that they must be in the living room. But when I got to where the living room branched off from the hall, all I saw were the back of the couch, the window onto the porch, and the pictures of Devi's family on a stand by the couch—basically the whole living room.

Devi's got some nice furniture, I thought.

But where were they?

I leaned against the wall—and that's when I saw them.

They were on the other side of the couch.

On the floor.

That's why I hadn't seen them before. They were shielded from view by the furniture.

Devi was on her stomach with her cheek flat on a sofa pillow. Her eyes were closed.

Don was kneeling next to her with his hands outstretched to her back, his fingers kneading her shoulders.

He lightly brushed her dark hair to the side, touched the flesh of her neck, massaged some more.

"Oh," she said. "Mmmmm. That's nice."

"You've got great hair," he said.

"Mmm."

Clapping my hand over my mouth, I retreated back into the shadows of the hallway.

I was wrong, I realized. What I'd said to Patel was a lie. I wasn't happy with this.

I was completely not happy with this.

Don had never given me a massage before!

This should have been me. I'd paid my dues. I'd waited for Don for a long time. Why should this girl be so lucky? Because she was Indian? Because she was professional? Because she was drop-dead gorgeous?

Man, I hated myself.

Even the wine couldn't get me over the feeling of seeing them like this…

I turned around and softly padded back to my room.

I did not pass Go.

I did not brush my teeth.

I went back to my bed, pulled the covers up over my eyes, and wished for sleep.

The last thing I heard from the living room was Don's soft voice, "Devi, can I tell you something," and Devi's purred reply, "Mmmm?"

CHAPTER TWENTY-THREE
SONGS OF LOVE,
SONGS OF PAIN

"OH MY GOD! Oh my God!"

"Mmm?"

It seemed like I had just gotten to sleep. I nudged my head deeper into my pillow.

"Don't just lie there saying "Mmmm"! Are you crazy? This is an emergency! It's a disaster! Wake up! Help me!" I was shaken ferociously, and when it was done, I was not quite as asleep.

I looked up at Don's face hovering above me, out of focus. I blinked, took in his worried blue eyes, his hair in disarray as if a bird had nested in it.

"Hurricane?" I mumbled.

"What? No, worse, yah? Now, wake up."

I was suddenly awake. I think it was the "yah" that did it. Don was back into faux Indian mode again, which couldn't be good. Nor could the fact that it was more over the top than ever.

"What's the matter?"

He didn't answer. Instead, he began pacing, stomping from one side of the room to the other and then back, with one hand over his mouth and the other on his waist, as if he were in the direst straits imaginable.

My first thought was that something bad had happened. "Where's Devi?"

"She's in her room. She doesn't want to talk to me."

"Why? What happened?"

He stopped pacing for a second. "I told her. I told her that I loved her."

"You told her?"

"Yes, yah? I just told you, yah? Didn't you hear me?"

"I thought you were going to wait for tomorrow. It was going to be like a birthday present."

"Well, I didn't, yah? I couldn't wait. And anyway, it was 12:01, yah?"

"Calm down. It can't be that bad."

"It can! It can!"

"Well, what did she say?"

"She didn't say anything!"

"What do you mean?"

"She cried. She didn't say anything because she was too busy crying."

I didn't know what to say to that.

"There I am pouring my heart out to the woman I love, and she cries."

"And then what?"

"Then nothing. That's it. She cries and then she says "Oh, Don," and then, "I don't know what to say," and then "I'd better go to bed.""

"She went to bed?"

"Yes, she went to bed!"

"Did you try to follow her?"

"Are you insane? It's too early for *that*!"

"No, I mean did you try to stop her? To talk to her?"

"No… should I have?"

"Well, no. Maybe. I don't know."

"You think I should have followed her."

"Calm down. I just woke up. I'm not thinking anything just yet."

"I think I should have followed her. Maybe she wanted me to kiss her! I'm going to go kiss her!"

"No! Stop! Wait. Let's think about this."

"Yeah, you're right. I can't kiss her. That wouldn't be right. I mean, they never kiss in Indian movies."

"Well, Devi *is* an American Indian. I mean... she's an Indo-American. I mean... *oh!*... well, you know what I mean! She's an Indian... you know... who's in America."

"So you think I should kiss her!"

"I don't know! I'm just saying... She's not one of the women in one of your movies. She's just a woman. Who knows what she wants?"

"So you're saying nobody knows what a woman wants."

"I'm not saying..."

"Shayla, just tell me what to *do!*"

Don was seriously conflicted, that was for sure. He looked like a cross between the puppy from the "Puppy Dog Eyes" poster I'd had when I was eight and David Banner about to turn into the Incredible Hulk. Like the puppy, his eyes were wide open and pleading, and he looked like he was about to cry. Like David Banner, he was full of tense energy, his hands stretched out, his arms trembling, as if standing still were the hardest thing in the world, as if he were about to explode... or turn green. I hadn't seen him look like this since the night I kissed him, and that was definitely a night I didn't want to remember right now.

I started talking: "Okay, for starters... sit down. Just chill. Maybe she just needs some time to think about what you said. She didn't know you loved her. She just thought you were a friend." *Like you thought about me.*

"Okay." Don sat and we were quiet for a few seconds.

Then he stood up.

"No," he said. "You were right. I should go to her. I should explain my love to her. But not with words this time... With a song! That's what Rahul would do."

"No, Don, that's not a good..."

But he had already stomped out of the room.

"Shayla?" Patel yawned loudly. "Everything okay? I just talked to you a couple of hours—"

"Patel, listen to me," I whispered. "Everything is not okay."

"What's up?" He suddenly sounded wide awake.

Down the hall, Don was knocking on Devi's door. "Devi?" he boomed, his old crazy confidence resurfaced.

I was sitting with my back to the wall by my slightly cracked bedroom door, through which I could only see Don, his arm outstretched. I could hear the knocking, but the crack wasn't wide enough to show me Devi's door or even his hand as it knocked. I leaned in closer.

"He's going to sing to her!" I hissed into my cell phone.

"What?"

"Don, look, I'm really tired. Let's talk in the morning." Devi spoke from inside her bedroom, and she really did sound tired.

"But there's something I need to tell you. I made a mistake."

"He told her he loved her, and she told him she needed to go to bed."

"A mistake?" A tinge of hopefulness in Devi's voice.

"She needed to go to bed?"

"Yeah, a mistake. What I told you before… What I meant was…"

"Oh my God…" Looking through the crack of the door, I could see from Don's posture what he was about to do, his legs and arms spread out, his head cocked to the side, his mouth opening for one big intake of air… and…

"Shayla, what…"

Cue music.

"…'s going…"

Don's mouth opened wide, and…

I love you, love you
Love you, love you
You are the moon

To my sun
I am the sun
To your moon
> *Your eyes are brown*
>> *My life is done…*

"Oh," said Patel.

The door swung open. "What the heck is wrong with you?" shouted Devi. "Are you singing a song from **Mere Dil Ko Kuch Chuhta Hai***?"*

"Yes… Do you like it?"

There was no sound at all from the hall now. I whispered into the cell, "She sounds really mad."

"I can hear," said Patel.

"Shayla?"

Whoops.

"Shayla, I can see you through that crack in the door. Can you come here, please?" Now Devi sounded mad at me.

"I've gotta go," I told Patel, and clicked off.

Clenching my teeth, I pushed my door open with my index finger.

What I saw was pretty much what I expected. Don was down on one knee with his hands outstretched to Devi, as if he were in the middle of proposing to her. He had a wide smile on his face, and was breathing a little hard, whether from being close to Devi or from singing his song I had no idea. Devi, on the other hand, was glaring—at *me*.

Sheepishly, I stood up and shuffled into the hall and toward them. I put a hand on Don's shoulder. "Hey, Don…"

I talked to Don only, although he was still staring at Devi longingly. I didn't look at Devi at all, but I could feel her eyes lasering into my back. *Set to kill*, as Don would have said, but I didn't care. I spoke only to Don. "Whatcha doin'?"

"I'm opening my heart to Devi through song so that she can see how much I care for her," came the reply.

I winced, but said, "Hey, how about you let us two

women talk for a bit? I'm sure there's a lot for us to talk about."

Don half turned his glance to me. "You're going to talk about me?"

I nodded.

Don looked thoughtful for a second, then he stood up. "Okay," he said. "You girls talk. I'll leave you alone." But he leaned his head up to me before he left and whispered in my ear, "Let me know what she says."

"Mm-hmm," I whispered back, knowing that Devi could hear everything.

"Goodnight!" Don said and vanished into his room.

Finally, I turned to Devi who stared back at me with venom in her eyes. Still, I noted that she was wearing a pair of striped pajamas and her hair was down, making her look even more beautiful.

"Uh," I said.

"Did you know that this was going to happen?" asked Devi.

"Devi…" I started. I remembered Don telling me on our drive that Devi had a temper.

"No… I mean, did you know that he was going to tell me he loved me? Did you know his plan?"

"Well, I thought he'd wait until morning…"

"You knew! Jeesh. You'd think you could have told me about this. I mean—"

"Listen, Devi, I'm sorry. I should have told you, but… well…"

I thought she was going to explode. Her anger was making her stick her head out, and her neck was long and straight, all which made her look something like a furious dark swan. She'd clamped her mouth shut, and her nostrils were dangerously flared. If she'd been a cartoon, steam would have been coming out of her ears.

This was the woman that Don loved…

I prepared myself for being chewed out…

But then Devi did something remarkable. In that same taut position, she closed her eyes, clenched her fists, and began to breathe deeply. She breathed in and out three times, and then opened her eyes. All the tension seemed to go out of her.

"Shayla, I'm sorry. I'm tense. Let's have a cup of tea and talk about this."

Suddenly, I realized what it was that Don liked about her.

CHAPTER TWENTY-FOUR
RATIONAL CONVERSATIONS

THE BLUE TEAPOT whistled on the stove and Devi came out of her room with her face shining from a slap of water and picked it up. She poured two mugs of fruity tea, and we sat across from each other at the kitchen table. She sat comfortably, crossing her legs below her Indian-style, and blowing on her tea to cool it. I applied a death grip to the handle of my own mug, but didn't lift it.

"All right," she said, calmly, taking a small sip of her tea. "Tell me."

"Well, there's a lot to tell."

"Tell it. All of it."

An hour later, Devi leaned back in her chair. Our tea cups were empty.

"Oh, and he says "yah" a lot," I concluded. "You know, like Rahul Ghosh does in that movie *Father/Friend,* where the guy gets reincarnated as his best friend's son. There's this one scene where Rahul Ghosh attacks his friend, and he's all like, 'You married your best friend's wife, yah, and now it's your duty, yah, to treat me as a son. You should be like a father to me, yah.'"

Devi regarded me coolly, slightly scrunching her eyebrows. I was embarrassed by how much I had gotten into describing the scene.

"I... uh... saw a few films on the way here. Don brought his VCR," I mumbled.

Devi shook her head, thoughtfully. "I guess," she said, ignoring that last little bit of unnecessary information, "I should have realized something was wrong. I read all of his letters, but something clearly changed in them in the spring. I don't know what exactly. I guess it was more like a feeling, but something definitely had changed. The dynamics were off somehow."

"I'm sorry to tell you."

For a few moments, she looked off into space, but then all of a sudden she became focused again. She looked at me purposefully. "The thing is, what do we do? I mean, we can't continue like this. I'm busy. As much as I love Don—as much as I love him *platonically*—I can't let this go on. But I don't want to hurt his feelings either."

Suddenly, I felt exhausted. Over the last few days, I had talked to Don about his problems, talked to Michael about his problems, and even rehashed all my own problems. And now here was Devi wanting to discuss solutions to more problems. Plus it was almost two in the morning. I just couldn't handle any more, at least not right at that moment. I reached my hand across the table. "Let's think of something in the morning," I said. "I mean, he's harmless. He won't do anything."

"Are you sure?"

"I'm sure." This I believed completely. Don may have been acting nuts, but he wasn't that kind of nuts.

Devi looked at me appraisingly. "Shayla, I have to ask you one thing."

"Okay."

"How long... have you been in love with Don?" she asked.

I gasped, and my mouth froze in that position for a second. Then I blustered, "How did you… I didn't…"

"No, you didn't say and I didn't know. I thought I'd say it and see how you reacted. It was an educated guess."

An educated guess that everybody'd been making. Was I that transparent?

"So you fooled me?" I felt stupid.

"Yes, in a way… Let's call it even."

"Okay," I said gratefully.

"We'll think of something in the morning."

It didn't take me long to think of something to do. What I did was call Patel. Somehow, over the course of this trip, I had gotten used to using him as a sounding board, and it felt completely natural to discuss the intricacies of my situation with him. As exhausted as I was, I *wanted* to talk to Patel.

He was happy to hear from me, even though it was so late, and after he had heard the story, he said he had the perfect solution.

"Have her tell him she has a boyfriend."

"But she doesn't." Devi had told me during our tea conversation that she wasn't that interested in a relationship, at least not until she finished her residency. It was just too hectic, and the hours too strange.

"Does Don know that?"

"Well, I guess not. She never mentioned it to him as far as I could tell… not at dinner at least, and by the way he was acting before, I'd say she definitely didn't."

"Good," said Patel.

"Why? What's up?"

"I've got a plan."

"A plan?"

"Yes, but I'll have to tell you about it in the morning. Just make sure that, if you see Devi before you talk to me, don't let her tell Don about not having a boyfriend."

"Okay…"

"All right. Well, there's a couple things I need to do

now, I guess. I'll talk to you first thing in the morning if that's all right."

I wanted to say no, that I wanted to hear what the plan was right away, but his tone made it pretty clear that he was ready to end the conversation. So…

"Yeah, that's alright," I said.

"And, Shayla…"

"Yes?"

"If you call again tonight, just leave a message. I won't be able to use my cell phone for a couple hours."

I hung up, and almost immediately fell into an exhausted sleep. Whatever Patel's plan might be, it could wait until the morning.

CHAPTER TWENTY-FIVE
GUESS WHO'S COMING TO BREAKFAST

I AWOKE TO loud voices streaming down from the living room/kitchen area.

Male voices.

10 a.m. said the alarm clock on the stand next to my bed.

I quickly pulled on my jeans and a T-shirt and walked down the hall toward the living room. Just as I was passing, Devi's bedroom door cracked open and she motioned agitatedly to me.

Who is Don talking to? she mouthed silently.

I don't know, I mouthed back.

It was clear that she had been listening and waiting for me to come out of my room before she ventured out. She was fully dressed, and her hair was perfectly washed and dried.

Is it safe? she mouthed.

I'll check.

I moved on to the end of the hall, where I stopped to survey the situation.

There was Don, leaning back in Devi's slat backed rocking chair, a glass of milk in one hand. Like Devi, he also was perfectly clean, his hair neatly parted, and surprise of surprises, he was fully decked out in his sherwani and kurta pajamas. He even had on the scarf and mojari shoes. He had obviously dressed up for Devi, and had been waiting for her to come out and see him like this, while she herself must have known he was out there and had been waiting for me to go out first so as not to be alone with him.

He raised his glass of milk to me and smiled.

"Shay!" he said. "Come in. I've gotten quite a shock this morning."

He didn't seem too shocked, though. In fact, he seemed remarkably relaxed, as if all the weight he'd had on his shoulders the night before had suddenly vanished.

"Come see who's here."

The other person was on the couch, with his back to me. All I saw was a head of black hair.

An oddly familiar head of black hair.

"This is Karan," Don said. "This is Devi's boyfriend."

"Devi's...?"

But she'd said...

The man on the couch turned to me, and I took in a sharp breath.

It was Patel.

CHAPTER TWENTY-SIX
THE PLAN,
IF YOU CAN CALL IT THAT

"B-BUT…" I STAMMERED.

"Ah, this must be the delightful Shayla." The man who was certainly Patel stood up and reached out a hand. I didn't take it. "Devi told me all about you last night. You're just as beautiful as she described."

Beautiful? That did it. This had to be a dream. I'd caught sight of my hair just before I left the bedroom. It was all Cyndi Lauper from the "Girls Just Wanna Have Fun" video, hair all matted on one side and the rest all hanging crazily down on the other.

I pointed a bewildered finger at Patel. "This is…" I said.

Luckily the Patel look-alike stopped me. I'm not sure what I was about to say, but I'm pretty sure that it wasn't the right thing.

"Don was just telling me how you came out for Devi's birthday. That's really nice of you."

I turned to Don.

"Don't be so shocked," said Don. "It's okay. I'm all

right."

"What… Really?" I asked.

Devi turned the corner, apparently feeling more powerful now that I had already entered. "Who is this in my house?" she demanded.

"It is I!" said Patel and before the angry, scolding look could leave her face, he stepped forward and embraced her. "I wanted to surprise you on your birthday, honey." He let her go and indicated the table, where twelve long stem roses resided in a red, heart-shaped vase. "Happy birthday!" he said.

"*Play along*," I mouthed.

Somehow we agreed to go out to breakfast, with me making all kinds of secret hand signals to Devi to get her to go along with the charade and pretend that Patel was her boyfriend. Finally, Devi went to her bedroom to get ready and Don, Patel, and I sat there.

I was eager to remove Don from the equation, so I said, "Don, no offense, but don't you think it would be better if you changed out of those clothes. I mean, we're probably not going to eat Indian food for breakfast."

"Shayla's right," said Patel. "Those are nice threads, my friend, but not right for where I plan on taking you."

"All right."

Don finished off his glass of milk and headed for his bedroom to change. I waited until I was sure he was in, and then I wheeled on Patel and hissed, "What are you doing here?"

"I told you I had a plan."

"Yeah, but I didn't think it would involve you actually being here!"

"To be honest, I was really worried about you last night. With all that Don was getting up to, I was afraid he might be dangerous. I had to come and see you."

"But… we hardly even know each other…"

"Oh, Shayla," Patel said. "Don't say that. We sat next to

each other for three months."

"But still…"

"Anyway, I hopped on a plane and was here on the red eye by 6 a.m. No big deal. I didn't really have any other plans for my Saturday as it was. My sister was having a baby shower, but I didn't really feel like doing that, so I'm kind of happy you gave me the excuse."

Was that a joke?

I searched for something to say. Couldn't find anything. Settled on: "And what's with the name? Karan?"

"That's my name."

"What? You're Patel."

"Shayla, Patel is my family name. I use it because most Americans get my first name wrong. It looks too much like Karen. Whoo—you wouldn't believe how much grief I got for *that* in elementary school."

"My God." I sat down across from him and bowed my head.

"What is it?" he asked, laying one protective hand on my shoulder.

"It's just…" I laughed, and by the look on his face, it was more of a panicked laugh than an amused one. "It's just everything I've known about people seems to have turned on its head. Don's not my pillar of strength. You're not Patel. What's next? Is my mom going to tell me I'm adopted?"

"Hang in there, Shayla. Just a little while. I need you to be a bit of a baazigar for the next few hours."

"A baazi-what?"

"Baazigar. It means juggler. For just a little while, pretend that I'm Devi's boyfriend and keep her pretending, too. In fact, you'd better go tell her what's going on. She looks like she's at the breaking point."

"And then?"

"And then… well, and then you and Don will drive home… and I'll fly home… and we'll hopefully leave this mess all patched up and nobody will have to visit a psychiatric ward. Not even Don."

"All right…"

Steeling myself, I got up to go and talk to Devi.

"Oh, and Shayla?"

"Yeah?"

"You might want to get ready too. I'm taking you out somewhere nice."

I felt my hair and was ashamed. "Where?" I asked.

"I have no idea. Do you know where Devi keeps her phone book?"

CHAPTER TWENTY-SEVEN
WHY IS IT ALWAYS BREAKFAST?

WE ATE BREAKFAST at the Tara Buffet, a fancy Southern colonial house that had been converted into a restaurant.

The waiter, Tyler, sat us at an empty table right in the middle of the dining hall. I looked around quickly to see if there might be another, less conspicuous table—a habit I'd picked up ever since Albeiro—but the restaurant was completely packed.

I was immediately thankful, however, that we were at a buffet. There was a little small talk about weather and what everybody did for a living, but mostly, since we didn't have to wait for service, we all just grabbed our plates and dug in.

Halfway into our breakfast, I was happy to note that things were going well, or at least as well as could be expected. Devi and Patel sat beside each other, eating in a leisurely manner, Patel acting comfortably in his role as the surprise boyfriend, and Devi only shooting the occasional perplexed look around the table.

Don, for his part, seemed completely at ease, and he

dived into his breakfast with gusto, as if he hadn't eaten for days.

I took the opportunity, though, as Don scarfed down his scrambled eggs and sausage, to lean in and whisper in his ear, "Are you really okay with this?"

"Yes," he answered aloud. "Of course. What could be better! I came offering love, but now I am free. Karan seems like a top chap! But... Devi, would you mind if I borrowed you for a second?"

Devi looked from Patel to me in apprehension.

"It's okay," said Patel. "Just don't go too far, love."

Looking nervous, she let Don lead her away toward the entrance. I watched protectively as they stepped outside. Don was surely taking her to the two big columns at the front of the restaurant, but what would he say, I wondered.

"Do you think they'll be all right?" I asked.

Patel scooted his chair close to me. "I have no idea," he said. "But, to be honest, Devi seems like the kind of person who can take care of herself."

I took his point. "It's sad, though. Don so wanted this to work."

"He's a romantic," mused Patel. "That's not a bad thing."

I nodded, then suddenly noticed how attentively Patel was looking at me.

"Uh…" I said.

"Shayla, you know I just flew from Seattle to Atlanta this morning, right?"

"Oh, of course," I said. "I never even said thank you, did I? I can't believe you…"

"Have you thought about why?"

"Um…"

I hadn't. Honestly, so much had been going on that I hadn't really had a chance to think at all.

Patel was staring at me.

My cheeks suddenly felt hot.

"Patel," I said.

"The truth is," he said, "you left so soon that I couldn't

tell you… I want… Well, I don't know how to say it, except…"

And he kissed me, right over my strawberry crepes.

"What the hell is this?! You rascal!!!"

Patel's lips disengaged from my own, just when I had been enjoying them.

I opened my eyes and saw Don leaning above us, one fist reached down and clasping Patel's collar.

Oh no, not another restaurant scene…

"Don…" I said.

And then Patel did something I had never seen him do, and have never seen him do since. He bobbed his head from side to side, put his hands together, and said, in absolute supplication, "Brother-ji, please don't hit me. I apologize for this."

Don's reaction was equally surprising. He completely backed off.

Don and Patel stared at each other, Don clenching and unclenching his fists.

"Would somebody mind telling me what's going on?" he asked. "Shayla, why on earth is Devi's boyfriend kissing you? What's going on, yah?"

"Uh…" I stammered.

"I'll tell you." The voice was strong and cold. Devi stood in the entrance. All eyes turned to her—and that included everybody in the restaurant, not just our table.

Oh no. Don'd driven her mad, too…

Devi took a deep breath, composing herself. She was obviously frustrated—*What had Don said to her out there?*—but she was doing a remarkable job of looking calm. Her words, when they came, were slow and deliberate, and they were addressed to Don:

"Your friend may not have the guts to tell you this, but I will…

"First off, you're insane, Don. There's something severely wrong with you. You are not Rahul Ghosh. You are not Indian—"

That's what he was talking to her about!

Devi continued:

"You are certainly not my type. Nothing personal, I've just always thought of you as a friend, and even if there was a *chance* of something more, even if I were to entertain the *idea* of dating you—and I mean dating you, not *marrying* you—"

Had he asked her to marry him!?

"Well, even in that case, I wouldn't do it just because you know all the lyrics to 'Bahut Bahut Danyavad'!"

My God, he'd been singing to her!!!

"Second…" she continued, and she sent one piercing glance Patel's way before turning back to Don. "This man is not my boyfriend. He's just pretending to be my boyfriend to help me, and presumably Shayla, out. They thought that if he pretended, you'd be satisfied and leave me alone. Well, I guess that's nice, but I can tell you myself. You're my friend, enough said. I'm trying to be a doctor; quite frankly, I can wait on boyfriends.

"Third, and this will be news for Patel, I'm sure. Don, Shayla is in love with you. She has been since seventh grade, or at least since some Spring Dance you guys went to. She told me last night. Presumably, this is *bad* news for Patel. Sorry.

"So, to sum up, Don, I'm sorry, but I'm not in love with you. Shayla is. Patel, Shayla's not in love with you. She's in love with Don. In the movies—the Indian movies, which you seem to know so well, Don—this wouldn't be a love triangle. It would be a love square, with each person looking at someone else, but with me looking at no one.

"In my professional opinion, you're all crazy, so I'm taking myself out of the equation. No more love square. I'll leave you three to be a triangle together.

"Now, here's what I'm going to do. I'm going to go home. You three stay, eat your breakfasts. Take your time. And then get a taxi and come by. When you get there, you'll find all of your stuff outside my locked door. Please. Don't knock."

She turned to walk away. Everybody in the restaurant clapped.

Don stood up.

"Don, don't…" I said.

"I have to, yah," he said. "Devi, wait!"

He ran after her, grabbed one of her hands just as she was about to step through the door. They stood like this for a second, her caught in mid-step, him holding onto her hand, both of them still facing forward.

If only there had been music!

Finally, Devi turned, her face set in exasperation. She glared at him, waiting.

Everybody in the restaurant gaped in anticipation. Some looked around to see if maybe Ashton Kutcher was hiding somewhere in the room.

"I…"

Don's breath caught. He looked down at his shoes, embarrassed.

"I know I'm not Indian. I just thought…

"You have no idea what happened. In Africa. It was bad.

"Rahul Ghosh saved me. I was wrong, but I wanted to be like him.

"I know I've been crazy… I know…"

Devi melted. She reached out one hand and placed it tenderly on Don's shoulder. "Thik hai," she said.

"Huh?" said Don.

"You're a terrible Indian," she said. "You don't really know any Hindi."

"I know."

Devi leaned forward and kissed Don lightly on the cheek. "But you're a good friend. Don't stop being that, okay? I don't want to lose you. Just… get yourself some help…"

Don nodded and he seemed to be fighting tears. "I'm sorry," he said, "really sorry, yah?"

Devi smiled softly. "A *really* terrible Indian," she

murmured. "You have no idea what 'yaar' means, do you?"

Don wrinkled his brow, confused.

"Look it up."

She gave him one last little pat on the shoulder, a sign of her affection, and also of finality. "Thank you for coming for my birthday," she said. "And call me when you reach Washington. I'd like to talk to you, but without…" she rolled her eyes to indicate the restaurant, Patel, me, "…all this."

And that's how Devi left.

She turned for the last time and walked away, past all the tables, through a crowd of curious, waiting people in the doorway, and then we all watched her through the glass windows as she walked to her car, got in, turned the ignition.

I'm pretty sure she wished she'd parked farther away.

"Devi," said Don.

He was still standing, his head hanging. He didn't sound Indian now. Not a bit.

He shook his head.

"She always was a straight shooter."

Outside the restaurant, on the other side of the window, Devi backed up her car and drove away.

CHAPTER TWENTY-EIGHT
THE WAY BACK

DON PAID FOR breakfast.

He didn't even sit down.

Head bowed in shame, he shuffled to the table, pulled his wallet from his slacks, and deposited a fifty dollar bill on the table—enough to pay for everything—then shambled out of the restaurant to search for a pay phone. Patel and I followed silently after him.

Devi was as good as her word. When we arrived at her apartment, all of our stuff was on her doorstep. Don searched for a note, but there was nothing.

We gathered our stuff and left in silence.

In the car, Patel drove, and I sat with Don in the back seat. He wouldn't look at me. Instead, he kept his face to the window, watching Atlanta fade away.

"Don," I said, "are you all right?"

He didn't turn, or say a word, just seemed lost in his own world.

When we stopped for gas, he asked to be alone, so I sat up front with Patel.

None of us spoke.

However, Devi's words kept circling through my thoughts. Don may have been depressed, and Patel may have been confused, but me…

I was about to explode.

Because here I was sitting in a car with two guys that loved me!

In the backseat was poor Don, seeming empty and wasted. He was neither the outgoing boy I had known in high school nor the eccentric lunatic that had taken me across the country for love—and yet I couldn't discount everything he had done for me in the past, couldn't disregard how I felt about him, how I'd always felt about him.

Next to me was Patel. I didn't know much about him, but I knew he cared for me. I remembered how he had always invited me to lunch, how he had talked to me in the break room, how he had always been happy to help me. I remembered the cake he brought me on my last day, how he'd been the only one who seemed like he would really miss me.

Why, I wondered.

Why did he like me?

And the answer, I realized suddenly, was exactly what Don and Patel had both said: I was a strong person. I was open-minded, caring, and giving. I had done my best to help Brad Newton when he needed it, and even if it hadn't worked out, I'd tried. I may have made mistakes with Don, too, but I had stuck with him through his toughest times, and I was still here now to see how they would turn out. I had lost my baby, the hardest thing that I'd ever endured, but I had survived that, too.

No matter what I may have felt about myself after that, I had survived.

And more than that, I was going to be okay.

That's what made me strong.

I'd just realized it.

I stole a glance at Patel, just as he rolled his eyes up to the rearview mirror. "Don, everything okay back there?" he asked. "See the roller coaster?"

We were passing Six Flags.

"Yeah. Thanks." The Indian accent was so completely gone now that I felt it must have flown back to India and lost its passport.

Without warning, a little flutter of excitement danced through my body. I turned to my window to hide a smile.

Calm, uncomplicated, honest.

These were all good qualities. Stable qualities.

Qualities that Patel had that I definitely liked.

And he also felt so strongly about me that he had flown to Atlanta to help me.

Could I take a chance?

Of course.

I was strong.

I reached across the seat and touched Patel's hand.

That night, we stayed at a divy hotel in Metropolis, Illinois. We had all wanted to get out of the South, even Don, who had been speaking in single syllables since we'd left. He was very clear about Atlanta. "Let's leave it as far behind us as possible," he'd said, when Patel asked somewhere around Chattanooga.

Metropolis, just across the Kentucky border, seemed to fit the bill.

"Metropolis," said the sign as we entered the little town, "Home of Superman."

We could all stand to feel a little more super…

Using Don's money, we rented two rooms, one for Patel and Don and one for me.

We retired, hoping to feel better in the morning.

I woke up to the sound of rain, proof perhaps that we were getting closer to home.

Somebody was knocking.

I jumped up. It must be Patel. He'd said he was going to wake me.

But it wasn't.

Standing in the doorway, framed by the rain pounding down behind him, was Don. He was wearing a ratty pair of blue jeans, a T-shirt, and Tevas sandals. He looked nothing like Rahul Ghosh at all.

"Can I come in?"

I moved aside silently.

"You've changed," I said.

Don went to the bed and sat down. "I've been an idiot," he said. "I'm sorry."

I waited for more.

He bowed his head.

"For everything," he said. "I'm sorry for everything."

"There's nothing to be…"

"No, there's everything. I'm sorry about Devi… and I'm sorry I dragged you through this."

"Don, it's okay…" I moved toward him, to hug him.

"Shay, no…"

He waved me off and I ended up just sitting on the bed next to him.

"I'm trying to tell you something important. It's about what happened in Africa. It's about what kind of man I am."

"What—?"

"I made a mistake, a really big mistake…"

He paused, and I waited for him to continue.

"I'm going to tell you something I haven't told anybody, not even my psychologist in D.C. She asked, but it was just too hard—"

"What was it? What did she want to talk to you about?"

"The thing that I was trying to ignore. The thing that really broke me…"

"What was that?"

"What happened to Jamie," he said.

CHAPTER TWENTY-NINE
WHAT HAPPENED IN AFRICA

"YOU'RE MY FRIEND.

"Like I told you during the Raksha Bandhan ceremony, you're my best friend, Shay. But I couldn't even tell you.

"I wanted to, but it was too much, because...

"Because what happened in Africa, it...

"It was too terrible...

"And it did make me crazy. If it didn't, I wanted it to.

"I'll tell you.

"Africa was fun. Tons of fun. Getting to know the Africans, and the people in the area. I lived in a village and I was the only American there, but there was a bigger city nearby—about ten miles away—with more volunteers. I'd ride my bike up to see them about once a month.

"There were three of them, Jamie and Gary and Marta. They all taught English there, Gary and Marta at the university, Jamie at the middle school. They lived in two little houses right next to each other.

"Gary and Marta were a little older, married. I spent most of my time with Jamie. It was always her house I stayed at.

"Jamie was great—a good friend, fun—but very different from me. A Lit major with no interest in *Star Trek*. Always reading Shakespeare or Chaucer or something. She was going to be a professor. But we clicked, Shay. When I visited, we'd always stay up all night talking about everything, just like you and I always used to.

"One night—this was April—I was visiting and we got together for a beer—the three of us—this little bar not far from their houses. It's where we always went, every time, just a little trail away from where they lived, a quarter mile at the most, lined by tall grass.

"It was so normal to us, Shay. We'd walked that trail so many times. So familiar.

"It was around six when we went there. We passed several people—women carrying water home, children sucking on mangoes… It was pleasant.

"At the bar, Gary and Marta stayed for a couple beers, but then they went home early, just as the sun was starting to set.

"Jamie and I, we stayed. We usually did. So much to talk about.

"We had flashlights, after all, and we'd be leaving just when it got dark.

"I don't know why; there was one thing different this time. Jamie was taking her time with that third beer, and I ordered a fourth. I'm usually pretty buzzed after three, but Jamie convinced me. 'What's the big deal?' she said. All we were going to do was walk home and go to sleep, maybe talk a little more.

"I wish I hadn't…

"When we left, we both were a little drunk. Not too much. I could walk. But we were silly. Everything was just a little out of focus. We were laughing, speaking loud, looking up at the stars. It wasn't that late, but it was already pitch dark. We shone our flashlights all around, up and down the tall grass. We were the only ones on the trail.

"'Look at the stars,' Jamie said. We both looked up. You can see the stars so well there, no streetlights at all.

Jamie laughed and spun in a circle, looking up, then stumbled. I caught her. 'You try it,' she said. She was giggling.

"I did...

"That's when they came out.

"Shay, the grass was tall and they just stepped out of it. I ended my twirl and stumbled, too dizzy. Jamie grabbed my arm and I steadied myself.

"I remember her touch. She was gripping me so tight.

"There were three of them—men—carrying machetes. I didn't recognize any of them. I remember they were smiling. It was really dark, but I saw the smiles. We stood next to each other, Jamie and me, facing those men.

"Jamie moved first—

"Oh, Shay, you would have liked Jamie; she was tough, like you.

"Perdon mois," she said and stepped forward to pass. I stepped forward, too.

"But the men didn't budge.

"The one in front—he was wearing blue jeans and a flower print vest—looked at me. 'Girlfriend?' he asked. Still that smile.

"Shay, I didn't know what to do. It was like I was in shock. Right then, I couldn't move. Couldn't speak. I was having trouble focusing, as if it wasn't real. It might have been the beer.

"It was Jamie who answered.

'Yes. He's my boyfriend.'

"The men... They laughed."

Don stopped. He swallowed hard.

"What did you do?"

Don closed his eyes, hardly breathing.

"Nothing," he said.

I waited.

"Neither of us did. It was like time was frozen. Just for that moment we were like prey, just waiting to see what happened."

"What happened?"

"The man—the one who spoke—came forward. He

touched Jamie's hair. I remember her flinch.

"'Leave me alone,' she said.

"The man laughed. He looked at me.

"That smile. He was still smiling.

"'I like this woman,' he said. 'I will pay you for one hour with your girlfriend. How much?'"

"Now I found my voice—finally—too late. 'No,' I said. I edged in front of Jamie. I'd block her.

"But I was useless.

"He hit me—one hit across the face with the flat of his palm—and it knocked me down—

"I've gone back over it in my mind, thinking what I could have done to change things, what I could have done differently. If we'd left earlier—if I'd have drunk less—if we'd been quieter on the trail—if I had answered more quickly when he'd asked if Jamie was my girlfriend—

"But now it was too late—

"I tried to stand up. He kicked me. 'Lie down,' he yelled. He kicked me again.

"I should have screamed for help. I should have told Jamie to run back to the bar when we'd had a chance.

"All three of them were kicking me now. There was nothing I could do Their feet just kept hitting me. By the time they were done, I could hardly move.

"But I heard it. I heard it all.

"I heard them grab Jamie. I heard her gasp.

"They dragged her into the long grass. She was struggling.

"I tried to stand—but the world was spinning—and one of them was still there. He kicked me again in the face. I almost passed out then, but not quite.

"I heard Jamie. She was calling me.

"I couldn't see.

"Her flashlight had dropped and it was shining in my face.

"I could hear the rustling of the grass and…

"…other noises…

"That's all I remember. I passed out.

"When I regained consciousness, she was shaking me. Her glasses were bent and there were streaks of tears on her face. They'd ripped her shirt. She was hugging it closed with one hand.

"The men were gone.

"'Are you all right?' I asked. I tried to stand but couldn't. My whole body ached. I was dizzy. I just wanted to lie back down, to go to sleep, right there in the dirt.

She helped me up and put my arm around her shoulder. It was all mechanical. She didn't say a thing. It was as if she wasn't really there. Her face was so blank, Shay.

She walked me back to her place. I wouldn't have been able to do it without her. She never said a word.

"When she got me to her house, she dropped me on the bed. It was a relief. I just wanted to sleep. But I asked again: 'Are you all right?' That's what I asked. The stupidest question in the world.

"I guess it didn't matter. She may not have even really heard what I asked. She did say, absently—I remember the absence in her eyes, as if she was just a shell—'Rest, Don. I'm going to Greg and Marta's.'

"That was the last I ever saw her.

"I passed out again there.

"Later, Greg came and he got me to the Peace Corps house in the capital. They took care of me. I was hurt, but there was nothing serious—nothing broken, nothing too damaged, at least not on my body.

"Jamie was already gone.

"She'd flown out on the first flight. She never came back."

Don closed his eyes, took a breath, leaned his head down to his hands, and slowly ran his fingers through his hair, across his cheek, down his neck, and then pressed them together against his nose and chin as if he were praying.

"I couldn't handle it. There was no one to talk to.

"I spent a week at the Peace Corps house getting better. They even flew in a Peace Corps psychologist to talk to me, but he wasn't much help. I didn't know how to express what

I felt. I was just numb, like a curtain had come down in my mind.

"After a week, they said I was fine to go back to my village. I wasn't. But I went anyway.

"At first, I just stayed in the village. I didn't want to see anyone, especially not Greg and Marta. I was ashamed. I blamed myself for everything. And I felt like they blamed me. It probably wasn't true, but that's how I felt.

"I stayed further and further away, stuck in my village, stuck in my hut. I didn't want to be seen unless it was absolutely necessary.

"I wanted to escape.

"Except for Thursdays. Thursday my village had market day and one vendor came with music.

"I badly needed music. It drowned out everything, all my bad thoughts.

"This vendor had all kinds of stuff. American, European, African, Hindi. I mostly chose African and Hindi. Those tapes were good because they were impossible to understand. You can't weep when you don't understand the words.

"It was the Indian tapes I liked most. They were so catchy, so hopeful. I felt so bad, but somehow they made me feel good, made me forget.

"That's what finally got me out of the village. I started obsessing, needing those tapes, so I went into town for more, got lost in them, and finally I went to see a movie. It was *Janm Ke Samay Badal Gaye*, and it showed me something.

"I didn't understand a word—there were no subtitles—but I understood it was about protection.

"The men were so strong, exactly the opposite of how I felt.

"Everything was opposite of me. They could dance, I can't... (even though you did try to teach me, remember?)... they could sing (Okay, I can do that)... they could protect. They were strong.

"I began to practice in my hut, to emulate them, especially Rahul Ghosh. He was my favorite. I came every week. I'd watch a movie a week, and I always was happiest if they were showing a Rahul film. I began to realize that this was what I wanted. A rebirth. To be like him.

"I wanted to be Rahul Ghosh. Strange, but I even wanted to show respect to my parents the way he did.

"Devi was sending me mail at the time... you were sending me mail, too, I know...

"But I began to fantasize.

"Devi had never been anything but a friend, but I felt...

"If I could be in her life, if I could be with her, I could recreate myself. I could be strong like Rahul.

"One day in the theater, it snapped. The redemption. It all snapped into place.

"Devi's birthday was coming up. I would be there.

"I went to Kat, the Peace Corps leader who lived in the regional house. I explained that I wasn't handling things well. I needed some time.

"By the time I got to the capital, I was hardly myself. I'd already started to speak in an accent. I'd already decided how things should be. I was already acting like Rahul Ghosh.

"So they sent me to D.C."

CHAPTER THIRTY
SALVATION

WE SAT IN silence, staring into the space in front of us, Don remembering, me considering the weight of the story he had just told.

It must have buried him, this shame. To keep it inside himself. To have no one to talk to, but to keep reliving it.

I knew what that felt like, that double pressure, one to escape from the secret, the other to suppress, to push it so far down inside that the shame and humiliation and guilt would disappear.

I knew what he felt, because I had felt the exact same way.

And I knew how important having somebody who understood it could be...

I reached out and placed my hand on his.

"It's terrible," I said. "Biribiri sounds terrible."

Don took a long, rattling breath, and then shook his head. "It wasn't." He turned his eyes to me, and they were bluer and deeper than ever. "It wasn't a bad place. It was wonderful. The people were wonderful. They treated me well. They loved me. No, I can't blame Biribiri for what happened. That could have happened here, it could have happened anywhere. It's just… It happened to me…"

His lips trembled. His forehead wrinkled.

"It happened to me and I'm so sorry."

His whole face seemed to implode. And then the tears came.

I held out my arms and he leaned into me, burying his face in my shoulder. "I'm just so, so sorry…"

"I know," I said, cradling his head in my arms. "I know. But it wasn't your fault."

I rocked him gently.

"That's what Jamie said, too," he said. I could feel his lips move as he spoke. "I talked to her once when I got back. She was getting better. She was dealing with it. She said it wasn't my fault—"

"Mmm," I said.

"Then she asked me not to call again. It wasn't me, she said. She was trying to put it all behind her, to forget…"

I didn't say anything for a while, just held onto him until I could feel his breathing slow, become normal.

I moved my lips next to his ear.

"Sometimes," I whispered, "no matter how strong you are, bad things happen."

I thought, then, about telling him everything.

About what happened to me.

He had told me his story, and the world hadn't ended.

He was going to be all right.

"Don," I said.

He moved back, out of my arms, and sat next to me. He wiped his eyes and gave a smile. It was a sad smile in a devastated face, but a smile nonetheless. Salt crystals clung to his eyelashes.

I was about to say.

And then I realized that I didn't need to.

Don was my friend. But he wasn't the one I needed to talk to.

There was another.

We sat together for a while, sharing silence, two friends

who had both known hurt, and come through it.

Finally, softly, Don spoke. "I guess," he said, "our adventure is over now."

I nodded.

"So—what are you going to do?"

"I don't know."

But I did have an idea…

"I know what you should do."

"What's that?"

"Go to Patel."

I gave him a sharp look.

Because that was my idea.

"He's a good guy. I can tell. You deserve that, Shay."

"What about you?"

"I'm going to the airport. I think my home time is over. I want to see that doctor in D.C. a couple more times, and then I'm ready to go back."

"Really?" I asked. I remembered why he had gone in the first place, to escape from his father.

"I want to go back," he said. "Maybe I went for the wrong reasons the first time, but now I really want to be there. I still have work to do in Biribiri. I'll go back and finish up… but as myself."

"And Rahul Ghosh…?"

"…is a great actor, but that's it. Don't worry. I'll see his movies, but I'm done being him. I'm me. I'll be okay."

There was a knock on the door.

Opening it revealed Patel. The rain was pounding the parking lot behind him, and his clothes were soaked, but he was able to produce a relatively dry tray with three hot coffees and a bag of donuts from beneath a soggy *Metropolis Planet* newspaper.

"Hungry?" he asked.

"Not really," said Don. "I've got to make a call. You guys talk."

"Who are you calling?" Patel sounded worried.

"My dad. I'm going to have him book my flight back to Africa. If you don't mind, I'll leave from here. You two can drive back together."

Don walked around him and out the door.

Patel pushed it closed behind him, frowning. He set the cups and donuts down on the table, looked at me.

"Is he really all right?"

"I think he's going to be just fine."

"How about you?"

"It looks," I said, "like Don has helped me out with Geometry all over again."

"Huh?"

"You know that triangle that Devi was talking about?"

Patel's eyes narrowed. "Yes," he said, cautiously.

"Well, now it's a straight line."

Patel watched me carefully. I stepped to him and took his hands in mine. "It leads to you."

He blinked.

"You mean it?" he asked.

"I mean it." I looked down at his hands and played with his fingers. "I definitely mean it.

"But come sit down," I said. "I want to tell you some things. Some things about me that I've never told anyone before. I want you to know who I am before we go any further."

Patel nodded. He came and sat on the bed beside me, regarding me intently, knowing that what I was about to say was important, maybe the most important thing he might ever hear.

And I told him. I told him everything. I left nothing out. It was the scariest thing I had ever done, to tell about Brad and what had happened, and how I had spent the last few years of my life thinking about him all the time.

I wasn't sure if Patel would still want to be with me after I was all done, but I kept going, resisting the impulse to stop and hide, looking down at the bed.

When I was done, Patel leaned forward and took my hand. He pulled me to him.

"It's all right," he said into my ear. "Everything is all right."

And he held me as I cried.
And he was there when I was done.
And he hasn't left me since.

EPILOGUE

Biribiri, West Africa
(Eight Months Later)

Khadiatou Camara, "Khadi" for short, walked down the unpaved street toward the theater, her sandaled feet kicking up dust. In one hand, she held two 500-franc coins her mother had given her, enjoying their slipperiness against her sweating palm. The fingers of her other hand were intertwined with the fingers of her friend Mariama. Today was special. It was Khadi's *anniversaire*, her birthday, and she was going with a school friend to the theater. She did not need to pull along any of her little brothers or sisters today.

Mariama was laughing good-spiritedly about how they had tricked another boy in their class, how they had flirted and flirted with him, and given him hope, and how he was probably at the taxi gare now, waiting for their appointment with him. He was going to take them to the waterfalls of Diabé for the day, he thought.

Who knew how long poor Amadou would wait for them? Poor buck-toothed Amadou, who was still remarkably handsome despite his buck teeth, who could still play football with the college students and give them competition. He wasn't unattractive, really. But this was part of the game. They were, after all, only fourteen. He would forgive them.

They made it to the theater and were about to pay Sidiki, who was at the door (and whom Mariama flirted with, shamelessly, batting her eyelids), when there was a call from across the street: "Khadi, Khadi!"

Aissatou, the vendor, was shouting at her, waving her little paring knife in the air above her orange bowl.

"Attend," Khadiatou said to Mariama and walked across the street, where Aissa was smiling.

"Inike," said Aissa.

"Inike."

"Tanate?"

"Tanate."

Khadiatou wondered what was up.

"L'americain," Aissa said softly, with a secret little smile. There was a man on the bench next to her. He was a little bit older, but he sat close and kept his eyes on her, soft and searching. He glanced at Khadi and smiled, but his eyes stayed with Aissa. Handsome, thought Khadi, and felt a quick, happy, warm feeling for her friend.

Aissa rolled her eyes toward the theater where Mariama waited, still flirting with Sidiki. Everybody seemed to be with a boy, thought Khadi. Maybe she would have to be nicer to Amadou…

"Il est la," said Aissa.

"Qua?" Khadi had no idea what she was talking about.

"The American. The American is there."

"Which American is there?" Why was Aissa talking to her like this, with all these secrets?

"You remember. It's the American. The same. Le fou Americain."

The crazy American.

Khadi opened her eyes wide in surprise. "Le fou

Americain! He has returned?"

"Yes. I said that. It's the same person."

Khadi forgot everything. The American was back!

"Merci, Aissa, merci beaucoup!"

Khadi rushed back across the street to Mariama, who was laughing at something Sidiki had said. "Let's go in," said Khadi, grabbing her friend's hand and pulling her, still chortling, to the entrance.

Inside, they found a seat, and then Khadi scanned the room.

She spotted him almost right away. He was in the first row, sitting with another American. The new teacher, Mademoiselle Karen. Mademoiselle Jamie had never come to an Indian movie before, but here was Mademoiselle Karen, sitting very close to him. And they were holding hands!

Khadi watched them for a few minutes, noting his body language. He didn't seem like before, tense and focused. Instead, he was relaxed, and all of his attention was on her teacher. Khadi shot a look at the entrance where Sidiki was still taking coins. She had a little time, and the American's comportment seemed normal enough. She decided to talk to him.

"Bonjour, Monsieur, Bonjour Mademoiselle Karen."

He spoke before her teacher could. "Bonjour. You're Khadi, aren't you?"

He'd addressed her in English! Khadi blushed, but responded softly, "You know me?"

"Of course. Your other teacher, Jamie, said that you were her favorite."

Khadi felt her skin rush with warmth.

"How is it going with Mademoiselle Jamie?"

"She returned to the United States," said the American, and then smiled gently when she frowned. "But she said that she was sorry."

"I would... like to write to her. Do you know her address?"

"No. I'm sorry."

Khadi lowered her eyes and stared at the floor.

"I am very sorry," said the American.

"It's okay," said Khadi.

Mademoiselle Karen touched his shoulder. "It's too bad. I know that Khadi was looking for an American pen pal to practice her English."

"Oh, is that it? I know just the person."

He took out a pen and a scrap of paper and began to write.

"She's my best friend, and she's very interested in international affairs. In fact, that's what she'll be studying at university. She just got accepted for next year." He handed the paper to Khadi. "She'd love to have an African pen pal," he said.

Khadi turned to Karen. "Do you feel safe with him?" she asked.

Immediately, she was embarrassed by her own question. She bit her tongue and looked down again, shyly. She'd been thinking about how the man had acted before in the theater, how wild he'd been, but she did not mean to cause offense.

Luckily, nobody took any.

"Yes," said Karen, with a glance at Don. "Yes. Absolutely safe."

"I won't let you down," he said, softly but firmly.

"Monsieur," said Khadi, eager to change the subject. "When I write to this person, I want to tell her who recommended her. I do not know your name." She had once, but she'd forgotten.

"Don. I am Don."

He reached out his hand, and she shook it. "Thank you, Monsieur," she said. "I will join my friend now."

"It's nice to finally meet you, Khadi."

It was only when she turned to go back to her seat next to Mariama that Khadi looked at the paper the American had given her. Above the address was the name of the lady who would be Khadi's pen pal:

SHAYLA PATEL.

***

Don watched Khadi leave with a smile and then touched Karen's hand. She was a new volunteer, had only just arrived in country while he was back in the states. Now, he was even thinking of staying an extra year, of extending his service, in order to be with her.

Then... and he hadn't told Karen this... he might ask her to go to India with him. If everything worked out. On his last visit to the Peace Corps house in the capital, he'd read that India was looking for help, that there might be jobs for foreigners in hospitals there. Perhaps, just perhaps, Karen would like to join him there. Who knew? After all, she liked Indian movies!

He gave her hand a squeeze, and felt her give a little squeeze in return. He smiled then, perhaps with that same smile that he'd had when, years earlier, he had dressed as a Klingon and met a girl he liked for the first time... and it was at that moment that a thought crossed his mind, an important thought. He was just starting to open his mouth, to tell the girl at his side...

Then the movie started, and he closed his mouth and watched.

With Karen's hand in his, he suddenly knew that there was plenty of time.

AFTERWORD
Loving Bollywood

"Bollywood" is the nickname for the Indian, or Hindi, film industry. The name is a cross between "Hollywood" and "Bombay," the city where Indian movies are made.*

—

I first heard the term "Bollywood" on a trip to Thies, Senegal, in 1997. As with most big cities in West Africa, there was a movie theater that showed Indian films, and my friend Ravi asked if I'd like to go. "Sure," I said, not knowing that the experience would change my life forever. Because that day I fell in love—completely, irrevocably— with Indian movies. And the seed was planted that would eventually grow into this novel.

You see, Bollywood movies are unique. Running around three hours apiece, they are predominantly musicals, with elaborate dance numbers that take one back to Big Band Hollywood films of the '30s and '40s. And the plotlines that come between the singing and dancing can truly be called epic, with each film covering a wide variety of genres and styles. Comedy, action, drama, and romance are often all mixed up in one film— a little bit of something for everybody. This mixture is called a *masala*, after the Indian culinary term for "a blending of spices."

My first film was definitely *masala*. It had heroes who fell in love, wooed their lovers with a song and dance, and then beat up bad guys in a sudden flurry of action as intense as a Chinese gangster movie, all before having a cozy little wedding scene. I absolutely loved it. I asked Ravi for some pointers on which movies would be fun to watch and quickly became an enthusiast.

And I'm not the only one. Worldwide, Indian movies are enormous. India has successfully exported its films around the world and built up a huge fan base. In fact, in many countries, Indian movies are just as popular as, or even

* "Bombay," of course, is now known as "Mumbai."

more popular than, movies from America, and it's not much of a surprise, either. India is a massive producer. They make more movies than any other country in the world (about twice as many movies per year as Hollywood), and the Indian box office is a strong competitor for Hollywood, often making more sales worldwide.

I didn't know any of this back in 1997, when Ravi showed me my first film. All I knew was that I loved watching the movies. My friends and family in America thought it was crazy—I went to Africa and came back loving Indian movies? What??? They knew as little about Bollywood's popularity in Africa and the world as I had.

But I know now. As a lover of Indian movies, I have joined a huge group of enthusiastic fans, which includes Ravi, the guy who invited me to my first film. I owe him thanks. Without that film, and all of the ones following it, I would never have thought to write a novel like this one, nor to have created a character like Don Smith. So thank you, Ravi, for sharing this with me.

Aap ki barii meharbanii hai.
(Thank you very much.)

INDIAN SUMMER

<u>OTHER STUFF</u>

THE MEANING OF "YAAR"

Throughout *Indian Summer*, Don often uses the term "Yah" at the end of his sentences as if it is the tag line "Yes?" or "Right?"

This is because Don is an idiot.

Okay, that's a bit harsh.

Don is not an idiot.

At least, probably not.

However, in his enthusiastic viewing of Indian cinema, he has completely failed to understand the usage of this particular popular word and instead imbued it with his own incorrect assumption.

"Yaar" (or "yar") doesn't mean "yes" at all, but instead is used as a term of endearment, particularly between males, along the same lines as "dude," "buddy," or "pal."

When Shayla describes Don's use of "yah" to Devi in Chapter 24, and makes specific reference to the fictional movie *Father/Friend*, Devi looks bemused. This is because Don and Shayla have both, in their misunderstanding of "yaar" to mean "yah," missed the somewhat ironic usage of the term in said film.

And that's all you need to know about "yaar," yar?

(If you don't mind me being informal here...)

BADLO, BADLO, BADLO:
ENGLISH LYRICS

Badlo, badlo, badlo
(Change, change, change)
Jo banna chahte ho
(To what you wanna be)
Badlo, badlo, badlo
(Change, change, change)
Apne ko badlo
(To what you want)

Rashtrapati banna hai to, badlo badlo badlo
(If you wanna be a president, change, change, change)
Hero banna hai to, badlo badlo badlo
(If you wanna be a superstar, change, change, change)
Govinda ki tarah nachna hai to, badlo badlo badlo
(If you wanna dance like Govinda, change change, change)
Tez gaadi chalani hai to, badlo badlo badlo
(If you wanna drive a fast car, change, change, change)

ACKNOWLEDGEMENTS

As Hilary Clinton once said (or used as a title of a book, at least), "It takes a village to raise a child." The same is true for writing a book, and this book owes a debt of gratitude to quite a neighborhood of people. (Sorry if I miss anyone!)

For her continued, and always continuing, support, I thank my wife Hyunji. It truly means everything.

For their work reading early drafts of the book and offering helpful insights and opinions: Jennifer Cozart, Darrin Drader, Dan McLachlan, Erik Uppenberg-Croone, Joan Shook, Bryan Winchell, and the wonderful Flat Cow Writers Group of Adarsh Char, Chris Quinn, Roxanne Russell, and Lora Schwenk.

For crucial help with Hindi translation: Adarsh Char, Mohsin Somani, and Dr. Michael Shapiro, the chair of the Department of Asian Languages and Literature at the University of Washington. Adarsh Char, in particular, did a wonderful job helping me create the Hindi songs I wanted to have, and now can't get out of my mind! (Sorry—I know you can't hear what I hear when you read the lyrics, but believe me, they are awesome.)

For other language assistance: Karen O'Brien, who helped me polish my withered French, and Kirok of L'Stok, who gets a special mention for pointing me in the right direction with my Klingon. (I can't remember how I found him now, but he's got a Web presence, and he's a great resource for all your Klingon needs.)

For expert advice on post traumatic stress disorder and dissociative identity disorder: Dr. Matthew Norman, whose expert advice showed me that I was on base with my characters' actions and opened up a new field of interest to me.

For creating a cover that I love: Jason Walton of Myriad Studios. For tweaking the images and colors, cleaning up the wraparound cover to make it flow naturally, and formatting the cover file to make it look perfect: Hyuna Shin of Hyuna

Shin Photography.

For their special help with making the cover: Don Hearn (cover model), Craig and Wing Livengood (pose recreations), Leslie Webb-Blanco (excellent cover mock ups and alternate covers which helped me conceptualize what I wanted on the front), and Torrence Webster (timely advice and calming words of wisdom.)

For help with formatting (thank God!): Scott Gray and Jason Matthews.

For his gracious permission to use the Website name "misterbook.com" in this book: Benjamin Azevedo, who owns the site. I was heartbroken when I found out that the fictitious name I'd come up with up got taken as I was drafting the book, but Mr. Azevedo kindly let me use it anyway. (Please note that the fictitious Misterbook is completely fictitious and not a representation of the real site at all.)

For providing a free Hindi font program that I used to create the title image for *Indian Summer*'s cover: www.hindifonts.net.

For his continued friendship and support: Ryan Boudinot, whose three excellent books (*The Littlest Hitler*, *Misconception*, and *Blueprints of the Afterlife*) should really be on everybody's bookshelves.

Also:

To the Monumental Works Group, whose support has been instrumental in getting this book out.

To Lisa Boynton of Ravens Books in Issaquah, WA, and the Pacific Northwest Writers Association (PNWA) for their support of local writers like myself.

To Ravi Goud, for introducing me to Hindi movies, and to all the people who have watched one or more of them with me.

And, finally, but very importantly, to Shah Rukh Khan. For the thrills.

ABOUT THE AUTHOR

DANIEL RIDER has taught English all over the world, including a stint in the Peace Corps during the late '90s, but left teaching in 2009 to pursue his writing dreams. Now he lives in Issaquah, Washington, where he divides his time between writing and being a stay-at-home dad to his two-year-old daughter.

CONNECT WITH DANIEL

Website: www.danielriderwrites.com

Blog: www.danielriderblogs.blogspot.com

The Monumental Works Group:
www.monumentalworksgroup.com/

Image by Leslie Webb-Blanco

www.ingramcontent.com/pod-product-compliance
Lightning Source LLC
Chambersburg PA
CBHW020914200626
46814CB00001BA/337